Type G

Thomas R. Morgan

This is a work of fiction. Names, characters, and incidents either are the product of the author's imagination or are used fictitiously. A few historical figures appear in the story, the incidents involving them are purely fictional, however. In all other cases any resemblance to actual persons, living or dead, is entirely coincidental.

Front cover: Pixabay, planet-1989837

Back cover: NASA Hubble STSci. Giant planet orbiting Beta Pictoris. News release ID: STScI-2014-08 Release Date: Jan 7, 2014.

The Gemini Planet Imager was used to image Beta Pictoris b, a planet orbiting the star Beta Pictoris. The bright star is hidden behind a mask in the center of the image to block out its glare.

For more information, visit Gemini Observatory's release at http://www.gemini.edu/node/12113

Foreword

I first became interested in science and in particular outer space as a child. It began from a combination of seeing the rings of Saturn through a neighbor's telescope and reading Robert Heinlein's *Have Spacesuit—Will Travel*. Growing up in the 1960s watching the Mercury, Gemini, and Apollo launches made it easy to stay excited about space travel. In high school I attempted to calculate the payload a Saturn V rocket could deliver to Mars. I could barely handle the calculus in the book I checked out of the library, but struggled through to an answer. The original *Star Trek* TV series also made a large impression on me at this same time.

This interest in science stayed with me through college where I studied physics and geology. I subsequently earned a Ph.D. in geophysics and embarked on a career as a research scientist.

In the late 1980's I began investigating a variety of fundamental questions concerning manned travel to the stars. What kind of ship would be needed, how could it be propelled, how would one navigate or communicate from star to star? One possible answer for the ship came from Arthur C. Clarke's Rama series. The general design described in *Type G* derives from the Rama ship. Propulsion concepts were influenced by Poul Anderson's *The Boat of a Million Years*.

There were additional questions, too. How would the aliens look, could they eat our food, would we infect one another? How could we determine if a planet orbiting another star had life on it, a civilization? Finally, what would the aliens' society be like, how would they govern themselves, how long would they live?

Lots of folks have been asking these and related questions for a long time. I did not have any expectations of answering them even in part. Rather, as a scientist I wanted to determine what the current level of knowledge was and try to sketch out the direction one might head in order to find the answers.

I asked these questions because I was curious about what the future holds for us. As the work evolved I began building a story based on what I had learned, what I thought that future might look like. This book is the result.

There are a few historical figures mentioned in the story. The dates correspond to the historical record, but the scenes in which they appear are made up. The science is as accurate as I could make it given the knowledge I was able to locate and my ability to comprehend it. Any errors are my own; corrections are welcome.

The action spans over three hundred years, starting nearly two hundred years in the past, ending more than one hundred years in the future. Interstellar distances are immense; the time to travel from one star to another—even with speculative technology a thousand plus years more advanced than what we have today—could take many decades. Consequently, the time line is long. The story unfolds slowly.

Its purpose is to look out into the future and speculate on where we are headed, what it might hold for us. As a result, to provoke thought. To get to know ourselves better.

Acknowledgements

I am indebted to Jon Praet and Laurel Barbieri for their guidance and encouragement. As someone who had never written fiction and especially dialog before, I received a great deal of wise assistance and expert critique from these two lifelong friends. Any remaining deficiencies are purely my own.

My wife, Diane's steady presence and quiet tolerance of my many hours spent researching and writing, plus additional hours listening to and discussing many elements of the story, were invaluable.

PART 1

A Crossing Ends

Chapter 1
A Joyous Occasion
(August 1823)

Henry and Lucy stood holding hands, their shoulders and hips gently touching as the attendant lifted their baby from the gestation chamber. Birth consisted of removing the fetus from the fluid in the chamber. The attendant cleared the infant's lungs, then neatly tied off and snipped the umbilical cord. Newborns usually starting breathing on their own, although sometimes a little assist was needed; a slap on the bottom. In this case the baby started breathing immediately. After a quick clean-up he was presented to the parents.

Natural childbirth was considered far too risky for both mother and child. The process had long ago been turned over to biosystems that did the job much better.

It was Tuesday, August 5, 1823. The baby was named John after Lucy's father. At 7 pounds, 11 ounces, and 21 inches long, John was ready for the world at 3:25 p.m. His parents had waited for this day for nine months. They were bringing him home to meet their combined families and his upbringing group. A gathering was scheduled for that evening. Lucy cradled John in her arms. Henry grabbed the basket of baby necessities as they headed for the lift down to the shuttle level. In about an hour, John was in his bassinet looking around inquisitively at his new home.

Henry and Lucy lived inside an enormous star ship. They had been together forty-eight years when it became Henry's turn to have a child. John had DNA from both parents but would be considered Henry's replacement. Lucy, who was ten years younger, would be not become eligible to produce her replacement until after their ship got to Alpha Centauri.

The conception process was straightforward. Germ cell DNA from both parents was screened for defects. Any needed repairs were made and the cells combined to produce a fertilized egg, which was gestated artificially until the fetus was ready for delivery. Women no longer had any greater participation in pregnancy than men.

The fertilized egg was carefully deposited in a gestation chamber, where it was provided with the necessary nutrients. It slowly grew from a single cell to a fully formed person. The fetus was closely monitored. It was given everything it needed to develop into a healthy baby.

Henry and Lucy intentionally had not screened for physical traits such as eye or hair color, or sex, nor had they asked to engineer for height or body frame type. All they wanted was a healthy child; beyond that, they preferred to let nature run its course.

In their society no one had a child of one's own in the sense that there was a nuclear family with two parents and several siblings. Instead, extended community units were the rule, with as many as sixty people involved in care and upbringing at one point or another during the years leading to maturity.

Guests started arriving around 6:00 p.m. Matilda, a petite redhead whom everyone called Mattie was already in the living room with her mate, Dave. They had arrived a few days earlier to help with the nursery duties. Mattie was Lucy's cousin. The two of them would be assisting in the first years of John's childhood. Mattie was scheduled to have a child in five years, so they would help with John in order to learn how to care for an infant. Lucy and Henry had done this a few years back when Lucy's friend Greta had had her baby.

There were close to thirty people at the party. The robots provided a splendid buffet dinner. They kept the drinks filled. Everyone took a turn at holding John, commenting on his good looks and alertness, as they did for every new baby. It was nearly midnight when the last guests departed. Henry settled into an easy chair in front of the picture window next to Caleb.

Caleb had been considered part of the family for many years. He was originally a colleague of Henry's father who had become a lifelong friend. He had been a member of Henry's upbringing group. Now he would be one of the older members of John's upbringing group.

The two men sat silently, gazing out across the midship landscape at the lights in the valley. Henry finally broke the silence.

"Thirty-five years of child-rearing and education ahead of us." He was quiet for a few minutes, then spoke again. "I wonder how it will turn out."

"Now, Henry, let's enjoy it as it unfolds. No sense in getting ahead of ourselves," replied Caleb.

"Actually, I was wondering how things with Sol c will turn out."

"So was I," said Caleb.

"But, of course, I am also concerned about Johnny, how he might fit in with what could await us there. I would never force him in a particular direction, I would be happy if he took an interest in something closely related to the ongoing investigations of that planet. He will be exposed to many new ideas by the time the ship leaves Alpha Centauri for the Solar System. He'll be a fully qualified adult by then."

"Now you *have* gotten ahead of events," said Caleb. "Give him a chance to learn how to ride a bike and have a couple girlfriends before getting him out of the house." He smiled.

They sat for a few minutes. Then Henry heard Caleb snoring. He got up and went to the nursery to look in on Johnny, who was sleeping peacefully. The two robots in close attendance whirred slightly as they turned to face him. Henry smiled. After a few moments he went back to shake Caleb, who woke with a slight start. The two of them retired to their respective bedrooms.

Raising a child was important business for the ship's inhabitants because they were likely to only have one or two children in their lifetime. This was especially true in Henry's case, since he had chosen to do a crossing with its tighter population controls.

There was no population expansion on the ship during the trip to Alpha Centauri, just replacement. Once at their destination, the population would increase, but others who had not yet had a child would be ahead of Henry. Lucy would have her replacement, Henry would probably not live long enough to have a second of his own if he remained with the ship. If, instead, he stayed at Alpha Centauri, he would be allowed to have another child. However, the communal manner in which their society raised and educated their offspring plus the length of their lives meant that anyone who wanted to would be able to experience the joy of many children.

John's upbringing group was starting out with a dozen people. Several worked with Henry, others were family or close friends. A few had originally been complete strangers. The group's number would vary with time as participants came and went with the child's changing needs. A core of half a dozen would remain until he reached majority. This was usually in a person's mid-thirties depending on their development rate, as determined by the personal evaluations of the group members. Each inhabitant of the ship must be carefully prepared for life in space. The ship's operational installations where they spent most of their lives contained facilities that to the uniformed could be dangerous or at times instantly lethal.

The interior living space, however, had familiar surroundings such as houses, fields, and woods that would look normal to anyone two hundred light-years back on their home planet, Teran. Typical daily activities, like playing in the yard, family outings, or visits with other children, filled Johnny's days. His early childhood was not particularly extraordinary, given that his entire world was inside a ship traveling at 10 percent of the speed of light.

Chapter 2
"What's Outside?"
(August 1828)

When Johnny, as everyone called him, reached five years of age, his educational program was accelerated. The upbringing group members, who were already keeping him busy with reading, vocabulary, counting games and other activities, began teaching him basic mathematics. They also introduced him to science. He went on field trips lead by various group members to farms, forests, the lake, nearby towns as well as to a couple of the surface operational installations. Often on these trips, they traveled in the underground shuttle system, but otherwise no direct action was taken to make him aware of their particular circumstance.

Johnny had limited access to the ship's library. This was not done to hide anything from him. His parents simply wanted to be the ones to present the facts of their existence in measured doses as he seemed ready for them, plus they wanted to make sure he got a complete, undistorted picture.

Henry opened the library window on the video wall and called up a general overview presentation. It began with a description of the ship's interior supported with plenty of pictures. Johnny got up a couple times to look closely at the images.

"You see," said Henry, "there is a lot more to our world than what you have experienced so far. More beneath your feet than the shuttle system. Most of the machinery that keeps our world running, right down to the flushing of toilets, is controlled by automated systems. Right now you do not have access permission to visit most of it, but you can view any part of it you want on the video wall. As you get older, you will be given increasing amounts of physical access."

"Another thing we have activated for you is access to the observation system," added Lucy. "This will allow you to see the public areas. They are continuously recorded."

"You mean I can see and hear what everyone is doing and saying?" Johnny asked.

"You can only view the public places. All conversation is personal. It cannot be accessed without the permission of the parties involved," she replied. "Our private areas are monitored too, by sensors in the walls, floors, and ceilings as well as by the robots. Your clothes also record your bodily functions like breathing and heartbeat. A continuous record of your personal activities is stored in the ship's archives."

"Everything I say or do anywhere I am goes in there?"

"Yes it does, dear," Lucy continued, "You will find later in life that sharing access to your records with friends and loved ones is a good way to maintain the memory of those you have separated from. Until you reach adulthood, your father and I will control your records. We can access them, however, we will not do this unless there is a vital need. The ship—they had been referring to it this way all along without actually telling him what it was—is complex. At times it can be a dangerous place. Until you have proven yourself to be a trustworthy adult, we will always have this access. Most of the time, if a real problem arises, the robots will respond quicker than either of us can. They are part of the ship's systems. They will know immediately if you get in trouble, either accidentally or by your own actions."

One of the robots always closely attended young children. These personal attendants were bipedal. They looked very much like people, but had a more durable outer covering than skin. They were also much stronger. There were many types of special purpose robots that came in a variety of shapes, sizes and modes of conveyance depending on their use. Johnny had named his most frequent mechanical companion Click for the sound one of its hips made when it walked. Lucy had long ago overruled the maintenance system's attempts to silence the noise. She thought the imperfection was endearing. It provided the robot with a bit of individuality. The robots had never been more than twenty or thirty feet away from Johnny, even when adults were present. At least one would still be near him, but they would now give him extra space.

His parents wanted to gauge Johnny's reaction to what he had just been told. Henry was getting ready to ask how he felt about it when Johnny said, "Okay, can I see what I did last week?"

"Yes, just ask the video screen," Lucy replied.

Johnny asked for the record of last Saturday's breakfast. He proceeded to watch himself eating pancakes. He seemed as fascinated by what was happening around him as in what he was actually doing in the images.

After ten minutes, Lucy broke in. "Well, that's enough for today. Why don't you spend time on your own with the recordings while we get some coffee?"

Johnny spent the next couple of hours absorbed in his changing appearance and behavior going back to his birth. Then he started accessing the ship's facilities.

"I guess we needn't have worried regarding his reaction," said Lucy. "It's funny how some kids really have a hard time coming to grips with the fact that they are being watched all the time, while others don't seem to be affected by it."

"Yes, he seems to have been waiting for it, half knowing what it was going to be. The way he has taken to the records access, I don't think we will have to be concerned with him being bored."

Until now Johnny had been unaware of what was in the ship's hull, except for the shuttle system. The next day, when he went out to play after his lessons, rather than spend time in the yard as he normally did, he disappeared.

Lucy tracked him down several hours later when it was time for dinner. He was twenty levels down inside the hull, within his permission zone but close to its limit, snooping in one of the computer installations.

A few mornings later, they sat down again in front of the display wall.

"Today we are going to tell you more about this world of ours," Henry announced.

Johnny's eyes lit up, he stopped fidgeting. Henry had his full attention.

The computer narrative began, "In order to sustain ourselves during the many years of travel between stars, we use a large and powerful ship, called a Main Ship because it is our main means of transport, also *main* is a synonym for *ocean*. In this case the ocean of deep space."

"What are oceans? What are stars?" Johnny asked.

"Let's watch for a few minutes, we'll see," Lucy replied, turning back to the narrative.

"On our ship we have worked continuously for several thousand years to get it to its present level of sophistication. The inside is a world as complete as one you would find on our home planet. Even with over a hundred thousand onboard, it is spacious enough to not feel crowded. In fact it seems nearly uninhabited if you travel around inside. There are a number of population centers spaced about the interior surface, where most of the crew lives. The intervening areas consisted of farms, parks, or forest preserves. The work areas and ship's systems are in the walls or hull, which is the half-mile-thick shell that separates the interior from the emptiness of space."

Henry broke in. "So you see, our home is a gigantic vehicle that is transporting us like the shuttle pods."

The narrative continued. "The result is a totally regulated living environment. We enjoy familiar day and night cycles plus longer seasonal variations in temperature. The ship's interior living space is large enough to support a complex weather system involving changing wind patterns, rain or snow."

Henry looked at Johnny to gauge his reaction.

"That's what we're inside of," Johnny exclaimed.

Henry was taken aback. "You already knew we were living in a ship?"

"Well, I knew we were living inside something, since no matter where you are, any which way you look, the ground in the distance is slightly higher."

Henry and Lucy traded surprised looks. Without any formal instruction, their child intuitively understood enough geometry to figure out at this early age the shape of his world.

"But what's outside?" Johnny asked.

"This is what's outside." Henry called for a display from one of the telescopes mounted on the outer hull. He toned down the intellectual level of the delivery, then told the narrative to continue.

"Space is basically nothing. No air, no people, just emptiness with widely scattered large bodies called stars that put out a bright light. We are traveling between two of these right now. Our ship keeps the nothingness out. It gives us a comfortable place to live. Around each star are smaller bodies that people can live on, called planets. We came from one of them and are heading to another."

Lucy picked up the discussion. "Over forty-five hundred years ago, our ancestors left a planet we call Teran that orbits the star Grian located in the northwest corner of the constellation Ara."

She pointed to a dim yellow spot surrounded by three fuzzy star clusters highlighted on the right center of the display.

"There have been many stops along the way at other stars," said the narrator. "The most recent was Epsilon Indi. We will be arriving at the next one in a little more than ten years. It is named Alpha Centauri AB. It is actually a double or binary star; the main one is called Alpha or A, the smaller is Beta or B."

"Wow, we came from one of those?" Johnny pointed to a dot on the screen.

"Let's take a look at it close up," said Henry.

The screen opened a display panel of their home planet's disk. They spent an hour navigating around it, looking at oceans, mountain ranges, cities, glaciers, and deserts. They zoomed in to see details until Johnny had gotten a good idea view of everything at ground level.

"Johnny, this has been a lot for you to absorb, think about what we have seen. Come up with some questions. Tell us what you want to study next," said Henry.

"Now we have a surprise for you," Lucy began. "In a couple of weeks, we will be launching a probe. It is a much smaller type of ship that we send out into space ahead of us. What would you say to a trip to the outer hull to see the launch firsthand?"

Henry added, "It will be a fun field trip. You'll get to directly see stars, plus the outside of the ship along with the launch."

"That would be the coolest!" Johnny responded. "What does a probe look like?"

"The probe is a cylinder five hundred feet long by two hundred feet in diameter. It is mostly engine with fuel storage in the center, surrounded by communications systems. Various orbiting satellites and surface landers to be used once the Solar System is reached are stowed inside or attached to the outside," Henry replied, thinking much of it probably went over Johnny's head.

Johnny did skip past the technical details of the probe. He went straight for the big question. "Solar System? What's that?"

"Aha," Henry said with a smile. "That got your attention. Sol is another star up ahead, beyond where we are headed right now. The Solar System is how we refer to that star and its planets. One day you will have the chance to go there with the ship"

Chapter 3
Last Probe
(September 1828)

Henry had been a member of the probe team since reaching majority. From the start, he showed a unique ability to ferret out the source of system faults. He was also an excellent organizer of both thoughts and activities. This made him a lucid presenter of his own and synthesizer of others' ideas, as well as an efficient manager of any task that came his way. He was recognized as a natural leader. Over the decades this was acknowledged by his colleagues. Henry was ultimately selected to be head of all probe-related activities, a post that brought him in contact with hundreds of his shipmates working on dozens of major launch vehicle projects, everything from propulsion to communications systems, launch scheduling, and resource allocation.

His was an important job. The probes were a vital link to the ship's destination. He felt the importance of his position and was aware of the respect he had earned, although he did not take himself that seriously. He was a modest person.

On launch day Johnny was up at dawn. They were going to the control facility on the exterior of the hull. Henry was bringing him on this special occasion to give him a first experience with space he would always remember.

Henry was in the bathroom shaving as Johnny came in, asking, "Dad, when do we go?"

"Now cool your thrusters, the launch isn't until 2:30 this afternoon, it will only take us an hour to get to the control center."

"But I can't wait to be weightless!" He had been reading-up on the environs of the outer hull launch facilities.

"You'll have plenty of time to float around. We'll leave after I help your mother get things ready for this evening."

"When will that be?"

"Okay, okay, we'll go at 10:00," Henry said with a mock look of exasperation.

They took the 10:25 shuttle from the station nearest their house. It carried them all the way to the terminus at the forward-end cap. From there they took the short lift ride to the surface station, where they got on one of the elevators that ran radially along the interior of the end cap. It carried them the twelve miles to the center of the cap in twenty minutes. The elevator cars had clear windows so passengers could view the interior as they rose. At the halfway point, Henry put on his magnetic boots. He told Johnny to do the same.

"But I want to float!"

"Suit yourself, keep in mind I'm not cleaning it up if you get sick," Henry replied calmly. "Lots of people get sick the first time they experience weightlessness. It can come on pretty quick."

Johnny reluctantly put on the boots.

As they ascended to the center of the end cap, the artificial gravity produced by the ship's spin slowly decreased to zero. This was the source of the weightlessness. Also because of the lack of spin, it was the access point for craft coming to and leaving the ship.

Once off the elevator, Henry guided his son along a series of corridors toward the launch control center.

"Now that we're near a bathroom, you can take the boots off for a while to see how you manage. Just don't float off too far," Henry instructed.

Johnny's boots were off in a flash. He proceed to bounce his way along by pushing off the floor, ceiling, and walls.

"How do you feel, do you want a bag?" Henry called after him.

"This is fun, I feel good—keep your bag."

This went on for ten minutes or so until the novelty wore off. Henry walked while Johnny floated the rest of the way.

"When you get more experienced with weightlessness, we'll take a float above the interior in enviro suits." Henry knew as soon as he spoke that he was in trouble.

"Can we do it on the way home?" Johnny asked.

"No, we won't have time. Besides, I said when you get older. We have a party later, remember?"

"How soon can we come back, then?"

Henry relented. "If you don't get sick before we leave, maybe in a couple weeks. Come on now—we're at the control room. Put your boots back on and keep them on. There are too many things to bump into, I wouldn't want you launching the shuttle prematurely." Henry smiled.

All he got in return was one of Johnny's *oh please* looks, but Johnny put the boots on.

Once in the control room, Henry sat down in one of the console chairs. He fixed his gaze on the wall screen, which showed a video image of the open launch bay doors. He watched intently for the probe to slide into view. The image filled the center of the ten-by-six-foot viewing area. Around the edges were smaller windows filled with telemetry readouts of the various probe systems with additional video images from different angles. The telemetry data glared back with its multicolored insistence. The exterior images were shades of gray. Henry thought to himself *space always seemed to be shades of gray when it was not plain black.*

They had been in the control room for forty-five minutes when Henry felt a tug on his arm. "Dad, how much longer?"

"It will be another hour or more, Johnny. Look, the launch bay doors are open."

Rocking forward in his swivel chair, Henry reached for his coffee container to take a swig. He had let it get cold. He called for added contrast on the image to highlight the bay doors. The console responded immediately to his voice command to ask if the lighting was sufficient. "A smidge more will do it," Henry said. Again the console responded, getting it just right. It knew him well enough to accurately determine what he meant by a "smidge."

"I see it—there it is!" Johnny exclaimed.

Slowly the probe emerged. It was covered with outgrowths of antennas, thrusters, and propulsion cones, it was designed purely for function. Not smooth or sleek, nothing painted on its exterior, simply the basic metallic colors of its components. There was no one out there to impress. It would not be seen again by eye for over a hundred years.

Light towers on the ship's hull surrounding the external camera mount illuminated the small craft's surface as it waited, poised to propel itself into the blackness beyond. Henry looked out past the open bay along the gray outer surface of their ship. Bathed in dull yellow light to a distance of a few hundred yards, it too was festooned with the projections of various types of equipment. The view along the hull then faded slowly to utter darkness. Henry could barely make out the form of a 25 meter radio dish at the limit of his field of view.

He watched the faint glow of the orientation thrusters as they fired to point the craft in the correct direction once it cleared the bay doors. This put the engine exhaust cones facing toward him. These were what he was most interested in. The bay doors slowly closed.

Henry's main purpose that day was to monitor the probe's engines to get a look at the performance data. A number of improvements had been made that his team expected would increase engine efficiency allowing the vehicle to get to full speed using half a percent less fuel.

One of the Terans' major occupations was to come up with ways to improve their propulsion systems. They were constantly sharing their discoveries with sister ships spread through that region of space via the communications links: an interstellar network of transceiver arrays, called High bandwidth Uplink Bases or HUBs for short, which relayed information around an interstellar network. Much of the time, the reports were so old the ship's own engineers and scientists had already made the same discovery. That was one of the advantages of having people onboard a completely automated, self-sufficient starship. In the instance of one report early in Henry's career, the sending ship had been only thirty light-years away on a parallel course. They combined ideas from it with their own to gain a significant engine efficiency increase.

Henry turned to Johnny. "Let's go downstairs to the bubble"—*down* being an arbitrary definition, given the lack of gravity, artificial or otherwise. He ushered Johnny to the tight spiral stairway in the far back corner of the room, then clasped the central column with one hand, nimbly swung himself around. Johnny followed awkwardly, owing to his short stature and the steep steps. The bare metal treads clanged underfoot as they descended.

The clear hemispherical viewing bubble projected directly into space. It was surrounded on all sides, except where it was attached to the hull, by the void. The stairs to the bubble did not quite reach to the bottom. After Henry hopped off the last one onto the floor pad used to protect part of the clear surface of the bubble from scratches and provide something for the gravity boots to stick to, he put out his hands to help Johnny down the last big step.

Being in the bubble gave the feeling of floating along with the probe that was hovering a hundred yards away. Johnny's mouth opened in awe as he stared out at it.

"What do you think?" Henry asked.

"Cool!"

"The launch sequence is controlled by the automatic systems. My participation is minimal. It could have been done from home, but I like coming to the outer hull to see our technology in action up close. I think it's cool, too."

"I see you boys made it to the bubble," said Lucy's voice over the intercom, calling from home. Without waiting for a reply, she added, "Make sure you get going right after the launch. People will be arriving soon, I don't want you to be late for your own party."

"Aye, aye, Captain," came Henry's cheerful reply.

To an outside viewer, it would look as if they were standing on the inside of the bubble's roof. It was twenty feet in diameter, though, so Henry could easily stand upright with plenty of clearance to see out without doing a headstand. He could walk around a bit but would not leave the pad. Johnny immediately began climbing up the interior of the bubble.

"Johnny, don't do that. You will leave fingerprints that will spoil the view. Take your boots off and float away from the sides."

Henry had done the same thing as a youngster to see how high he could get before losing traction. He knew it was difficult to climb too high. Johnny would soon tire of the game.

Henry turned off the lights in the control room above, along with the external floodlights, to put the bubble in total darkness surrounded by thousands of stars off in the deep. The view always made him shudder at first. It was similar to going outside the hull in an enviro-suit, just roomier and much safer. Henry stood gazing out. Over the millennia his people had traveled through that space; he had crossed a portion of it.

Johnny, as Henry had expected, soon quit climbing the wall and joined him watching for the engines to ignite.

Henry explained, "The probe is now in launch position. Once the final checkouts are done, it will move out slowly until it is clear of the collector screens, at three thousand miles. Then it will bring its engines up to full power for the main acceleration phase."

As the engines powered up, they began to push the small craft forward. From inside the dome, Henry watched it move slowly away to begin its voyage. It looked lonely, but he knew it would soon rendezvous with eight companions exactly like itself.

He told Johnny, "Together with shipboard systems such as the telescope arrays, the probes provide critical information concerning the ship's heading. As our Main Ship travels to its next destination, they are sent out ahead to gather data. This final one is the last of nine that have been launched in recent weeks. Once it reaches full speed, all nine will join up to coast in formation in a Y pattern."

As the probe's engine glow faded in the distance, Henry said, "Let's get back upstairs, I want to look at the readings on the console one last time."

Neither really wanted to leave, so they lingered a little longer. Finally Henry motioned to the stairs, Johnny reluctantly followed.

The last probe of the chain between Alpha Centauri and Sol was away. Henry took a final look into the vast emptiness as he climbed back up the spiral stairs.

On the way up, he explained to his son their purpose. "We select star system stops in advance based on remote astronomical observations. It is the probe data, however, that allows us to evaluate a system and determine what can be done there."

Johnny nodded slightly, it was obvious his attention was still down below in the bubble.

When Johnny was older he would be better prepared to understand the technical aspects, he would learn much more about the probes, how they worked, and what they were used for.

Henry concluded, "We are nearing the end of our trip to Alpha Centauri. Our deceleration into the system will begin soon. A few years after deceleration is finished, we will start receiving close-up data from the first group sent out long ago that are now approaching Sol. The satellites and landers they deploy will send back data from Sol's planets via the probe-to-probe communication chain."

Back at the console, he looked at a set of telemetry displays to see if there were any anomalies and get an initial reading on engine efficiency. The probe's main engine was operating as planned. This was not a surprise, a failure had not occurred in hundreds of years. In fact, the launch team's participation was marginal, as the process was highly automated. They mainly watched what was going on and responded to the system's request for final approval to launch. The launch leader had given that approval, although it was mostly a formality.

"Time to go, son," said Henry. "We don't want to be late for our guests."

Chapter 4
Retirement Party
(September 1828)

Confirmation appeared on the living room wall display that the last of the Sol probes was clear of the collector screens. It was safely accelerating away from the Main Ship. Henry picked up his drink from the coffee table and sat back in the easy chair. All the probes needed for the Alpha Centauri–Sol chain had been launched. The initial ones, launched so many years ago, were most of the way to the Solar System. In fourteen years the Terans would receive the first data from Sol relayed back along the communication chain. Then they would get a look, albeit a remote one via photographs, at the surfaces of Sol's planets and moons.

Through the years Henry had made better use of his intelligence than most of his peers. However, he did not think of himself as that much brighter than normal. He knew he had a good memory, he had learned how to maximize use of it. A good deal of science and engineering work was seeing patterns or connections among seemingly unrelated phenomena. That he could recall more of these more quickly and hold them together in his mind longer than others is what let him see things ahead of others, or to see what they did not see at all. What they might call quick-wittedness or brilliance, he considered a lot of constant work absorbing data and making it intelligible. His one gift, a good memory, is what he felt allowed him to stand out.

As with all work teams on the ship, the ones he oversaw were completely self-organizing. No one was ever assigned to anything in Teran society. If someone wanted to be on a particular team, they were on it. All they had to do was show up. This did not mean they could do absolutely anything they wanted. If a team member did not have sufficient skills, the team would guide him or her to the necessary educational resources and mentor them as they learned. No one got to do interesting things without first proving their ability.

Teams were run democratically, selecting their leaders and deciding how to meet the obligations they had agreed to with teams they interacted with. Henry had been chosen leader in probe propulsion this way years ago. He had been chosen that same way every step up the administrative ladder.

Together, the teams formed a well-established hierarchy that had been constructed, reconstructed, and fine-tuned over the millennia since the Main Ship's original launch. The various teams met periodically to coordinate on issues where their systems interfaced. As with all other ship's systems, the organization of the probe teams was a high-level blueprint for how they were constructed. It provided overall probe program structure. Henry was at the top of that hierarchy, placed there by those who worked on the program.

He liked the technical part of his work, but was never comfortable with the people aspects. He had an easy, open manner and got along with nearly everyone; he just had a difficult time being hard on people when necessary.

When the infrequent dispute occurred, or on occasions when a deadline was missed, Henry was the one who had to step in to make things right. Deadlines were the toughest situation for everyone. The probes had to go out on a rigid schedule in order to maintain uniform spacing between them, thus assuring the integrity of the communication chain. The future of the mission to the next star completely depended on this. What made it doubly difficult was that probe launches were almost the only major activity of the ship that required adherence to such a tight schedule. Since no one was practiced in meeting tight deadlines in their everyday lives, new team members found it difficult to adapt sometimes. This gave team leaders at all levels headaches.

Even when they were on or ahead of schedule, one never could be sure when something unexpected or overlooked would crop up. Henry was where the big problems came for final resolution. He was not good at giving bad news or cracking down, consequently he avoided it as much as possible. Neither did he like being told what to do, so in turn did not dictate to others what to do. He would rather keep after poor performers, individuals or teams, until things got better or they got tired of his persistence and let someone else take over. On top of this, he always had a backup plan.

Most activities were duplicated in various ways by other groups. If a failure occurred somewhere, there was always an alternative that could be brought in to fill the gap. It was Henry's job to keep on top of the teams' activities, anticipate problems, and have a plan to switch to one of the alternatives when necessary. Doing so did not happen often, when it did there were always ruffled feathers in the team whose role was supplanted by another. Dealing with often highly opinionated experts, he had to master the fine arts of diplomacy. He also put things back as they were as soon as possible. People were always given another chance. It was up to management to provide the tools and environment necessary for those doing the real work to succeed. If they did not, he felt it was his failure, not theirs.

With the launch of the final probe, Henry was out of a job—at least to the extent that none would be launched until after the next departure, when they would begin forming the chain between Sol and Epsilon Eridani. In a little over two years they would start the five-year deceleration into the Alpha Centauri system, where the Main Ship would remain for forty-five years. That meant it would be sixty years before the next probe launch. Henry was still young at one hundred. The Main Ship was large and comfortable. He had nearly one hundred thousand companions. Soon there would be plenty of data relayed back along the communication chain to work on during the years of preparation for the forty-five-year trip to Sol.

Henry smiled as he looked around the living room. *Who am I kidding?* He said to himself. He would not go on to Sol. If he did, he would be over two hundred years old when they got there. He would probably not be in any shape to enjoy the sights of a planetary system. No, he would do that now at Alpha Centauri while he was still fit enough to be able to get the most out of visiting unfamiliar worlds. He would not be launching any more probes. This phase of his life was now behind him. He would move on to something else. What that might be, he had no idea. He knew it would come to him as long as he allowed himself to be open to possibilities.

His son would get the chance to go on to Sol. Henry would have his time on a habitable planet in the Alpha Centauri system. He had been born before they left the Epsilon Indi system and had the brief opportunity to visit its third planet when he was John's age. He had enjoyed several marvelous adventures on that planet's surface, exploring much of it with his parents. He never ceased to marvel at the variety of the place, the differences in climate, the variability of the weather, the complexity of the environment, the things that the persistent forces of nature could accomplish with sufficient time.

In spite of this, his parents' decision to leave had been an easy one. They both had spent the first part of their lives at Delta Pavonis. Then they went together on the crossing to Epsilon Indi. Henry was his father's second child, coming late in his parents' lives. They had gone on to Alpha Centauri so Henry could take his turn at setting off into the vastness of space as the original crew of the Main Ship had done over a score of generations ago. After all, if they had not gone with the ship, he never would have met Lucy.

Henry let his mind wander back to the day they had met fifty-three years earlier, when he was a young member of the probe propulsion sub-team. Lucy had been living and working in the farming zone in the middle of the ship's cylinder. Her family had been in the same location for many generations. She spent most of her time outdoors managing the fields and livestock. Given their different backgrounds, the two would not have been likely to cross paths unless they had close common relatives, friends, or teammates. Their meeting was a coincidence that came about because of Henry's running.

At the time he was in the habit of doing twenty-mile runs alternate Restday mornings. He would pick two points on the ship's interior surface that were roughly that distance apart, take the shuttle to one, then run to the other. One late summer day when he was a little past halfway, running along a quiet dirt road beside a ripened field of wheat, he spotted a large harvesting machine moving over it. He had seen harvesters before, but this one had a young woman lying on top. She appeared to be sunbathing. What really got his interest was that it looked like she was au naturel. Henry was paying more attention to her than where he was running, and put his foot in a rut. He went down with a yelp. He felt his ankle; it was sore but did not appear to be broken.

Henry did not take a robot with him when he ran, so he was starting to think about what to do next when he saw one coming toward him. The harvester had stopped, the girl was nowhere to be seen. He figured either she or the harvester had seen him and sent the robot. It soon confirmed that his injury was a sprain. After his ankle had been wrapped, he stood on it. He could walk slowly, but that was it. He would not be able make it to the nearest shuttle entrance, wherever it was, under his own power.

Finally a slightly frazzled female face appeared on the robot's view screen. "Are you okay?" she inquired.

"Thanks for stopping," Henry answered. "It's just a sprain, I am in a bit of a quandary on how to get home though. I can't walk far in my present state."

"I'll give you a lift," she responded cheerily.

"I wouldn't want to tie up your harvester for that," Henry answered. "Maybe your robot can carry me to the closest shuttle port?"

"I have a cart. I'll be right there," she answered.

Sure enough, a small cart emerged from the side of the harvester. It drove across the field toward him.

"Sorry for the delay and my somewhat shabby appearance," the girl said as the cart came to a stop. "This was all I had with me. I had to throw it on quickly."

"I know," said Henry sheepishly. "I spotted you on top of the machine." Henry thought she had a nice figure. He had noticed that her tan covered her whole body.

The two mile ride to her family's farm took thirty minutes. She went slowly along the rough road to avoid bouncing his foot too much. They talked about themselves. He learned something of harvesters and farming, she of probes and propulsion systems. That they liked one another immediately was obvious to both. They dropped subtle hints that they were unattached.

When they got to the farmhouse, Lucy's mother was there to greet them at the door. The farm team was already inside, gathering for Restday dinner. This was a tradition they held, like many others in the ship. Henry's family group usually did the same later in the afternoon. Lucy's mother invited him to stay. She insisted, actually, claiming he should rest his foot. He videoed with his own family and excused himself from their dinner. They already knew what had happened from the robot that attended him. They had also been contacted by Lucy's mother as soon as she saw them approaching the farmhouse. Henry's mom said for him to have a good dinner and look for a change of clothes in the farmhouse lift closet in a few minutes.

Except for their initial meeting, things progressed much as most courtships on the ship. Lucy came to Restday dinner with his family group the next weekend. Then they began to see each other on a regular basis. Mostly they met someplace to go for long walks. They talked about whatever came into their minds. There was never any strain in the conversation. They both had a wide variety of interests; there was enough overlap and separation to make things new yet familiar at the same time. Eventually, the members of the two family groups got to meet one another, then they simply began living together.

A toy truck bounced off Henry's foot jolting him out of his daydreaming. He became aware of the other people in the room. Many were members of the probe team, others were families and friends. He had invited them to his home for a celebration of the launch of the last of the Sol series. He also wanted to pass the word that he was retiring. The various sub-teams would continue on, even without launches, but a new overall leader would be selected. There was always monitoring of the communication chain to do plus R&D on the various probe systems. For him, however, it was the natural point to make his departure.

As the host, Henry knew he had certain social responsibilities, accordingly he got up out of the chair to mingle. They were an informal, casually dressed crowd. He was accorded no special treatment because he was the overall leader. He had been chosen by the team members, they could just as easily replace him. As leader he felt he should do some leading, so he had organized the gathering, which was turning boisterous as they watched a replay of the vehicle emerging from the launch bay, orienting itself, and moving away from the ship. Then came the spot of light that was the probe's main engine as it sped into the deep.

Henry scooped up the toy truck's owner. He walked over to the child's father, saying, "Little Jake, either you are the biggest three-year-old in recent history, or I need a new exercise program!"

Jake Senior responded, "It was a good idea to get the team together along with Johnny's upbringing group."

Jacob Senior had been born near the end of the crossing from Delta Pavonis to Epsilon Indi. He was thirty-seven years older than Henry. Their families had been close for generations, serving together in many upbringing groups.

Little Jake was now sitting high atop his father's shoulders. With Lucy and Johnny by his side, Henry called for everyone's attention. He proposed a toast to the team and the successful launch of the last probe. "Hear, hear!" echoed all around. Jake Senior got one hand free as he steadied his son to lift his glass to the upbringing group. Henry then guided everyone out to the patio surrounding the swimming pool where the barbecue was being prepared by the robots. It was a balmy, late summer day. The pool was well used by the kids—both big and small.

Like the probe launches, every routine aspect of life onboard the Main Ship was automated. Robots took care of numerous small personal tasks. Every resident had a personal robotic assistant that dealt with everything from household chores to emergency medical response. In a situation such as the party, several robots would prepare the meal while the rest served drinks or hors d'oeuvres. Two or three robots would stand by on the sidelines.

The festivities were well along before Henry finally got a chance to take a breather. He ambled over to a pair of chairs on the far side of the pool that were positioned under a large willow tree. One was already occupied by the Little Jake's "uncle," Caleb, who spoke up as Henry approached. Technically Caleb and Little Jake were cousins, however, because of the limitations on having offspring, there could be large age differences between siblings. Jake Senior and Caleb's mother were brother and sister, she was seventy-three years older than Jake, putting Caleb more in Jake Senior's generation; hence the title "uncle."

"Come, sit awhile," Caleb offered. "We haven't spoken in quite some time, Henry." It had been several months since their last video chat. The most recent in person had been three years ago.

"You're right, Cal, but then you don't get down here much, neither one of us seems to be very good at making video calls. It was good of you to make the trip."

Caleb lived at the far-forward end of the ship in a forested area that was lightly inhabited. He was every bit the recluse, rarely venturing away from his cabin in the woods. When he did, it was usually not without purpose.

"Happy to. I always like to come down to see how things are where the action is," Caleb replied wryly.

The two men talked for a while longer of life's comings and goings, who had died, the new baby the Harwins had, how they were feeling. Finally, after a lull in the conversation, Henry asked if there was anything in particular on Caleb's mind.

"Well, yes, there is, but let's not talk about it right now," said Caleb. "What I would like, which was part of the reason I came down here, was to invite you up to the woods for a while. What do you say?"

Henry's face broke into a big smile. "Nothing would please me more. We've decided, or rather Lucy insisted, it was a good time for me to take time off and relax. Plus I've reached an obvious crossroad. It's time for me to make a change. Going up to your place would be the perfect prescription."

Henry thought, *Caleb is a wise man*; as in the past, he seemed to know what Henry needed before Henry knew himself.

Mentors often came from a child's upbringing group; someone with whom the child shared common interests and developed an especially strong bond, as with parents. While most members of the upbringing group generally ceased playing guiding roles in a person's life once majority was reached, Caleb had remained close; emotionally, if not physically in Henry's case. This was especially true since Henry's father and mother had passed away many years ago. Going up to the woods for a visit with Caleb would be the perfect change of pace.

During the Terans' long lifetimes, it was not unusual for someone to make several changes in career along the way. Frequently the shift was dramatic, involving many years of study before becoming proficient enough to be a contributing member of a new work team. At Henry's age, it was late for what would be his first change.

He had focused on engineering after his upbringing, going on to become one of the ship's primary propulsion experts. He had been at it for nearly seventy years. They had accomplished much in that time. One of the early significant achievements came at the launch of the initial probe to Sol. They had successfully applied several new concepts Henry had played a part in working out, which resulted in a full 1 percent speed increase that would cut seven months off the trip. They had labored long to accomplish this. It consumed most of his attention during those early days on the propulsion sub-team. They had been well along to the breakthrough when a report from Main Ship (MS) 27 had come in. It allowed them to quickly converge on a solution and implement it in time for the launch. Their result was even better than MS27's, as often happened when independent collaborators shared ideas. They had sent off a report of their own, which in turn would undoubtedly be improved upon by the MS27 crew, as well as others.

Today's launch was a milestone for Henry. There would always be a continuing need for better probe propulsion, navigation systems, and other systems' improvements, but there would be less opportunity to apply any new advances for a very long time.

"I'll pack in the morning to head back up with you," Henry offered. "Do you mind if I bring a small companion?"

"Of course not. In fact I was hoping you would want to bring him along. Come by Jake's place for lunch, we can take a midafternoon shuttle. Don't forget to bring that old fly rod your dad gave you," Caleb finished.

Henry got up to hunt down Johnny, but Johnny found him first.

"Dad, who was that man you were talking to?"

"That was your uncle Caleb. You met him before, you were just too young to remember. He invited us to his place for a visit."

"Is it someplace neat?"

"Well, I don't know whether it is neat, but I think you would like it. It is in the woods at the far end of the ship. Uncle Caleb lives up there in a cabin."

"Sure, can we go to the end cap?"

"Absolutely. Let's go say hello and thank him for the invitation."

After thanking Uncle Caleb, Johnny took off to tell his mother.

Chapter 5
A Rustic Retreat
(October 1828)

Early the next morning, Click got out their travel bags. Henry watched the robot pack as he pointed out some special items he wanted included, especially the fly rod. The robot was good at anticipating his desires. It had already taken it out of the closet. Click must have heard him talking to Caleb the night before, Henry thought. Then again, he didn't recall seeing Click nearby at that particular time. Outside the house, the robot normally stayed close, inside it roamed around. It probably did a download from the house systems and picked up on the fly rod comment in its nightly review. *Not having to sleep does have its advantages*, Henry thought with a smile to himself.

Click put the bags on the lift platform in the closet by the back door and communicated their destination, Caleb's cabin, to the delivery system. Once the door was closed, the lift descended, sending the bags on their way.

The lift platforms were entry points to the subsurface transport system. The lift descended twenty feet to the first subsurface level of the ship. At this point a service robot picked up the object and wheeled it to a transport tube. The first level was an array of tubes running in multiple directions from one end of the ship to the other. Small magnetically levitated capsules ran along in the tubes at speeds up to 200 miles per hour. The baggage was already moving in this manner. Occasionally people, especially teenagers, would use the lift and tube system for the fun of it or to be by themselves. Mostly people used the shuttle system. Robots used either, depending on the circumstances.

The passenger shuttles were larger, consequently there were usually other folks traveling together for at least part of the ride, large parties did not have to split up on longer runs. There were fewer entry and exit points though. The descent was farther down to the third level, a hundred feet below the surface. The intervening second level was used for utilities.

The two travelers went out the back door of their home, Click followed. They mounted bicycles for the ride to Jake's that would take twenty minutes, arriving well in time for lunch.

"Eleven thirty, good timing," called out Jake Senior as Henry and Johnny came up the alleyway beside the house. The robots were starting to set out lunch fixings on the patio table.

They parked their bikes against the fence and walked to the small group that included Jake, his wife, son, and Caleb, along with Little Jake's dog, Comet, an aptly named greyhound given its long tail. He immediately came up to Johnny. The boy was soon absorbed in playing with him.

Click went directly to Caleb's robot, which Johnny had recently named Clack for the sound one of its fingers made whenever it closed its left hand tightly. The robots conferred briefly. Click then went in the back door and got onto the lift platform. It would go on ahead to the house in the woods to prepare things, while Clack accompanied them on the passenger shuttle. The two robots decided between themselves to do this. Clack would stay with them, since it was more familiar with the older man, who was naturally a greater health risk. Clack could better attend to his medical needs in the unlikely event of an emergency, as well as Henry or Johnny if need be.

Click had received a download of the layout of the house, its surroundings, along with instructions on what Caleb wanted in the way of preparations for their arrival. The baggage would be taken to the bedrooms. Their things would be put away. The video wall would be activated with their new messages laid out in the prescribed manner. A fire would be started, since the outside temperature would be in the 40s when they arrived, there might be a frost that night. The beds would be freshly made and dinner started in time for their arrival. The robot had plenty of time to do this, since it would be most of the way to the Caleb's house by the time they started lunch.

After lunch the whole group, dog and robots included, walked the two blocks to the shuttle station. Henry and Johnny walked their bikes. They said their good-byes as the travelers descended to the shuttle level. A twenty-minute trip got them to the forward-end station nearest Caleb's forest house. Henry and Johnny biked the two miles to the house while Caleb followed on foot with Clack.

Henry looked forward to the next three weeks. He was anxious to get settled in. Caleb was happy to be going home. He enjoyed coming down to the midsection of the ship occasionally to see family or friends, but preferred they come to him. He enjoyed the solitude of his retreat.

Caleb had long ago given up life in town. He liked the quiet of his cabin in the woods. It wasn't that he disliked people or society, he simply liked solitude better. It gave him the time and space to do what he really wanted to do, think.

He had earned the right to do what he wanted. He spent his youth working on a series of teams looking after a number of the ship's systems. It was not strictly required, but was expected, everyone learned early on that they owed service to the ship. Knowledge of how it worked, how to fix things when they broke had to be maintained across the generations for safety reasons. In each area Caleb had worked, he had quickly become recognized as a supreme technical expert. Even now, years after he'd left the last team, he got frequent questions on technical matters as well as personal messages asking how he was doing.

He spent time tending his apple orchard. Most of his days were passed in unhurried reading and thought, however.

In recent years these thoughts had often turned to Sol c. As the ship journeyed toward Alpha Centauri, increasing amounts of telescope time was being allotted to Sol and its planets. The Terans had an enormous amount of information about the Alpha Centauri system from decades of satellite observations, landers, and probe transmissions, so the telescopes were no longer needed there. Yet arrival at Sol was many years in the future. Although Caleb might not live long enough to get there, it seemed to be absorbing more of his time.

The planet Sol c in particular had fascinated him from the point where they were close enough to begin resolving the planetary disk. The third planet outward from Sol, it was the only one in the star's habitable zone. Sol c's rotational axis had an advantageous amount of tilt, an atmosphere rich in oxygen, which almost always indicated biologic activity, and water. Plus it had a large moon relative to its size to stabilize its rotational tilt.

With a star 4.5 billion years in age with stable luminosity, it was likely biological activity had been established for a long time on Sol c, and evolutionary processes had had the chance to produce sophisticated life forms.

Caleb began by reading all he could find in the archives on habitable planets visited by their ship and the others scattered among the stars surrounding Teran. Not many planets with any biological activity, even fewer with higher life forms, had been found. None had anything more than the most primitive vertebrates confined to the seas. There always seemed to be something wrong. The star's output was not stable enough for long enough periods. The planet's orbit was unstable due to the influence of nearby companion stars. The star system was too young; not enough time had passed for evolution to make much progress. Or the planet's rotational axis was unstable, resulting in frequent, wild climatic shifts. It was always something. He often wondered how life had managed to sustain itself to the point of evolving sentient beings on his own home planet. The answer in this case was a stable star, a planet of ideal size and location, a stable rotational axis, and lots of time. Five billion years of it, in fact.

Now he thought he might be looking at another such planet. It was not one particular thing concerning Sol c that was key; his realization of its potential did not happen suddenly. As he watched the planet, analyzed the data, researched other worlds, the feeling grew that this world was different. Different from the others that had been visited before, different from his home world, as well.

Caleb could be a patient man when necessary. He had to be, since they were moving slowly toward Sol c via Alpha Centauri, the telescope images increased in resolution at a snail's pace. As he watched and waited, every year revealed something new. First, they had been able to differentiated land from oceans. Then the continents began to take shape, although their edges were indistinct. The atmosphere could now be studied in greater detail; large cloud masses and major weather systems could be analyzed with a variety of instruments.

Caleb persisted. He continually cajoled the telescope teams into accepting project proposals allocating larger amounts of time to observing Sol c. He enlisted a number of his old friends to take up the challenge, as well. They formed a team meeting weekly via video conference to share information with the well-established teams whose missions were to conduct scientific studies of the Solar System. Caleb's team was a little different. They poking their noses in anything that struck their fancy rather than being dedicated to a particular discipline such as, planetary evolution, or orbital dynamics.

The proposals took a lot of effort to prepare. Telescope time was allotted based strictly on peer review; anyone onboard the ship could submit one. The process was intensely competitive. Caleb's team of five had many decades of scientific experience, they could consistently write good proposals that would get the attention of the reviewers, although not always their approval. The main problem was his team's objectives were all over the place. There was no apparently consistent pattern or trend to what they were doing, it seemed as if they were throwing darts with bad aim.

These appearances were not deceiving. The team really did not have a set plan. They freely admitted they had no clear picture of the path ahead. In part it was because the entire team was made up of cantankerous loners like Caleb, who long ago had stopped worrying what anyone else thought of them. It was also because the five of them were a long way through lives that had been widely varied. They had been broadly exposed to the process of solving complicated problems. Their motto was "No preconceived notions about anything." Nothing was too crazy to consider, failure was welcomed as a learning opportunity. The bigger the failure, the better. It was the best way to learn.

Their approach and attitude did not completely align with the expectations of the peer review committees, which were typically made up of younger, specialized authorities. Every review seemed to end up with a lot of questions, sometimes rancor. One such review session had taken place two weeks ago. The team's latest proposal once again had made the short list. As in the past, there had been questions on objectives, how they fit in with a coherent program of research. Once again the team had had to explain why their program was not coherent; in fact, why it would deliberately continue to be so. Caleb and his friends were not doing systematic research. Rather they were on an exploratory mission. Even though they had their suspicions about where their work was headed, they wanted to remain as open minded as possible to new, unexpected discoveries.

Chapter 6
The End Cap
(October 1828)

Henry woke up as per usual at first light, 6:30 a.m. He liked to get up early, even if he had nothing much in particular planned for the day. He did not hear Johnny yet, he would let the boy sleep.

First light varied during the course of the 401-day year, but only by an hour. Last light varied more, from 7:00 p.m. to 10:00 p.m. The Terans had scheduled the Main Ship's lighting system this way partly to break up the monotony of a constant regimen, partly to maintain the illusion of changing seasons. They varied the temperature to match, again, not by as much as one would normally encounter on the surface of a habitable planet.

The living space of the ship was maintained to resemble the climate at mid-latitudes on the continental interior of Teran; an average daily high of 75 degrees to low of 40 degrees. During the year the high could swing from 55 to 95, the low from 20 to 60. A major difference from their home world was that they avoided drastic daily variations, keeping the low range warmer. Rain was usually scheduled to come at night, although the occasional afternoon shower was thrown in on the hottest days of summer. The forward end where Caleb lived was elevated above the central region. It was kept cooler; it often snowed there on the colder nights.

The aft end of the ship was warmer and dryer, almost a desert in places.

Henry got out of bed, put on his robe, and headed to the bathroom. After relieving himself, followed by a splash of water on his face, he made his way to the kitchen for breakfast. Caleb was still asleep, so he sat down by himself to start in on his usual cold cereal with milk and fruit. He thought this morning he would begin with a simple walk in the woods. He had a lot to talk about with Caleb, but didn't feel like it yet. In fact he didn't feel any pressure to do much of anything.

After finishing breakfast, he went in to wake up Johnny. Once the boy had eaten, Henry proposed a hike. Johnny ran back to the bedroom to get dressed.

Henry was a tall man, considerably taller and more muscular than average, at the same time he was on the slender side. He believed in regular, strenuous exercise, maintaining his regimen of walking, running, biking, and weight training well into middle age, past the point where most others had stopped such pursuits. He also kept his reflexes sharp by regularly playing ball games on a competitive basis with men and women half his age.

They headed out the door in old clothes and hiking boots. Johnny wanted to see the end cap so they would travel uphill in that direction, but Henry would not tell him right away that it was their destination.

He was not sure the boy could handle the four miles and one thousand feet of elevation gain involved. If it turned out to be too much, they would circle around in the woods back to the cabin. Later they could take a cart some or all of the way to allow Johnny to get to the cap.

Henry found the path end ward at the bottom of the small road that led up to the cabin. As they walked, time seemed to stand still. His awareness was focused on the trees and bushes along the trail, the occasional bird singing in the distance. The air fresh and cool. It was not tough for him to figure out why Caleb loved this place immensely. Henry did, as well. He cherished the time he spent up here, but he also needed human contact, much more than his friend. That was why he lived down on the plains at midship with most everyone else. It was the best place for him at this time of his life, the best place to do the work he enjoyed so much. Maybe someday that would change, he allowed himself to surmise.

As distance on the trail accumulated, Johnny showed no sign of tiring. He was turning out to be a good hiking companion. He stayed with the pace Henry set without complaint. He asked questions about things they saw along the trail but did not chatter a lot, which was remarkable for a child of five. Henry already knew that his son was mature for his age. He was quickly moving beyond the behavior of typical children.

The air warmed as midmorning approached. They took a break along a small stream for a drink of water. No sign of Click, but Henry knew the robot was nearby in case it was needed. They carried their own provisions, so would probably not see the robot all day. *Another forty-five minutes and we should be close*, he guessed. He looked ahead on the trail, up above the treetops, he could not yet see it. The end cap, the ship's forward bulkhead, was up there somewhere. It was the same color as the sky, Henry knew it could be tough to spot until they were almost up to it.

Finally the trees ended, the trail stopped in front of a pitch of broken rock. The end cap was in sight a few hundred yards away.

"Wow!" Johnny exclaimed. "It's the end cap! Why didn't you tell me we were coming here?"

"I wanted it to be a surprise," Henry replied. "Frankly, I was not sure you could make it all the way on the trail, I did not want you to be disappointed if you could not. I see now I needn't have worried."

Johnny made a face, as if to say, *what are you talking about? This was easy.*

Oh, he is already starting to act like a teenager, Henry thought. *What are we in for?*

They scrambled up on the rocks to the catwalk that ringed the end cap. They turned to look out on the interior of the ship, or at least the portion they could see. Henry pulled out his binoculars. In the far distance he could see Lake Soliton and the beginnings of drier grazing land beyond. He could not see the aft end of the ship. It was a hundred miles away. He drew his gaze in toward the foreground. At twenty miles he could barely make out the buildings of the town they had left the previous afternoon. He saw smaller garden plots on the immediate outskirts with larger farm fields stretching out in all directions.

He followed the interior curvature up to the left spotting the next town over from theirs. At night, when the artificial sunlight was off, he could have followed the curvature to the town directly opposite, then completed the circle to arrive back where he started. If they followed the catwalk halfway around the end cap, their view would be the reverse. Ninety-five years onboard, Henry still marveled at the thought.

Despite spending that much time on the ship, living his life in a society for which such things had been second nature for millennia, he couldn't help feeling a tingle or two when confronted with such stark evidence of the reality of their situation: inside a spinning cylinder one hundred miles long, twenty-five miles in diameter traveling at one-tenth the speed of light. Though the technology was impressive, the thought of where they were always frightened him a bit. Healthy reactions, he allowed. If one was not at least a little awed, it would be a sure sign of pending senility, while the fear showed that one was sane.

After spending over an hour sightseeing on the catwalk, they descended to take a longer, indirect path home, which Johnny handled with ease.

The next several days passed in much the same way as the first; a morning walk, the afternoon spent reading or keeping in touch with friends and family, the evenings reminiscing with Caleb.

Johnny spent much of his time roaming nearby with Caleb's dog, always followed by Click to answer his frequent questions and keep an eye on him. In the evenings, Johnny sat in front of the video wall working on his lessons.

During the morning walks, Henry's mind turned frequently to the question of what he wanted to do next. It was not that remaining with the probe team was so unappealing. The group had been together for many years;

he knew its members well. They worked together effort-lessly. He enjoyed the work and liked the people, staying with it would be easy. Yet, he knew he was at a crossroads, it was time to change, but to what?

He liked to do things that provided tangible feedback. Propulsion engineering had been the perfect area for this when he reached the end of his upbringing period at age thirty-five. The ship had left Epsilon Indi thirty years before, it would be ten years until the first Sol probe set was sent out. At that point they were applying anything and everything new they had learned to eke out the last bit of performance from the propulsion system to boost the probes to the highest speed possible. It was an exciting time to be working on the probes, it had a natural appeal for him.

He knew change would not be easy, mainly because he didn't really have any other serious interests. His hobbies ran toward physical activities rather than useful crafts or the arts. Most people acquired a couple of side interests along the way. When they found themselves at a natural career checkpoint, especially after their first career, they frequently slid right into one of these, making it a full-time pursuit. In this way many second careers involved things such as painting, music, carpentry, or horticulture. In a lifetime as long as the Terans', there would be plenty of time later on to take up another, more technical endeavor. Henry's exclusive focus on his work meant he was now the proverbial clean slate. Everything and nothing had appeal. It would take time, long talks with Lucy, plus guidance from Caleb to sort it out.

Finally, on the last night of the week, Henry broached the subject with Caleb at the end of dinner. They had gotten up from the table to move closer to the warmth of the fire. Henry paused a moment, then said quietly, "Cal, how did you go about deciding to switch careers? After a week, I feel at a loss on how to proceed. The only thing I have concluded is that I do need and want to make a change." He would never ask directly for a recommendation. Besides, Caleb would never directly make one. That was not how the mentoring process worked, although he was sure Caleb had some ideas, perhaps a very specific area that would best suit Henry's character and abilities as well as the ship's needs.

"Henry, I would look to where we are going," Caleb replied after a bit.

"The Alpha Centauri system?"

"No. After that."

"Sol. I'm not going to Sol."

"I was thinking more along the lines of what may need to be done before anyone gets there."

That was all Caleb said. He turned away from the fire, walked a few steps to one of the rockers behind them, and sat down. Henry remained standing for several minutes before finally doing the same.

He started talking as he sat. "Well, I guess it's the third planet, the one with the oxygen you are thinking of. That star, Sol, 4.5 billion years old; surely a lot of time for things to happen on that planet. But we know almost nothing about it."

"Much preparation will be needed," was Caleb's only response. He left it at that for the evening.

The next day Henry went walking alone to think. As he strolled through the apple orchards, he wondered, *what makes Caleb think Sol's third planet would need such attention? We have little information, mainly telescope images and spectroscopy results showing a variety of chemicals present in the planet's atmosphere. We won't get any probe reports until after the Main Ship gets to Alpha Centauri.*

In many ways Sol was similar to Alpha Centauri A. Both stars were spectral type G2, luminosity class V. Sol was slightly smaller, and two-thirds as bright. It was younger, at 4.5 billion years versus 5.0 billion. The main difference was Alpha Centauri A's two companion stars. Proxima Centauri was a much smaller dwarf that orbited A and B at a distance of a quarter light-year. A and B themselves were separated by two to three light-hours. Both had small ensembles of inner stony planets. Due to their separation distance, each was positioned with respect to the other where an outer gas giant planet would ordinarily be located. A and B each had a planet in its habitable zone.

The planet at Alpha Centauri A harbored a well-established set of primitive life forms. It had an atmosphere with elevated oxygen levels, liquid water, reasonably uniform temperatures and weather conditions—vital for supporting hydrocarbon-based life, the only type of life they knew. The planet had an essentially circular orbit, which assured uniform heating from the star, which itself was not violent. At five billion years of age, it had several billion years of stable life remaining before its hydrogen was exhausted and it swelled up into a red giant. When that happened, the inner two planets would be engulfed, the life-bearing one would be roasted to a crisp.

Data from the orbiters told them a green carpet of life had crept from the shores of the seas outward across the broad, flat coastal zone. The mountain foothills were beginning to be assaulted. In the lowlands extensive forests of tree ferns up to a hundred feet tall flourished. They were practically impenetrable to the robot landers, and populated by crawling and flying insects the size of a Teran's arm.

This had been going on for hundreds of millions of years, yet the land was only partly covered by life. Oxygen levels were just getting to the point where larger oxygen-breathing life forms could survive and begin to flourish.

The planet had been lucky. Its major continents had either formed in or drifted to the equatorial regions. Subsequent tectonic drift had kept them at low latitudes or returned them there if they wandered away. Such a configuration kept the planet's temperature relatively uniform, since cold waters at high latitudes were free to circulate to be warmed at low latitudes.

The planet in Alpha Centauri B's habitable zone had not been as fortunate. Its landmasses were concentrated at or near high latitudes, the south pole was completely covered by one. To compound matters, the planet's rotational axis was steeply inclined, lying almost on its side. As a result, a large part of one hemisphere was always in sunlight while the other was in perpetual darkness for half the year. There were no seasons, only an enormous climatic transition from north to south. With polar continents blocking effective ocean circulation, global climate had become highly unbalanced. Even so, the orbiters found evidence of abundant single-celled life forms. Not much to show for five billion years, though.

Proxima Centauri was still bleaker. Because of its small size and low heat output, its habitable zone was close in to the star. So close, in fact, that its one potentially life-bearing planet's rotation was gravitationally locked. It completed three rotations on its axis for every two trips around the star. It was a barren, lifeless rock, its atmosphere and oceans having long ago been stripped away by the star's solar wind.

The Main Ship would stop at Alpha Centauri A, its third planet would become the center of the Terans' attention. They would build a HUB, construct habitats, the ship would be prepared for the trip to Sol.

"What did Caleb suspect concerning Sol c?" Henry repeated to himself. He figured it might be interesting to find out, subsequently he got to work examining the available data.

Chapter 7
Lessons
(October 1828)

The next day Henry decided to spend some more time alone. Johnny and Caleb went out together.

"Well, how do you like life in the woods, Johnny?" Caleb asked as they strolled off from the cabin.

"It's so cool," Johnny replied.

"Yes, I suppose so," Caleb said. "Lots of new things to see and do. How are your lessons going? Are you able to keep up given the distractions?"

"My lessons are going okay, but I was wondering. What were you doing on the video wall?"

"I'm doing my lessons, too."

"Really? I thought you were retired."

"I am, even so, I still do lessons. Why are you surprised? I'm sure you've seen your father doing his."

"Well, yes, but he's on the probe team, they have lots to do," Johnny said.

"Don't you have things you just enjoy doing?" Caleb asked.

"Yes, I like to read about dinosaurs. I found them in the library after Mom and Dad gave me access."

"I know you do, I've been watching."

"What is it you like to do, Uncle Caleb?"

"Well, what you saw me doing was research on the planets at Sol, but what I most like to do is study old things too. It's called history."

"Wow, history is all about dinosaurs?"

"Well, not just dinosaurs. There is a lot that happened long ago and not so long ago that is as interesting as dinosaurs."

"Would you give me a history lesson when we get back?" Johnny asked.

"Certainly, I would love to," Caleb answered.

Back at the cabin, Johnny and Caleb sat down for a lunch of ham-and-cheese sandwiches. Johnny had a glass of milk, Caleb a cup of coffee. After getting some chocolate chip cookies for dessert, they walked over to the video wall.

"Lesson one," Caleb began as they sat down. "Where do you want to begin?"

"With the dinosaurs," Johnny said.

"That was a long, long time ago. Why don't we start with something a bit more recent, such as when our ship started out?"

"Okay, tell me why we left Teran."

"Sure, let's start with a little on space travel and why the ship was built. The most fundamental aspect of outer space is that there is lot of it. So much that it is practically the only thing out there—I bet you already knew that."

"I saw it out in the dome at the probe launch." Johnny replied excitedly.

"You know, then, that it is mostly empty, lacking anything except occasional small particles. Distances between bigger objects, namely stars, are immense.

"Now, when planning a trip through deep space, you want, as with any trip, to avoid boredom as much as possible. Otherwise the passengers get restless. Pleasant surroundings with plenty of distracting in-route activities can help relieve the tedium of particularly featureless stretches, therefore we built this big ship to live in while traveling. But ultimately you must get somewhere. The most successful voyages get to a place that is interesting and entertaining as quickly as possible. You also have to get someplace useful, since any traveler eventually must replenish consumables. In outer space interesting, entertaining and useful places to visit usually involve stars."

"So that's why we're going to Alpha Centauri?"

"Yes, stars in this part of the Milky Way galaxy tend to be spaced roughly eight light-years apart. Do you know what a light-year is?"

"No, I know what a year is and I know what light is, but not both together."

"Okay, let's do a little experiment. Turn off the display screen, then turn it back on."

Johnny did as he was asked.

"Now," said Caleb, "how long did it take between when you turned the screen back on and you saw what was in the screen?"

"No time at all, it happened at once."

"That was how it appeared because light moves extremely fast. Much faster than our ship. In fact, if this display was back on Epsilon Indi, it would take eight years for its light to get to us here. We call that distance eight light-years, one-eighth of it is one light-year."

"It's a big distance, then?"

"Yes, very big. It takes light many years to travel between stars. Even this amount of time between stops can be too much for some travelers, so why go when you know it will take much, much longer?"

"To see things?" Johnny replied.

"Yes, if you had asked the people involved, they would have given a dozen or more familiar reasons: adventure, curiosity, or escape. Like your hike to the end cap, they wanted to see things, new things. Together, everyone in our planet wide society decided long ago to send these ships out to the stars because we are looking for something. It is a search, one in which everyone who goes knows they will not return home. In this respect we are similar to emigrants, leaving for good to travel to an unknown land. We are on a search for new life, other life on planets around distant stars. Such as the planet at Epsilon Indi that the ship left from."

"Why not stay there, since it had life on it?" Johnny asked.

"A reasonable question—you are quite a bright five-year-old. The life on Epsilon Indi is not very intelligent. We are looking for life like us that can build a civilization. Some of us have continued on with the ship to keep searching.

"You can read more on the ship's travels, but you know the launch of the ship was not the beginning. As you get older, you will read about Teran, its history and the events that led to the launch of this ship and many others. If you want we can talk over these things as your lessons progress."

"I would like that a lot," Johnny said.

Just then they heard the screen door slam. It was Henry coming in from his walk. "I see you two have been occupying yourselves nicely," he said.

"Uncle Caleb has been giving me history lessons."

"Well, Cal, working on another convert, huh?" Henry kidded. Caleb's interest in history was widely known, he talked about it to anyone who would listen.

"No recruiting necessary. He was already studying it. Didn't you know?"

"I guess the launch distracted me from keeping close tabs on what he has been up to. I'll have to ask his mother, although she has not mentioned it. So, Johnny, you have taken an interest in history. When did this start?"

"With dinosaurs, Dad. They're cool. Then I sort of started looking around at other stuff from way back then."

Henry smiled and shook his head.

Chapter 8
Sol c
(November 1828)

Henry ended up spending six weeks with Caleb. Johnny went back home to Lucy after the first two; he was missing his mother and playmates; he needed to spend time with the rest of his upbringing group. Henry's time was consumed by looking at everything he could find on Sol's third planet.

They knew the basic physical properties of the star: size, age, spectral class, luminosity. It was similar to their home star in many respects. Of the third planet there was less information, gathered exclusively from the telescope arrays, as the probes were not yet close enough to produce useful details. It had a circular orbit that was at the right distance from the star to allow for the presence of liquid water, plus it had an oxygen-nitrogen atmosphere.

The ship's telescope systems comprised groups of individual instruments spread out in wide arrays in the space surrounding the ship. There were microwave, infrared, optical, ultraviolet, gamma ray, and X-ray telescopes. Their combined detectors covered the entire electromagnetic spectrum. They could be used singly or in combination to observe any astronomical phenomena. To look at a planet near to another star required the highest resolution possible, an entire array would need to be used at its fullest capacity.

Consequently, they could examine any object in the sky in a wide variety of ways to determine its size, shape, and composition. The resolution obtained depended on the wavelength of the energy being received and the diameter of the telescope array. In the case of optical observations, when the data from the individual instruments was combined, that diameter was close to five thousand miles. Even so, when pointing at a planet in orbit around a star that was five light-years away, they could not make out much surface detail.

From that distance their visible-light telescopes were capable of seeing features that were in principle two miles across. Because of the planet's atmosphere, however, this lower limit was reduced to four miles except at high surface elevations where there was little moisture in the air. Visible-light images allowed them to identify major surface features such as mountain ranges, oceans, deserts, and large green areas covering major portions of the land that were probably savannas or forests. They also revealed the south polar ice cap. Because of the direction of the ship's approach, they could not see the northern polar region. Nor could they see any of the northern hemisphere above 30 degrees latitude.

One specific thing they were interested in was surface brightness or albedo, a measure of how much of the incident light from Sol was reflected and at what wavelengths. This would tell them something on surface composition and temperature. Early on they were satisfied with a general reading that could tell them about the existence of water in the atmosphere. This was an important first step toward determining the planet's moisture level. As they got closer, more detailed measurements became possible. They were able to see large cloud systems leading to an understanding of weather patterns.

From the telescopes they could analyze the atmosphere using spectroscopy. Because molecular compounds emit light at characteristic wavelengths, called colors in the optical region, the various compounds could be detected by studying the emission lines they formed on the recorded spectra. Sol c's atmosphere contained the expected amounts of water vapor, oxygen, nitrogen, carbon dioxide, ozone, plus trace compounds such as nitrous oxide, methane, and sulfur dioxide.

Another thing they established was the presence of radiation belts around the planet, which revealed the presence of a strong magnetic field. This was important for life because it helped shield the surface from harmful radiation. It also indicated the presence of a dynamic planetary interior of flowing material and the high likelihood of drifting tectonic plates. The absence of plate tectonics on such a planet usually meant, from the Terans' experience, a world covered by a half mile or more of water. A lack of continental development, movement and eventual collisions, resulting in recycling of large amounts of crustal material to form mountains, meant the surface would always remain flat and below sea level. If the occasional isolated volcano emerged, it would be quickly leveled by erosion.

Henry knew well that making optical images of a planet was a difficult process. It involved blocking or otherwise avoiding the intense light from the planet's nearby star. Early on the image of Sol's third planet was a fuzzy spot. The Terans kept having problems locating the planet, because it was never quite where they expected it to be. They suspected that a companion was perturbing its orbit slightly; unfortunately, since they were approaching the plane of the Solar System at an angle from below, they could not use standard transit methods to detect it. They did computer modeling of possible two- and multi-body combinations but could never come up with a result that matched the observed perturbations. Then as they got closer, an image showed a second, close by fuzzy spot.

This came as a surprise. Not that a companion had been detected, because they had expected something for a while, but because they were able to observe it at all. It had to be a major fraction of the size of the main planet to be detectable at that distance. They reran the two-body model with a range of extremely large companions, quickly getting a good match. The planet's moon was over two thousand miles in diameter, much larger than any they had previously found orbiting an inner planet. Moons this size had been found frequently with outer gas giants, this occurrence, however, was unprecedented. Teran had a pair of more modest sized moons, neither more than five hundred miles in diameter.

As they got closer, the presence of a large moon was a startling discovery. The moon's gravitational influence made for a very stable system. This planet would not suffer from wide variations in its rotational tilt. Such variations led to extremely volatile climates that inhibited the development and evolution of life.

Henry said to Caleb, "Aside from that big moon, it looks pretty normal for a large inner planet, not that different from Alpha Centauri A c."

"There are subtle differences," Caleb replied.

He didn't say what they were—which was like Caleb. Henry thought Caleb already had it figured out, ever the teacher, he wanted Henry to discovery it on his own.

Henry got back to work. That is, he went for a walk to think about the problem, or, rather, to deliberately not think about the problem. His mind was full of data; lots of small conclusions and connections, just no big picture. He needed to clear his head to let his subconscious work for a while. Something would pop up soon enough. It always did.

Hours later, Henry rushed in the house straight to the video wall. He went feverishly to work and continued past midnight.

The next morning at breakfast with Caleb, he announced his conclusion, which was really his dilemma. "The presence of trace compounds such as carbon monoxide, nitrous oxide, and sulfur dioxide are not unusual for a planet of this type. The overall amounts are within the range of what we have seen elsewhere. What is unusual is the distribution and concentration of sulfur dioxide. There are a couple areas of concentration that are fairly small, right at the limit of resolution for the strongest sulfur dioxide absorption lines. At roughly twenty miles across, they all occur along seacoasts."

"What does this mean?" asked Caleb. "Volcanic activity is the most obvious explanation, but no evidence of volcanic activity shows up anywhere near these locations on the—admittedly low resolution—visible imagery of the surface."

"Yes," said Henry, "that is the dilemma."

For the next three years they would be able to do additional observing. However, once the Main Ship began its deceleration phase, continuing until it was stationed in orbit at Alpha Centauri A, they would have no new information from the telescope arrays. The last data they would have on Sol c would be obtained immediately before the arrays were shut down.

During deceleration, the telescope arrays would have to be brought back to the Main Ship and docked on the exterior of the hull. They could not reliably maintain the accurate alignment of the individual telescopes in the array formation while decelerating. They would not be able to do any high resolution observing. Over the five years of the deceleration, they would be completely refurbished.

The arrays would be redeployed while at Alpha Centauri, little new information concerning Sol would be added, however. At four-plus light-years they would still be too far away. The arrays would be stowed again for acceleration. Once the acceleration phase at the beginning of the crossing from Alpha Centauri to Sol was completed, followed by a few weeks of testing and calibration, they would be ready to begin serious observing again.

Long before that they would start getting much higher resolution, close-up probe data, which would definitively settle the question of what kind of life forms inhabited the planet.

Before leaving Caleb's, Henry made contact with several members of the astrophysics group that concentrated on studies of planets orbiting nearby stars. There was an entire subgroup devoted to Sol c, he joined up. He knew little about astronomy or planetary physics but was familiar with instrumentation in general and well versed in computational science. None of this really mattered, though. Henry was interested, that was all the existing team members needed to hear. He would learn as he went. Besides, joining a team was only a formality. He could have easily gone off on his own, but he liked working in a group, preferring to be part of a formal organization.

Henry busied himself with studying the characteristics of Teran and the many other planets encountered during the past five thousand years by the ships in the fleet. He also spent a lot of time looking through the data archives to get familiar with the types of observations that could be done at various distances so he would know when they would be able to detect specific phenomena. This would tell them something on what to expect. Nevertheless, he knew there would be surprises.

Chapter 9
Air Pollution
(March 1829)

It had been right in front of him from the start, Henry realized.

Like many people, when Henry took a break from working on a difficult problem, in this case, the five days attending a conference of the Sol c investigative groups, it frequently resulted in a fresh look at the problem. Often this led to new ideas that could restart stalled progress.

He had spent much of his time in the four months leading up to the conference studying reports produced by the teams doing investigative studies, including Caleb's. Now he reimmersed himself in the raw data.

Finally he was sure he knew what Caleb had been talking about. He sent Caleb a v-mail before leaving for the forward end of the ship.

Henry arrived late in the afternoon, Caleb was out. *Probably pruning in the orchard*, Henry thought. It was early March, a great time to be up in the woods. Crisp, clear mornings with cool, sunny afternoons. He was looking forward to some fresh maple syrup from the sap that was finishing its run.

He spotted a note displayed on the kitchen table where it was sure to be seen: "Henry, I'll be along by 6:30 for dinner. Make yourself at home."

Henry did just that; or, rather, Clack did, getting Henry's stuff put away in the guestroom. Henry went out onto the porch to enjoy the remaining afternoon sunshine.

"So, Cal," Henry declared as he pushed himself back from the dinner table, "let's talk about the atmospheric gases."

They had spent the meal discussing family, friends, and of course the maple sap harvest. Caleb knew why Henry was there; he had viewed his v-mail that morning.

Caleb got up. "Let's sit by the fireplace," he suggested.

It cooled off quickly in the evenings at this point in the early spring. Clack finished clearing the table, then came over to build a fire on the hearth when it noticed them heading that way.

"Bet you missed it the first couple times through the data. I certainly did," Caleb began. "What finally clinched it for you?"

"The carbon dioxide, sulfur dioxide, and methane levels in the atmosphere," Henry replied. "Once I realized they could be accounted for by glaciation cycles, everything fell into place.

"During periods of glaciation, concentrations of carbon dioxide and methane in the atmosphere naturally moved down. In the times between glaciations they rose back up. In contrast, sulfur dioxide levels should remain low and fairly steady with the occasional spike from a large volcanic eruption. There ought to be a fairly uniform distribution with the only concentrated areas around and downwind of active volcanoes. Instead, there seems to be small, steady, low-level sources of the three gases in a few specific locations along the seacoasts. It took a lot of time to come up with a plausible explanation.

"After eliminating everything the study teams had thought of, such as grazing animals, or increased venting from volcanic activity, I concluded that it had to be from burning coal. Now, there are many natural ways coal-burning could occur, but there is one other—industrialization. The latest spectra show the trends continuing. Sulfur dioxide, carbon dioxide, and methane rising together in these locations. I think we are looking at air pollution."

Caleb now spoke. "Yes, I think it's a dead lock for nascent industrialization. I thought so when you were up here last. I spent hours with the Teran history records looking over the same data. I was able to confirm that when we began industrialization, coal use increased dramatically. The absolute levels and rates of increase of those gases are very similar to what we are seeing from Sol c. I'd bet they are still in the early stages. Rail transportation is probably just starting."

"It never occurred to me to look in the Teran records for analogs," Henry replied. "What made you think of it?"

"Now, Henry, I'm surprised at you," Caleb chided. "I tried, with little success, to get you to study history when you were a boy."

"Yeah, yeah . . . it rated right up there with piano lessons and lima beans. I was always more interested in sports."

"Cal, I can start contacting the analysis groups in the morning. So far none of them have made the sulfur dioxide–methane–carbon dioxide connection. At least, they have not made anything public."

"Before you do," said Caleb, "I need to introduce you to some friends of mine. We call ourselves the Geezers. We've have been working on this problem for a long time. I'll set up a video conference for tomorrow afternoon."

The two old friends then passed a quiet evening reading in front of the fire.

Henry helped out with the sugaring for a while in the morning, then went for a walk before lunch. In the afternoon, they had the video conference with the Geezers. After introductions, Caleb brought Henry up to speed on what they had been doing, covering the details of their latest telescope array proposal, which was due for another review in two weeks. He then ran through Henry's progress.

The Geezers knew who Henry was. This was not because he was close to Caleb. Henry's reputation as a leader and organizer was common knowledge on the ship. After a short discussion they agreed that Henry would join their group but also continue his work with the Sol c group. They considered a second independent line of investigation a sensible way to ensure multiple viewpoints.

Chapter 10
Caleb's Proposal
(March 1829)

Caleb opened a window on the video wall for the telescope array conference, which he called the mini inquisition. He understood why the time allocation committee had to scrutinize every request, that didn't mean he had to like it. If only they didn't feel the need to quiz him and his colleagues at length on every detail. He supposed he should be happy the proposals were not rejected out of hand.

"Caleb," began the central figure of the three facing him on the screen. "An investigation of air pollution. You have outdone yourself this time—five hundred hours in five-hour increments over one hundred days, and not any one hundred days, the last hundred before we bring in the arrays."

Helen, the committee member who had spoken, never asked questions. She simply made statements. It always disconcerted Caleb, he usually responded to whatever she said last, ignoring the rest.

"We will be looking for very weak spectral lines in a fairly small area," said Caleb. "These spectral lines will be buried in the background noise due to the low concentrations of gases we are expecting. We need as much observing time as possible to build up signal to noise, the longer we wait to start, the closer we get to Sol c and the better the resolution.

That's why we want to crowd right up to the shutdown of the arrays."

The committee member to Helen's right joined in. "Yes, that much is obvious, but you are asking for a lot of time. We are a bit puzzled by the five-hour increments. What exactly are you expecting to find?"

At least he asked a question, Caleb thought, then said, "We don't know yet what we are looking for. That's why we want the time. What we do know is where we want to look. The anomalies are in a specific area of one of the triangular continents. The planet's rotation combined with our angle of approach forces us to observe during those hours when we are most directly pointed at the anomalies. Obviously it does us no good to record data when the continent is on the opposite side out of sight."

Caleb went on to describe the rotational and orbital dynamics involved, which explained the need for a five-hour window and why it had to be constantly shifted. He finished by saying that the modeling data in the proposal indicated they would need at least three hundred hours of clear observing to obtain the resolution they needed. Given the general weather patterns on that part of the planet, it would take five hundred hours of observing to get three hundred usable hours.

The discussion went on for another thirty minutes, with the team members adding comments along the way. Ultimately it came down to whether Caleb's group could convince the committee that what they were doing would produce more-important results than other proposals competing for the same period. Even a negative result would do, provided a useful or interesting question was addressed. The problem was, they were proposing to investigate what they were calling an "air pollution anomaly." They were speculating that the source of the anomaly could be industrial in nature. It was a big leap from measurements of a few common gases in the air to the presence of beings advanced enough to produce significant amounts of industrial air pollutants.

The committee signed off, the video-con window closed. Caleb stayed on a few minutes for some final words with his teammates. He got up to walk out onto the porch, talking to himself as he sat down in the rocker.

"They'll let us know in a few weeks. Until then, we'll have to keep our fingers crossed. I sure wish we had something else to go on to build our case." He put his head back and dozed off in the late afternoon warmth.

He was startled awake an hour later by the chiming of the message bell. He had it set to do this for a few select correspondents. He immediately went inside to see who it was. Helen's face was on the screen, she began to talk as soon as Caleb walked in front of the video wall.

"Caleb, I wanted to contact you personally, in an unofficial capacity. The three of us want to grant your time, we will recommend it to the whole screening committee, however, we already know that in its current state it is not likely to be approved. I want to run a proposition by you."

Caleb nodded his head in assent.

"I believe we can get it accepted on a contingency basis," Helen continued, "if additional supporting data can be provided by the time you want to start observing. This means you will need to find evidence that gives us an idea of what the air pollution anomalies might mean, how they can be connected to industrial sources."

"Sounds like we don't have much of a choice, I guess we will accept," Caleb replied after a moment. The team had discussed this possibility several times and were already in agreement.

"You are right. I'll inform the rest of the subcommittee then take it to the main committee for final approval."

"I'll tell the others we have more work to do," Caleb responded.

"Good luck!" Helen said as she signed off.

"The good news is we have two years to come up with something," Caleb muttered to himself.

Chapter 11
More Evidence
(1829 - 1832)

Biological evolution was present on Sol c. Most likely it had been going on for a very long time, given the stability of Sol during the past several billion years. Caleb's team was proposing to investigate what they believed to be direct evidence of an industrialized civilization. If confirmed, it would be a dramatic event. Neither they nor any of their sister ships, at least none within the limits of communication at light speed, had encountered higher-level conscious beings. The most advanced had been large sea creatures. The land-based biological systems observed to date had not evolved past basic plant forms, vegetation was abundant only within a few hundred feet of sea level.

Caleb had been focusing his attention on a particular area of the farther-south-reaching continent. There were two locations along the eastern coast near 35 degrees south latitude that showed peculiar spectroscopic anomalies. He knew that all molecules absorbed and readmitted photons, light, at characteristic frequencies. These showed up as lines on a spectrograph, the combination of lines for a given molecule acted like a fingerprint. The atmosphere in the areas he was studying contained barely detectible, elevated amounts of carbon dioxide, methane, and sulfur dioxide. The areas were close to the coasts. Given the low resolution of the images, it was difficult to tell if they were on land or sea or both.

Volcanic activity was a prime candidate as a source of the gases. There were numerous active volcanoes along the western coast of the continent, they were identifiable by their gaseous plumes, which could be tracked as they spread and dispersed. The anomalies Caleb was studying, while not much more intense than the dispersed volcanic plumes, seemed to be fairly stationary. They disappeared after strong weather events, signaled by movement of dense clouds across the region. But the plumes soon returned, indicating that the carbon dioxide, sulfur dioxide, and methane were being produced locally.

Since there was no volcanic activity in the area, this could not be the source of the anomalies. Natural organic processes in combination with combustion of plant and animal material or fossil fuels could also account for these trace gases. Swamps could be responsible for the methane. Plants, trees, and burning coal could account for the rest. Perhaps there were coal deposits at the surface or oil seeps that had been ignited by lightning or forest fires. Large herds of grazing animals were an alternative possible source of methane. However, there was no seasonal movement of the gas, as might be expected from migrating herds. The location remained constant.

Caleb sat in front of the wall screen reading from the dozens of windows he had opened. They overlapped, sometimes completely hiding one another. All were from the history archives, accounts of civilization on Teran along with old reports of chemical analyses of its atmosphere from numerous different places and times.

Caleb was sure he was seeing isolated areas of industrial air pollution. His many hours of reading, cross referencing, and doing supporting calculations convinced him that the evidence was good, but not compelling. He bookmarked the key data and closed his work folders. He would rest for a few days, putting aside active research, to let his subconscious mind turn things over while he tended to other matters.

Henry, as well, continued to think about the atmospheric data from Sol c. He agreed that it looked a lot like pollution. He had not read much history, but he quickly became enthralled by their home planet's industrialization era. He found it a fascinating time of invention, introduction of revolutionary new technologies, with fantastic stories of the people who had made it happen. Resources had been exploited, vast new markets had been created, fortunes made and lost. It was a time of enormous change, constant risk taking, rapid rises and sudden falls. It was also a time of incredible ruin for the planet. Little regard had been given to the quality of its land, water, and air, which were sacrificed in the name of progress. It was those times he sought out now in the archives.

It took him a few days to find what he was looking for: air-quality reports from major cities that broke down the different chemical pollutants. Sulfur dioxide, methane, and carbon dioxide led the list. There were a number of trace gases including nitrous oxide, carbon monoxide, ozone, and a large number of volatile organic compounds, or VOCs for short.

The VOCs in particular were among the expected standard pollutants produced by an emerging industrial society that used plant or animal oils, or fossil fuels for most heating, lighting, cooking, and transportation. Caleb's Geezers had found hints of a number of organic compounds, but the spectral lines were extremely weak. It had been difficult to identify specific ones with any certainty. Concentrations of these gases should have been detectable, given a large enough population with a high density combined with a significant level of industrialization. Henry turned to a couple of friends who, like Caleb, were interested in the history of their home planet.

Barry's and Sandy's faces popped up on the screen at 4:00 that afternoon as Henry sat down in his easy chair. "Thanks for linking in on such short notice," he said.

"My pleasure," Barry cheerily shot back. "I was just reading."

Sandy responded that she was happy to talk with them, apologizing for making them wait until 4:00. She had been doing lessons with her niece. They spent a few minutes catching up. Sandy's niece was the prime topic; everyone was always interested to hear from someone active in an upbringing group.

Henry then quickly reviewed the files he had forwarded. Sandy had not had a chance to look at them, Barry had already given them a quick read. He pointed out the similarities between the Sol c data and the industrial pollution data from back home.

"Well, the gases present on Sol c match the pollutants from the industrial age of Teran, but there are alternative explanations for their presence," Barry pointed out.

"Yes. What do the planetary chemists say?" asked Sandy.

Henry reviewed the section of Caleb's observation proposal that discussed possible sources. "This was supplied by the chemists. The gases can all be explained by one or more natural mechanism, although we don't see any evidence of these mechanisms in the locations where we are detecting them," he said.

Sandy summarized, "The only gases we can identify are consistent with, but cannot be used to definitively identify an industrial source. I think we should focus on the VOCs. There are many VOCs, certain ones or combinations might indicate a unique source."

"Caleb and I have discussed this a couple of times," Henry said, "We cannot identify any one VOC in particular because there are very few spectral lines that are strong enough. We can see a line that could be hexane, but companion lines that would confirm it are below the noise level. Sometimes there are two good lines that can be either one VOC or parts of two different ones. There is not enough good data to narrow it down to one particular compound."

Sandy replied, "I think it might be useful to study home world VOC data in general during the whole of the period of our early industrial growth phase beginning with matching pollutants with sources without reference to anything else."

"Yes," said Barry. "That way we can build a time line of compounds to expect as industrialization progresses. Each point in time will have a characteristic set of spectral lines that represents the major chemical compounds that are present. We then compare against the lines we see from the Sol c data. We won't see all the lines, but the best match with the strong ones we do see should tell us roughly where they are on the industrialization time line."

"So we work the problem indirectly from the Teran history data. Makes sense to me," Henry replied enthusiastically. "I'll get started right away."

"Don't forget us," Barry shot back.

"Yeah," said Sandy. "You have really teased us with this project."

"Okay, then," answered Henry. "Let's go."

It took the better part of three weeks working together to slowly unravel the constituents of the Teran data by isolating each source and analyzing them one by one, then building a profile of VOCs as industrialization developed. For instance, the era of intense gasoline-powered internal combustion engine use produced a distinct profile of pollutants, once the technology was adopted and as long as it was used, those gases would be present. The Sol c data did not include all the necessary VOCs in concentrations that matched the profile, since several key strong spectral lines that should have been detected were missing, therefore it had to predate gasoline-powered engine use. They did the same analysis on dozens of additional pollution producing technologies from power generation to transportation, heating and cooking, plus a long list of industrial processes.

As they progressed, they found they had eliminated all of the industrial technologies present in the city pollution reports from back home. They were starting to get a little desperate. What had they missed? They had succeeded in proving only that if it was pollution from an industrial society, it was at its earliest stages. Coal was probably being used for heat, and possibly for steam-powered engines. The methane was most likely produced by livestock. The presence of so many animals and related meat cooking might partially account for the animal oil pollutants they suspected. Finally, more digging provided the answer.

At the beginning of Teran's industrial revolution, various types of nonpetroleum fuels had been used on a wide scale for illumination. In the cities that participated early in the industrial era, the streets, homes, and factories had been lit with oil lamps. Some of this oil came from coal, a lot from alcohol- or turpentine-based products. A good deal also came from animal fats, especially large ocean creatures. This was the key. They now had a theory that could explain the types and relative amounts of gases seen in the VOC spectral lines in Caleb's Sol c data. They were observing the pollutants of an early industrial city with large stockyards, widespread use of coal fired engines for transportation and manufacturing, combined with alcohol, turpentine, and animal oil burning for cooking and illumination. Using the known detection threshold of the telescopes' spectrometers, they could estimate the size of the population by comparison to Teran statistics. The two suspected cities would have from 100,000 to 150,000 inhabitants.

They now had a hypothesis concerning a specific mechanism behind the pollution data they wanted to collect with the proposed array time. It could be related to known events in their home planet's past and calibrated with historical data to draw general conclusions about conditions on Sol c. They also had an alteration to Caleb's plan. Local nighttime observations should be added. We expect certain of the pollutants will increase after dark, peaking in the evening, then decline as cooking and lighting subsided. This type of prediction was vital for any theory's success. If it made a prediction that was verified, the theory gained credence.

Caleb's group got the five hundred hours of telescope time. Henry and his friends had come through; their analysis was compelling. They had a detailed theory with testable predictions that could be used to prove whether or not there was an early-stage industrial civilization on Sol c.

Once their observing began, things proceeded slowly. Nothing happened fast in astronomical research. They would have to accumulate data across numerous observing windows to get distinct results that would not be considered noise. This was complicated by the fact that not all of their hours were usable owing to the occasional presence of dense clouds in the region of interest. They needed clear, calm air to get the best data.

As the months progressed, a picture emerged that confirmed their theory, right down to the daily variation through the evening. The pollutants were concentrated in two specific areas that were becoming distinct as data was accumulated. In addition, it was clear that the sources of the pollution were always within the local region. The pollutants were not being conducted in from somewhere else.

Another group using the optical telescope array was studying the same region at the same time. This came about as a direct result of Caleb's updated proposal. The optical array committee took the extraordinary step of overriding time already allocated in order to attempt to determine if they could directly visualize the constructs of any nascent civilization that might be present. In January of 1832 the evidence was clear. They were able to detect, through accumulation of many hours of recording, a diffuse area of light during the local nighttime. At first it was an amorphous patch that could have been from a forest fire. But the patch persisted much longer than a fire would. They suspected they were seeing city lights.

Chapter 12
Star Travel
(July 1832)

Caleb's observations were completed at the end of June shortly before the array was brought in for the deceleration to Alpha Centauri A.

Johnny was approaching his ninth birthday and was able to travel by himself to Caleb's cabin. He went there often to see his uncle. Caleb had been progressively expanding his education in science, engineering, and, of course, history.

"Uncle Caleb, I want to know more about the ship. Tell me how it works. I also want to know everything on the probes."

"Well, those are pretty big areas. Suppose we start with an overview," Caleb replied.

They started the narrative.

"Every component of every subsystem of every shipboard system has several groups of crew members devoted to maintaining them, as well as developing new and better versions. These days, changes come slowly, in small increments. Propulsion is extremely important, for example, since it is the system most directly connected to the time it takes to get from one star to the next. The Main Ship can now reach a cruising speed of 0.1c or 10 percent of the speed of light within five years after departure, at which point our fuel supply allotted for the acceleration phase is exhausted.

Even at this speed, it takes decades to get from one star to another. Nevertheless it is an enormous improvement over the first ship's propulsion system. After it was launched five thousand years ago, it took almost eight hundred years to travel the nine and a half light-years to our nearest neighboring star. This was more than three of our life spans."

"Oh, Uncle Caleb. I already know that stuff."

"Then let's step it up a bit," Caleb replied, smiling. "I guess I should not have expected to get away with that, huh?"

He skipped ahead to the next section.

"At our current speed, hospitable long-lived stars with planets in the habitable zone are close enough together, roughly five to fifteen light-years in this region of the Milky Way, to complete a crossing between stars in less than half an average lifetime. Now we can make the journey plus spend part of our lives at a star with a planetary system. This way no one misses out on either experience. In the beginning, one generation in four got to spend a part of their lives at a planet. As a result, we devoted a great deal of time and effort early on to constructing and perfecting an onboard environment that was comfortable and self-sustaining. It turned out that these two goals were not mutually exclusive. In fact they were complementary.

"Eventually, we got the speed problem under control. We could endure the time it took to travel from star to star, but there were other problems with traveling in deep space. The stars are constantly on the move. Worse still, not at uniform rates or along easily predictable paths.

"Turning, doing a midcourse correction, takes so much power that aside from minor shifts in direction we cannot do it unassisted; that is, only with the ship's engines. We need the strength of the gravity field around a star or large planet to do major course changes. Accurately navigating toward the destination star in an efficient manner is, therefore, very important. You would think that since you could look directly at a star through a telescope, you could quickly figure out the direction to head in order to get to it. Unfortunately, you are aiming at a moving target. It is not at that location anymore, it has moved on during the time it took its light to get to you and it will move further during the time it takes to get to it. You need to aim not where the star is when you start heading for it, but where it is going to be years in the future when you finally reach it."

"How is that, a bit more to your liking?" Caleb joshed.

"Wow, traveling to a star is like trying to hit a rabbit with my slingshot!"

"That is quite a perceptive analogy," Caleb replied with a bit of astonishment, thinking, *he is as bright as his father says he is, I suppose he also knows the meaning of an analogy.* He let the narrative run to see how much more the boy could grasp.

"The motion of the target star has to be studied in detail for a long period; an accurate projection of its path must be made so it can be intersected at the correct point in space and time. Unfortunately, the path that a star travels is not always regular and exactly predictable. It can be influenced by surrounding visible stars or objects that are less obvious. In the end you start tracking the target long in advance, along with the stars near it. In the case of our present target, we have been studying its path for thousands of years. You then make your best effort at predicting its future path and depart for the expected intersection point.

"You never get it exactly right, but you can get close enough so that a few minor midcourse corrections are all that are needed. The difficulties are not over, however. Just as the target star's path through the cosmos is affected by other bodies, so is your path while you are heading for it. Again, you try to account for perturbations as much as possible. To make things easier, we send out unmanned spacecraft ahead of time, studying their paths in order to minimize the guesswork when the time comes to make the trip. This is one of the purposes of the probes."

"So, it is not as easy as aiming at a rabbit," Johnny commented. "On the ship we get to make changes partway there. With the rabbit it is all or nothing from the start."

"Yes, then what happens to the rabbit when your aim is not right?" Caleb asked.

"You miss. The stone flies on by and hits something else."

"As it is with a probe," Caleb said. "If the first one or two miss, it is not a catastrophe, although we work hard to avoid it. This has not happened in a long time. There are more following, and we can make corrections based on the mistakes. Missing with the ship would not be a good outcome."

Caleb sat quietly for a minute pondering the consequences of his final statement. Johnny was silent too. One of the great risks of their collective undertaking had hit home.

Chapter 13
Destinations in Space
(September 1833)

The lessons continued with the earliest days of astronomy, an overview of the Terans' quest to learn what was out in space and expanded on earlier presentations on the mission of the Main Ship and its journeys.

Caleb started the narrative as John sat down on the sofa in front of the video screen. Yes, Johnny was John now. At the age of ten, he no longer thought it appropriate to be addressed in the diminutive, he let everyone know it.

John's upbringing group allowed the boy a large amount of input on the direction of his studies, but they made sure the important facts were included. The lesson program was coherent and complete. They selected a level of difficulty they felt John could manage without either becoming bored because it was too basic or overly frustrated because of its difficulty. John got as much as he could handle, given his age though, he would be sheltered from being overwhelmed.

This lesson began with a topic the boy was highly interested in. A voice began the narrative while images were displayed to illustrate important points. Periodically Caleb or John paused the recording to look at detailed images or read captions.

"Back on our home planet long before space travel, speculation on the origins of the lights we saw in the night sky had gone on for millennia. Questions about whether or not we were alone in the universe were as inevitable as a look upward into that darkness. Our ancient ancestors originally observed the night sky with their naked eyes. They puzzled over the nature of objects they saw, kept track of their movements, and named them. Eventually they built small telescopes to get a better look at the points of light. This revealed objects they had not been able to see with their unaided eyes. Next they built larger telescopes, the distances they saw grew farther, the objects more numerous and fantastic. Ultimately, the telescopes were placed in outer space beyond the distorting effects of the planet's atmosphere, their range and resolution grew greater again. Yet, in spite of these technical advances, no signs of life were found.

"Hundreds of years were spent observing nearby stars, we were able to find planets orbiting many of them. At first we found gas giants so large they were almost stars themselves. A little more mass and they would be able to ignite a nuclear fusion engine in their interiors. As our instruments improved in resolving power and sensitivity, we were able to identify and directly view smaller planets, and determine the rough composition of their atmospheres. We found no planets with over 5 or 6 percent oxygen in their atmosphere, unlike our world that had 20 percent. The presence of even these low levels was a sign that some kinds of living organisms might have evolved on these other worlds.

"We also used telescopes that could observe the heavens at frequencies in the radio portion of the electromagnetic spectrum. Initially we observed at certain key frequencies where important physical phenomena could be studied. The small frequency windows were expanded, and recorded simultaneously across the entire radio, microwave, infrared, and optical range up to the gamma ray region. This revealed new interesting physics. We used the same instruments to search for signals that might have been created by intelligent life. Nearby stars were examined, then more distant ones, until the entire sky had been studied. We never found anything that remotely resembled a coherent signal or message."

John paused the narrative to ask, "Are our telescopes the same as the ones used back then?"

"Essentially, yes," replied Caleb. "Ours are bigger and we have figured out how to make them a lot more sensitive, but the basic principles remain the same. John, there is an important point to be made here. The reason we can use these same principles from way back then, a long way away, is that physics does not change, at least we have never see any evidence that it does. No matter where or when you look, it is the same. Remember we are seeing things way back in time when we look at distant stars and galaxies."

They went back to the lesson.

"The search was expanded outward, eventually studying the million or so stars within five hundred light-years of Teran. No signs were found of alien civilizations; at least, not any advanced enough to broadcast. If others were within those five hundred light-years, they were either not sending signals or their own society was still too technologically unsophisticated to detect what was being sent.

"While we scanned the heavens, we also explored our own planetary system, sending unmanned and manned ships to the ten planets, their moons, the major asteroids, comets, even large bodies in the zone of icy objects swirling beyond the outermost planet. We learned how to build unmanned, self-sustaining space vehicles that could repair themselves. We constructed manned ones with complete recycling of vital life-supporting materials. The vessels steadily grew larger until they could hold thousands of inhabitants, and were rotated to produce artificial gravity. They were put in orbit around our star as permanent space habitats and became home for millions.

"We were able to maintain any climate we wanted inside the habitats. Some were like South Seas islands, always warm and breezy with lots of light. Additional habitats were wet and forested, while others were open and dry like the plains. People could easily move from one to another. Most found a suitable place and stayed put. Farming or raising livestock was not necessary, because food production was done by automated systems. Even so, many preferred to provide for themselves. There was plenty of time to do different things; the choice was left to each individual.

"Our ancestors came to prefer these space habitats because they were very safe, much safer than living on the planet with the unpredictable natural disasters that could happen. With our biologically engineered life span that typically exceeded 250 years, accidents became the main cause of premature death. The monitoring systems in the habitats prevented practically all accidents and completely eliminated the possibility of natural disaster.

"Eventually most people came to live off the home world, our attention then focused on restoring the planet. After several millennia of abuse from civilization, its agricultural, industrial, and technological development, it was time to repair the damage. It was largely returned to its original condition before the advent of civilization. It now serves as a giant environmental laboratory and eco-resort.

"Finally we got to the point where our cumulative steps led us to exhaust the possibilities in our own star's planetary system. Unmanned craft were sent to several of the nearest stars. None of their planets were particularly well suited to the development of hydrocarbon-based life, but they were the easiest to get to. No signs of life were found."

Caleb interjected, "Pay close attention to this next part; it involves the forerunners of what your father did for many years."

"Oh, the probes. I remember seeing the last one launched!" John exclaimed.

"We sent out the unmanned ships in a series at five-year intervals in order to form a continuous chain. This was done partly for communications purposes. Rather than build a single ship with a large and powerful enough transmission capability to reach the entire distance to home, it was more efficient to send a sequence of smaller ones that could communicate only part of the total distance. In this manner signals were relayed from one to another in both directions along the chain.

"This approach also allowed us to apply new technologies every five years. Even though we did have the basic means of upgrading after launch, unexpected events were often beyond the capabilities of the onboard systems. In this way advances could be incorporated into each new craft prior to launch.

"The successors to these original unmanned craft are what we now call probes. They are cylindrically shaped, the forward end having large dish antennas and a particle collector to provide supplemental fuel for the engines. Mounted on the rear is the engine exhaust cone surrounded by dish antennas equal in size to those on the forward one. These features mimic on a smaller scale the appearance and function of similar ones on the Main Ship

"At present they, too, can reach a velocity of 0.1c on their own, which when launched from the Main Ship also traveling at 0.1c means they can achieve 0.2c. After five years of slow acceleration, they turn off their engines and coast."

Caleb added, "The probe you saw launched, after accelerating to cruising speed, coasted past Alpha Centauri A, where it, along with its eight companions, recently did a gravitationally assisted course correction and got a velocity boost. Now they are coasting on to Sol, their final destination."

The narrative continued. "Initially, getting information back from the unmanned craft was slow. It took hundreds of years to get to a star, and then receive returning data. Although these early unmanned ships were sophisticated, possessing many intelligent capabilities, they had their limitations. If manned ships were used, we could not only cut the time to discovery, but be able to decide immediately on site how next to proceed when unexpected things turned up. What came next was an enormous leap. We outfitted one of our habitat vessels with the most powerful propulsion system we could build, pointed it toward the nearest star, and set off. Then we did it again and again until over fifty ships were headed toward various stars. Failing to detect civilization remotely from home, dissatisfied with the disconnectedness of unmanned ships, we decided to search directly.

"Main Ship number 19, MS19, is the designation of this vessel. Other Main Ships are heading away from Teran on different trajectories. The ships are numbered consecutively according to original launch date. The Main Ships are moving outward in slightly different directions, although they are concentrated in the galactic plane where most of the stars are located. We receive a constant flow of data from back home via the transceiver at our most recent stop, Epsilon Indi. The signal contains everything from scientific and engineering reports to history—there is no news. By the time we receive information here, it is all history.

"The radio wave dish antennas on each of the nine probes traveling together combine to form the main transmitter and receiver arrays used to relay communications outbound from the Main Ship and inbound from probes formations farther along the chain. The waist of each craft is covered with maneuvering thrusters and smaller antennas pointed in different directions. These are used to maintain communication among the nine probes of the formation. They have to keep their relative positions within the group plus their front-back pointing directions with respect to the next probe formation along the chain with great accuracy.

To do this they constantly monitor and adjust their positions. At the same time, they are continuously receiving and recording incoming signals from both directions. Before these signals are retransmitted, each of the nine compares its acquired signal with the others, sharing any discrepancies. They then collectively decide on a single set of fixes to apply to repair flaws while boosting the signal strength and retransmitting. This happens in real time, in both directions, at data rates of several terabits per second.

"Within each probe there are redundant systems performing the same error detection and repair operations on the signals. A given probe could lose 90 percent of these systems and function reliably. The nine probe formation could successfully retransmit signals in both directions even if it lost six of the probes. The formations are spaced along the chain in such a way that the complete loss of an entire formation will not interrupt the flow of information, only reduce its rate. The loss of two consecutive formations will not cause a complete breakdown.

"The number of formations is such that they completely fill the route between the star system we are approaching and the next one on our itinerary. As each formation reaches the far end, it refuels from the stellar wind, uses the star's gravitational well to turn and heads back in the direction it came, thus maintaining and reinforcing the chain. The first formation in the current series was launched fifty-one years ago, timed in order to arrive at Sol a few years after the Main Ship gets to Alpha Centauri. At this point the chain of probe formations will extend from one star system to the next.

"Once the Main Ship begins decelerating and while it is parked in the Alpha Centauri system, it will no longer be able to add new formations to the chain. To keep the chain full, we start redirecting probe formations in the already established Epsilon Indi to Alpha Centauri chain to not turn at Alpha Centauri, instead we let them continue on to fill in behind the existing formations. It will take over 180 years to completely drain the original chain between Epsilon Indi and Alpha Centauri. Long before that we will no longer be dependent on them for communication, because the much larger, more powerful HUB transceiver system at Alpha Centauri will be communicating directly with the HUB at Epsilon Indi. The probe chain will continue to play a vital role in maintaining the pointing direction of the HUB transceivers, however. New ones will eventually be sent out, the original probes will be recovered and studied in order to make improvements for the future. This exquisitely choreographed parade extends across fifteen light-years of space and hundreds of years.

"It is planned so the Main Ship will begin receiving returning data from the next destination prior to setting out for it. Major bodies in a destination star system are visited by satellites and landers launched from the probes as they enter a star's neighborhood. Planets with oxygen atmospheres are given the highest priority, their surfaces are surveyed in detail from orbit as well as by landers. Observational data is beamed back for evaluation, providing details needed to plan the habitat, communication HUB, and other development projects undertaken once we arrive. We will never actually heavily populate any planet. Rather, we will live in orbiting habitats with the option to make periodic visits to the surface." Each star and its planetary system we visit becomes another home for a part of the Teran race.

Chapter 14
Habitable Planets
(October 1833)

The lessons continued.

"Right now all we know about the Solar system is what we can discover via the Main Ship's telescopes," Caleb began.

"And we think there are other people there," John interrupted. "Dad told me of your air pollution study."

"Well, yes, that's right. Lots of folks are working on the project, there is indeed a strong possibility that some sort of civilized creatures inhabit the third planet." Caleb replied.

"What do you think they look like?" John asked.

"Well, we are certain they are carbon based, given the similarities of the planet's surface environment to Teran. They could resemble us quite a bit. At least insofar as they might be bipedal, have one head, two eyes, and so forth. You never know. They might be covered in feathers or be ten feet tall!"

"Why carbon based?"

"The complex compounds we see from the spectroscopy are carbon chain molecules. It is all we have ever seen on planets with life forms present. Carbon is the only atom that can form so many types of complex molecules with long chains in them. This complexity eventually gives rise to life. Without it there would be no way to construct the code in

DNA to build a sophisticated life form and pass along the instructions to future generations.

"Now, let's get to the lesson. Today we are going to look at the conditions that need to exist for a planet with life on it to come about."

Caleb started the lesson dialogue.

"The star Sol is a mature, stable, average size yellow sun much like Alpha Centauri A, Epsilon Indi, Delta Pavonis, and the one that warms our home world. We have determined the configuration of Sol's planetary system, the individual planets, and basic atmospheric composition. There are four outer gas giants and four inner stony planets, one with an atmosphere rich in oxygen. There is just one reason in our experience that a planet would have an abundance of oxygen: It is alive.

"We know some general aspects of the planet's southern half, the only part we can see. We have little detail of its surface or that of the other bodies in the system, we will get this information from the satellites placed by the probes. We have the capability to launch landers, but these will not be used because we suspect the presence of an early stage industrial civilization.

"Stars come in a wide range of sizes, colors, and compositions that can be used to characterize their life cycle. Those that are large are made almost entirely of hydrogen and helium. These are the Giant and Supergiant stars that have relatively short, violent life spans; frequently ending their lives in a cataclysmic explosion called a supernova, leaving a neutron star or a black hole behind. Smaller stars with a few percent of elements other than hydrogen or helium are stable and longer lived. They can grow to be extremely hot, and are blue in color. These two groups make up only a small portion of the stellar population, but they are most of the ones we can easily observe. Most stars are much smaller, relatively cool, dwarf stars with long, stable lives. In this group is our own star. It is classified G5 V, meaning it is a Type G star of medium temperature. The V designation comes from its luminosity and means it is in the main sequence of very stable, long-lived stars. This plus neighboring types, F and K, combine the twin properties of long, stable lives, billions of years, and sufficient energy output to warm and sustain life on sizable inner planets.

"In addition, many stars have companions associated with them. Fully half the stars in the galaxy are gravitationally bound with one or more other stars. If the companions are too close, planetary orbits can become oblong or erratic, stable conditions cannot be sustained for a long enough period for life to arise and evolve. Their large gravitational fields will severely disrupt the orbits of any planets that may be present or prevent them from forming altogether.

"To maintain relatively well behaved weather conditions on the entire surface during the course of a year, a planet's orbit must be nearly circular. Its distance from the star, and therefore the amount of heating provided by the star, may not vary greatly over its orbit.

"We have discovered that most stars have planetary systems consisting of two or three gas giants and several smaller, stony planets composed in large part of silicates. At least one of the stony planets is usually located in the habitable zone. It is called habitable because it is the right distance from the star where water, if it is present, can exist in liquid form. This is not to be confused with inhabited from the standpoint of complex, oxygen-breathing life forms.

"Finally there are the small, dim stars. These also invariably have planetary systems with at least one planet in the star's habitable zone. The difficulty for sustained development of life on these planets is that the habitable zone is close-in to the star due to its weak heat output. Planets in the habitable zone of such Type M stars eventually become gravitationally locked with the star like the situation at Proxima Centauri. As a result, one side of the planet is always facing the star while the other faces the cold of deep space. The effect on planetary climate and evolution of life is inevitably terminal.

"This means we have to focus our search on stars that are Spectral Type G, Class V or similar with no companion stars that are too close. This still leaves us with lots of stars to visit. They will inevitably be surrounded by variously sized bodies composed of useful materials we need for maintenance, construction, and resupply. Many will harbor fantastic vistas of mountain ranges, impact craters, or ring systems. Occasionally one will have substantial amounts of frozen or liquid water.

"In our travels to date, we and our colleagues on companion ships have found a number of habitable planets; some that were already inhabited. They all have significant amounts of oxygen in their atmospheres. This is because it appears that the only way a planet can possess more than trace amounts of oxygen is through biotic activity. A planet has to undergo trillions of generations of anaerobic bacterial, oxygen-producing activity spread across hundreds of millions of years to get such an atmosphere. This assumes the surface of the planet has a stable environment over this long period. The liquid water can't be entirely frozen or boiled off part of the time. This, unfortunately, is what happens to many inner planets with liquid oceans.

"In fact the third planet at Delta Pavonis, the stop before the most recent one at Epsilon Indi, is one such example of failed development. It is inhabited solely by single-celled organisms and the most basic of multicellular plants, enough to make large areas of shallow seas and low-lying wetlands blue-green. The planet has considerable oxygen in its atmosphere—8.6 percent—but we doubt that evolution will progress to the point where complex land animals will arise.

"The problem is that the planet's rotational axis is inherently unstable. A rotating body of any size has a natural tendency to wobble. It happens with spinning tops and it happens to planets. The wobble increases as the body's rotation slows with time due to gravitational drag from its parent star and nearby large planets. A planet with a large wobble is in danger of having an unstable environment. During the course of time, the planet's rotational axis can wander, changing orientation—so much so that it might at one point be aligned perpendicular to the plane of the planet's orbit about its star, while one or two hundred thousand years later it could be in line with its orbit, thus alternately pointing one of the poles directly at the star.

"This in itself is not necessarily a problem for sustained evolution. If the continents on the planet are distributed favorably, it is possible that ocean and wind circulation will be able to keep the worldwide climate relatively uniform and comfortable. The planet in question, however, has the unfortunate luck to have its major continents in high latitudes and at the poles. The ramifications for worldwide climate are immense, varying with time from large tropical regions to global deep freeze. Evolution takes a long time, it needs stability. A stable climate, with gradual changes over many millions of years, can be tolerated. Unless continental drift significantly rearranges the planet's landmasses to the middle or low latitudes, it is fated to experience little in the way of sustained development of higher life forms.

"One way out of the problem is to have a large moon. A planet with a moon that is large compared to its own size will have a much more stable rotational configuration. As its spin slows with time, the presence of the moon will help maintain that stability. The rotational axis will remain in a small range, uniform surface temperatures can prevail for long periods. Such planets, in spite of the number of stars with stony planets in the habitable zone, are rare. Since leaving our home world, we and our sister ships have visited hundreds of stars but have encountered only a handful.

"Consequently, most of the time we have to content ourselves with stopping in places that are less than desirable from a habitability perspective, although each system has turned out to be uniquely fascinating. So fascinating that portions of the crew have willingly stayed behind to build habitation facilities in orbit, and, when possible, visit planetary surfaces.

"We are closing in on Alpha Centauri. A communications HUB will be established there that will allow our signals to reach back to Epsilon Indi. Sol is next. Because of the suspected presence of a civilization, it will most likely not become a major installation like Alpha Centauri or Epsilon Indi. We will need to keep clear of Sol c and not leave anything behind that could reveal our presence, at least not before they are ready for contact.

Chapter 15
HUBs and Probes
(October 1833)

"John, you know what a HUB is, don't you?" Caleb asked.

"Sure, everyone does. It's a huge, ugly biosphere."

"Well, yes, that is the fun name we use for it, do you know what it does?" said Caleb.

"I think it's for deep-space communications."

"Yes, that's right. For direct star-to-star communications. Go ahead, begin the lesson."

John started the narrative.

"Interstellar communications is another hard problem to solve, like housing, propulsion, or navigation. Even at the speed of light, it takes years to send a message from one destination star to the next; plus an equal amount of time to get a reply. The biggest headache with communications is the amount of information that can be sent.

"A signal can be easily transmitted and received across interstellar distances. That was the rationale behind our long years of searching for intelligent life with radio telescopes. With relatively low power transmitters, a simple message of a repeating series of on-off or single-bit elements can be sent. This type of message takes up a very narrow range or band of frequency. The receiver sits and listens. By accumulating many, many copies of the repeating message, the receiving party can overcome the interfering effects of extraneous radio noise. There is a lot of it coming from the cosmic microwave background — the remnants of the big bang — exploding stars, black holes in the centers of galaxies, and a host of other exotic phenomena. Eventually you can understand the message.

"To send larger amounts of data in a shorter period of time, you have to reduce the number of repeats and boost the transmitting power to make up for the smaller number of duplications that are added together to overcome the interfering noise. Alternatively, you could transmit different content at multiple frequencies; that is, spread a complicated message across a wider range of frequencies. We learned how to do that in the early days of digital communications millennia ago.

"Because of size and power considerations, there are limits to the strength of the signal we can send from the ship, therefore we spread or multiplex our messages over a wide band of frequencies. It is also done in a coded fashion so the content is mixed up and duplicated a number of times. This way, if some of the frequencies are lost or corrupted, the entire content can usually be recovered. In the end, the signal sent out looks much like noise. To someone with no knowledge of the method used to scramble the content, it would be practically impossible to decipher. In fact, it would take a great deal of computerized signal processing along with a lot of luck to determine that it was a message and not simply random noise.

"Using almost the entire radio band from a hundred million cycles to several trillion cycles in the near infrared in very small increments of a few cycles, we are able to pack a tremendous amount of data into the transmission. Sophisticated processing equipment on the receiving end is used to decode the message and assemble a coherent result.

"We build the largest transmitters practical, continually work on making the receivers more sensitive, and leave the rest to the signal processing systems. In this way we can send large amounts of data across tens of light-years of interstellar space. Now, however, you have to navigate the communication signal.

"The transmitted signals are sent out in a narrow beam aimed at the receiver to maximize the message content given the available transmit power. The more we concentrate the signal in a particular direction, the stronger it will be at the receiver for a given level of transmit power. The stronger the signal at the receiver, the easier it is to detect in the presence of noise. Fewer duplicate copies are needed as a result. Hence, greater data transfer.

"Unfortunately, the narrower the beam, the better the pointing of your receiver toward the transmitter has to be, because for the same types of signal strength reasons, the receiver can detect signals only in a very narrow beam. The two narrow beams have to be closely aligned and kept that way in order to successfully send and receive data. In addition, the larger the distance between the two, the tougher it is to keep them properly pointed at each other for the same reasons that ship navigation gets so tricky. Everything is moving, and the motion is not always perfectly predictable. You don't want to lose the signal, because it can be exceedingly difficult to get back in alignment.

"This makes it highly unlikely that someone else will accidentally run across our messages. You would have to be right in the signal's path with your receiver pointed at the transmitter's location, or else you would never encounter the communication. We realized long ago that this is probably the reason we never intercepted any alien communications, assuming they were being sent. The chances of crossing a transmission beam while being pointed in the correct direction to receive it are astonishingly small. Someone would have to be deliberately coming right toward you to have a chance of detecting their transmissions. Then they would also have the problem of decoding the message without any knowledge of how it had been encoded.

"Behind us at Epsilon Indi are a large, powerful transmitter and an equally large, very sensitive receiver. In fact, there are two of each mounted on the HUBs orbiting Epsilon Indi: one set to send and receive directly with our ship heading to Alpha Centauri, the other to communicate back with the prior destination, Delta Pavonis. Being stationary, that is, not onboard a starship, the HUB transceivers can be much larger.

"Conversations using these communications beams, in the sense of asking a question and getting a reply, are out of the question because of the time delays involved. We do, however, send data both ways in an effort to maintain contact between those who stayed behind and those of us who went on ahead. Like many immigrants, we want to maintain ties with those we are separated from. As in the days of wooden sailing vessels, the separations are almost invariably permanent, which often heightens the desire for some kind of contact.

"The communications also allow us to pool our knowledge and experience. New discoveries in propulsion, communications and numerous other fields are shared constantly over this long-range network that stretches back to Teran two hundred light-years away, and outward from it to ships similar to ours traveling on different trajectories. It is surprising how many hundred-year-old reports on the net contain useful information.

"The communications facilities at Epsilon Indi were finished before we left. They were brought to full power early in the current crossing to Alpha Centauri. The ship carries a more modest sized set of transmitters and receivers.

"Along the route to Alpha Centauri is the previously emplaced string of small transceiver stations, the probe chain, spaced a tenth of a light-year apart, constantly circulating between Epsilon Indi and Alpha Centauri. Even though the HUBs can communicate directly from star to star, we still maintain the probe chain in between the stars. We use them to help hold the HUB transceivers in alignment with one another.

"At the HUB we continually project the path of our target, the HUB we are communicating with, using observations of the time variation of its location."

John interrupted, "I remember my old slingshot and rabbit analogy. You can't simply point at the star where it is now."

"That's right," said Caleb. "For a star eight light-years away, we see it where it was eight years ago. It takes that long for its light to get to us. By that time it has moved. During transmission we need to point to where it is going to be in another eight years, because our signal will take that long to get to it. Therefore, the HUB transmitter has to point where it is going to be in sixteen years to transmit in the correct direction—the eight years it has already moved plus the eight years it will take for the signal to reach it. Receiving is a lot easier, you simply have to point the receiver array at the visible location of the star."

The narrative resumed. "Our ships, including the probes, keep track of their location in space by continuously observing X-ray pulsars. These are variable stars whose output oscillates rapidly. The probes continuously compare their positions with their predicted path and the target star location. They make course corrections as needed. This data is sent back so we can compare it with our predictions of where the probes are and use the differences to refine our prediction methods of their future motion as well as the target star.

"When they are sent out to the next destination star, the probes carry a large amount of observational equipment. They carry telescopes and spectrometers that operate in various bands of the electromagnetic spectrum. In addition, they have smaller satellites and landers onboard that can be released to do closer inspections of the planets, moons, and additional bodies of the destination star system.

"We have already studied the Alpha Centauri system extensively. This was done on the journey to Epsilon Indi. Now on the way to Alpha Centauri, we are studying the next destination. Accordingly, while traveling to one destination star, we study the one after at the same time by sending out probes to it. As a result we will be familiar with the next destination before we set out for it. A large amount of data has already been obtained on the Centauri star system. We have a detailed understanding of what we will find once we get there.

"The next several years will be spent decelerating and completing the journey to Alpha Centauri, followed by fifty years constructing the communications station, the HUB, and habitat stations. Part of the crew will stay behind to staff the HUB or live in the habitats. They will have a number of planets to explore. Eventually, long after this ship leaves for Sol, another Main Ship will be built and sent out to other nearby stars. This will give succeeding generations an opportunity to explore different worlds and perhaps have a chance to set foot on a green, living planet such as the one waiting for us at Alpha Centauri."

Chapter 16
Decision Time
(December 1833)

The observational results generated by Caleb's team were followed closely by the inhabitants of the ship. In the months since his group began posting reports on industrial air pollution on Sol c, a constant stream of messages, comments and side analyses grew in volume to the point where they were starting to crowd out other conversations on the network. The question of whether they were seeing direct evidence of civilization on Sol c became the hot topic. A consensus about how to proceed in the face of this discovery was beginning to form in the governance postings.

"John, in light of current events, today I think we ought to take up the topic of how the ship's population governs itself," Caleb said by way of introducing the next lesson.

John squirmed a bit in his seat. Caleb smiled and went on.

"It is important to realize that we are completely autonomous. It is impossible for anyone from outside, be they another ship or our home planet, to impose their will on us. We are on our own and govern ourselves in all matters. Decisions are made collectively via the governance monitor site. You have access to it, but currently cannot post anything. Have you spent much time on the site?"

"No, it's kind of boring, especially since I can't interact with it," John answered.

"Yes, I felt the same way at your age, nevertheless, it is important to spend time on the site every few days, even if all you do is read the summary. There is a lot going on right now, we are approaching a big decision. You should learn how the process functions, how we work together to come to a consensus. Besides, we listen to you. Your opinions will be represented through us."

John became more attentive as he straightened-up.

"Input on the governance site is constantly analyzed by the computer system. It classifies comments, queries, replies, and, yes, rants too. Summaries and statistics are produced so everyone can follow the trends or read the intermediate conclusions of a particular discussion. It is a giant town meeting involving all the adults on the ship. Anyone can start a discussion, everyone is free to join in or ignore it as they see fit. Local issues that apply to a few people or a particular group get resolved when that group gains a consensus. Topics with wider affect get the attention of a large portion or sometimes all of the ship's adult population. When a particularly important discussion approaches a consensus, we usually call for a vote. Often, however, the consensus is so strong that a vote is not necessary, we simply go ahead with whatever view dominates.

"There are also a number of fixed decisions that were agreed upon long ago. In fact, none of the current crew of the ship were alive when the agreements were made. Now, I said earlier that we are completely autonomous; no one can impose their will on us. Nevertheless, we continue to accept these fixed decisions because they are either in our best interests or they make very good sense. It is possible at any time for someone to open an issue on one of them, but this has never been done since the ship's launch.

"The major fixed decisions are:

"(1) Our trajectory heading out from Teran is set within a solid angle with a defined direction. Other Main Ships have their own fixed sector. This was done to allow each Main Ship to travel within a unique sector of space of sufficient size for it to determine and maintain a path from one Type F, G, or K star to another in trips under twenty light-years.

"(2) We will not interfere with any emerging civilizations we might encounter. We will keep ourselves hidden until they find us or we have studied them sufficiently to determine they are ready for contact.

"(3) We carry no weapons or military defenses of any kind. We will not develop any in the future. It was recognized early on in our exploration of space that the power and materials required for weaponry on a scale large enough to be effective was not workable from a basic physics and engineering perspective. We will take our chances that we can avoid any less-developed, hostile civilizations by not landing on their planet. We will take our chances that any more-advanced civilization will have already adopted this same philosophy."

"So," John interjected, "I guess the second one is behind the hot governance issue going on right now?"

"Yes. It is actually the first time one of the big three has come up for us. A couple ships have wrestled with the first one, there are also a few previous instances of the second being an issue when planets with life on them have been encountered. However, we are, as far as we know, the first ship to encounter what appears to be sentient beings with some sort of organized civilization.

"Now, John, follow the discussion until we reach a consensus, then we will get back together to talk about it."

As postings on the governance site mounted, calls increased dramatically for an immediate decision on the first probe formation that was fast approaching Sol. If the Terans wanted to redirect its activities toward or perhaps away from Sol c, they would have to transmit the signal within six months. After that, there would not be enough time for the signal to reach it before it started sending out satellites and landers.

There were two sets of opinions. One was that the probes should be directed to maintain a large distance from Sol c, at least until it could be established that its population had not yet invented telescopes and radar. The Terans could not risk detection of one of them by the planet's population, owing to consensus directive (2): no contact until they could establish that the others were ready. The definition of *ready* included a list of social, technical, and supplementary criteria that exceeded three hundred items. They were specific and demanding. A common joke among the ship's crew was that they would have to avoid their own home planet because it could not pass these stringent standards. Ultimately, a ship's consensus would decide.

The second set of opinions wanted to redirect the probe formation for the same reasons plus cease transmissions to and from it. If the Sol c inhabitants had radio and related technologies, they might be able to detect the Terans' communication beam, since it swept across the planet. Therefore, the second group advocated turning off the forward beam immediately after the redirection signal was sent.

Caleb and Henry had opinions, too, but they were in a third, small minority. They thought there was little chance the inhabitants of Sol c had radar, which would be needed to detect the probe signals from the planet's surface. The society would not be advanced enough. Henry, along with Barry and Sandy, did additional comparative studies using Teran history. These suggested it would be hundreds of years before Sol c's civilization arrived at the stage where they could detect the ship's probes or beam if they developed at the same rate as Teran's civilization had. Caleb, Henry and their colleagues felt there was nothing to worry about. The consensus shifted in that direction as the ship's crew read, and considered their minority postings. In the end a clear agreement in favor of this approach was reached, a consensus was declared.

"Uncle Caleb, why were so many people wrong at the beginning?" John asked when they resumed his lessons.

"John, they were not wrong. These discussions have nothing to do with whether anyone is right or wrong. They are concerned with seeking what is most sensible given what we know. It takes time for the pertinent information to come out. For everyone to mull it over. Opinions can be unmade and remade as easily as they are made. A consensus forms when opinions stabilize on an outcome."

"How do you know what is 'sensible'?" John asked.

"Ah, that's a tough one. It comes from a lot of things. Experience, knowledge, practice. Mainly it comes from carefully collecting as much information as practical then analyzing it in an open and honest manner. If you take care in what you are doing—this applies to everything you do, not just issue postings—and always try to do the best you can by not taking the easy way out or cutting corners, you will be well on your way."

"It sounds hard," said John.

"It is, but don't worry. Whether you know it or not, you have already made a good start. It shows in your studies," Caleb finished.

A second part of Caleb's postings included a recommendation that the probes be directed to increase their attention to Sol c, but under no circumstance should they send landers. Satellites would be put in Sol c orbits high enough to avoid being spotted from the ground. The other planets would get orbiting satellites but no landers. The Terans did not want to leave any trace of their presence, not even tracks or exhaust blast marks.

The communication beam from the Main Ship to the probes would be left on. These conditions were agreed to.

There was also discussion on the Main Ship's course. Their next destination after Sol, Epsilon Eridani, was 12.6 light-years directly from Alpha Centauri. This was a journey of 130 years. Unfortunately, it would take much extra time to set a probe chain to it, whereas the existing probes going to Sol could be diverted as planned to Epsilon Eridani with no delay of the Main Ship's schedule. Consequently, they really had no choice. The existing probe chain defined their route.

It was 4.4 light-years to Sol, Epsilon Eridani was another 10.5 light-years from there, for a total journey of 14.9 light-years. A flyby of Sol would allow them to replenish their fuel and, along with using the star's gravity well, give them a speed boost resulting in a 140 year trip. The question was whether or not to stop at Sol, adding time to the trip to Epsilon Eridani; and if they did stop, whether or how they should limit their activities.

Since their arrival at Sol was decades in the future, the discussion centered on ethical issues regarding establishing contact. A clear consensus reaffirming noninterference set in from the start.

Chapter 17
Deceleration Finished
(1838)

The countdown was nearing the last few minutes before engine shutdown. Everyone was watching a video screen somewhere, either at home with friends and neighbors, out in the plazas with large groups of partiers, or in the control center where engineers were monitoring critical systems.

John was at the plaza by Jake senior's house. He had come to town with his parents especially for the big event. "Almost time!" he yelled. The clock was down to the last twenty seconds. At five seconds to go, a slight vibration would be felt, then at zero, it would stop.

"There it is!" he yelled again, but no one was listening. They were too busy filling champagne glasses, dancing, hugging one another.

Up on the screen, the tilt meter next to the countdown clock moved from an angle of two degrees to zero as the engine's thrust subsided. They had finished deceleration into Alpha Centauri.

After half an hour, Henry downed one final glass of bubbly and began the five block walk from the plaza to Jake's with Lucy. The rest of the clan would follow at their own pace.

Back at Jake's home he saw that preparations for the party were done. He checked with Click to get a last minute update on the guest list.

John was already there and had Alpha Centauri A in a window on the display. The star was the brightest one in the sky yet small enough to be a dot with fuzzy edges. The fourth planet was not visible except with a telescope. Alpha Centauri B could be spotted if you knew exactly where to look.

This gathering would mark both the end of their 102-year trip and the beginning of the ship's forty-five year stay in the Centauri system.

They would maneuver the ship into position in orbit around Alpha Centauri A between the third planet and Alpha Centauri B. The Main Ship had to be far enough away from both stars so that stellar flares would not be disruptive, but sufficiently close to harvest enough particles from the stellar wind for fuel. As well, materials for building the HUB and habitats had to be near at hand. These materials would come from asteroids circulating between their location and Alpha Centauri B.

As soon as the Main Ship reached its new temporary home location, the arrays would be sent back out. This returned the data transmission rate to and from Epsilon Indi and the Sol probe chain back to its normal level.

Everything was timed to be completed shortly before the first group of probes, sent out long ago and already in the Solar System, sent out their sub-probes. It would be a couple of months before these satellites and landers reached the planets and went into orbit. At that point they would begin to send back data from the whole surface of Sol c instead of just the southern part. The sub-probes were too small to have wide array capabilities, hence imaging was relatively low resolution. In orbit, however, a few hundred miles above the surface, satellites sent from the sub-probes would be close enough for extremely high resolution imagery. There was, of course, the ever present four-year plus time delay. The Terans would have to wait it out before they would begin to get better data as the sub-probes rendezvoused with the planets and other objects in the Solar System.

Chapter 18
Sol c, Up Close
(1842)

Henry sat down in front of the video wall to eat lunch while watching the transmissions from the first Sol c satellite. It was heading directly in toward the region Caleb's team had studied prior to the shutdown of the arrays. New spectroscopic data was already confirming their findings. As the craft closed in, the blue southern oceans distinguished themselves from the green and brown continents. No doubt there was a lot of vegetation covering major portions of the land, Henry thought, but the planet appeared to be largely covered by water. In addition, the enormous ice cap covering the southern pole came into stark focus.

Three weeks later, Henry was back in front of the video wall, this time the room was full of people. His entire team was there including John, even Caleb had made the trip down from the forward end. In a little over an hour, the satellite would go into low orbit around Sol c. In the coming hours, they would start to get a detailed look at the planet's surface. In reality, the craft had been in orbit for four years, or so they hoped, faithfully sending back data. It had taken the signal that long to transit the distance back to Alpha Centauri. They would finally see it for the first time today.

The satellite made its final course adjustment to begin its swing into orbit from south to north. This initial orbit happened to pass across the main southern ocean; as the orbit progressed, all the Terans saw was more and more water. At last the west coast of a northern continent came into view. The orbit traversed southwest to northeast, passing south of the North Pole. Just as the South Pole, the north one was covered by large ice sheets. After giving another brief glimpse of water, the satellite was back over land, as it turned out, another even larger northern continent that extended on for most of the rest of the orbit.

There were lots of clouds below, as a result, ground images were not great for much of this area. As time went by the satellite's orbit would slowly precess around the planet, crossing directly above the entire surface. After many orbits the viewers would eventually build a cloud-free set of images.

The gathering started breaking up near the end of the second orbit. Each one took ninety minutes, the hour was getting late. Henry and Caleb stayed up to the middle of the third orbit then called it quits.

The following morning the pair was right back at the video wall watching the probe images of different resolution and fields of view, they reveled in reading the data streams from the sensors. It was now the middle of the ninth orbit and viewing was much clearer. The eastern side of the large northern continent was almost cloud free, it looked much drier. The whole northern hemisphere was turning out to be the mirror opposite of the southern. It was largely covered by land instead of sea.

At night, additional spectroscopic data provided localized readings of carbon dioxide, sulfur dioxide, methane gases, and VOCs mimicking those from the original observations of the southern hemisphere. The concentrations were sprinkled across the landmass, but were mainly by seacoasts.

Some of last night's crowd had returned. As the robots were bringing in brunch, one of them jumped up from his chair, hastening over to the video wall. He pointed at something on the southeast side of the field of view.

"Do you see this?" he nearly yelled.

From the high resolution images it could be seen that the satellite was coming up to and crossing above a long, narrow linear feature that appeared to be a wall. It was not completely intact, giving the appearance of being quite old. Someone, however, had built it. The immediate, stunning conclusion was that the planet was, or at least had been, inhabited by an organized civilization for a long time.

The satellite passed farther along the wall on the next orbit. This time the viewers were in for an even greater surprise. South of the wall was the unmistakable street grid of a large city. Its pollution readings were strong, proving that it was currently inhabited.

For a few minutes, Henry and his guests were completely occupied with the images of the city. Then someone noticed that the message window was lit up with traffic. In less than ten minutes, it seemed that everyone on the ship knew what the satellite had seen.

The communication system was nearly overloaded; it was barely able to keep up with sorting and classifying the statements, opinions, questions, and comments coming in.

They now had direct visual evidence of an intelligent civilization; it was no longer a theory based on the presence of certain gases in the atmosphere.

Again the issue of contact came up on the governance postings; after much discussion, the consensus was to do nothing and wait. To abandon the trip and redirect to Epsilon Eridani would require setting a new probe chain. If they started immediately, it would take 130 years, delaying the Main Ship launch by almost eighty. No one liked that option. They were going to Sol. They determine exactly how much or little they would do there as more became known about Sol c.

Chapter 19
Comparative History
(1845)

With the confirmation of a civilization on Sol c, John began devouring the reports that were coming out, extending his reading to include the range of Teran's history that paralleled what they were seeing at Sol c. He concentrated on comparing this newly discovered society to the Teran past. He enlisted a great deal of help from Caleb, who had been doing the same since the possibility of industrialization on the planet had been discovered.

"John, it's time to talk about comparative history. How have your readings been going?" Caleb asked.

"I'm way ahead of you, Uncle Caleb. I've covered everything from three hundred years before to fifty years past the current state on Sol c in our home world records."

Caleb grinned.

John had demonstrated again what those who took part in his upbringing had seen while he was growing up. It had been clear early on that young John was a self-contained, highly independent individual with already well developed abilities to concentrate and learn. Not a classic recluse such as Caleb, but certainly happy to spend time on his own mostly reading or, like his father, running.

John's independence sometimes put him at odds with his upbringing group—everyone except Caleb, that is. They also wanted to spend time with him outside his formal instruction sessions. The problem was John would frequently run through his lessons in advance. It didn't matter much whether he liked the subject or not. He did the work quickly and correctly. He just as quickly went off to run or hide himself away to read or to investigate a part of the ship he had not seen yet. The upbringing group, Henry included, did not see as much of John as they wanted; as John moved into his teens, he became even more independent. Often they would have to track him down with the ship's location system to find out what he was up to.

History was his favorite subject; all kinds of history, from the geology, paleontology and archeology of the deep Teran past to the most recent accounts of destinations encountered by sister ships. As time passed he became increasingly dependent on Caleb for guidance. Caleb understood what John needed. Ironically he was the one member of the upbringing group who felt John should be left alone if that was what he wanted, but he probably saw more of him than anyone else.

In spite of his independence, John was not rebellious. Though it would have been impossible for him to access anything that was off-limits, he rarely tried to enter areas of the ship's interior that were restricted to minors. Any attempted infractions were always inadvertent, stemming from his desire to investigate different systems or find new hideouts where he could read and think without being disturbed.

Through his years of studying the history of Teran, John had been playing with the socioeconomic modeling and simulation tools available on the ship's computer systems. These programs had been largely forgotten over the centuries. He found them by accident when he began trying to figure out if he could somehow predict or at least partially anticipate the development path that might be occurring on Sol c.

The first problem was to get Teran and Sol c aligned in time; that is, to figure out the point in the Teran past that corresponded to the present situation on Sol c. It was easy enough to get information on Teran. Information from Sol c however, consisted of images and remote sensing data collected from orbit. This data provided limited direct or indirect information on what was happening on the surface. It took John a while to deduce what was going on from that data and get the two planets' stories aligned

He built on the old programs, adding new features and analytical techniques to handle the specific types of data available from Sol c. As he improved the modeling programs, he back-tested them on Teran data. He was able to successfully predict his home world's development with 95 percent confidence as far as fifty years into the future, provided he stuck to macro trends like population growth and industrial growth. Predictions of specifics, like the discovery of a given new technology, were much less reliable.

Sol c and Teran were similar in size, differing by a few percent in diameter. Oceans predominated on both planets. Teran's surface was 65 percent ocean while Sol c was 70 percent covered by water. The most striking difference was the way the continents were arranged. Teran had one large landmass that roughly girdled the middle latitudes, although it did not go completely around the planet. There were two smaller continents, one at the north pole that was uninhabitable because of the arctic conditions, and a smaller island continent in the southern ocean that came within eight hundred miles of the main one at the point of closest approach.

Sol c, on the other hand, had two distinct major continental masses separated by thousands of miles of ocean at its middle latitudes and by hostile arctic conditions in the polar regions. One was two north-south lobes connected by a narrow land bridge north of the equator. The whole thing ran nearly from pole to pole. The second primarily ran east-west with a large southern spur in the west and an island arc leading to a small continent off the southeastern corner.

The difference in the distribution of the landmasses between the two worlds would be critical as civilization developed. The Terans knew from their archaeological records that agricultural development, the initiating technology for civilization, had occurred in the temperate regions in areas with abundant naturally occurring seed plants that could be domesticated. The dominant east-west trend of the main continent on Teran favored the rapid spread of cultivation to all areas that could sustain it; this led to fairly uniform, relatively rapid development across the planet. The same would likely have happened on the east-west landmass on Sol c. The separate north-south one would turn out to be a different story.

John theorized that the north-south orientation of the other major pair of continents would inhibit, if not prevent altogether, the widespread development of agriculture, thereby arresting the progress of civilization. The reason for this was simple. A native seed plant that was domesticated and put in production could be easily introduced to new areas so long as the climatic conditions remained nearly the same. This was generally true on any planet as one moved in an east-west direction. Going north-south, however, one often quickly moved away from favorable conditions. Sometimes a different seed plant could be found that would be successful in the new area, but here, too, geography worked against that possibility. The number of available seed plants was a direct function of the size of the temperate zone. On a continent that was oriented north-south, the number would be much smaller; there would likely be fewer plants available for exploitation. With fewer seed plants, it was less likely one could be mass cultivated in each set of conditions.

John surmised that it was on the larger, east-west landmass that sustained expansion of civilization initially occurred. Since they had positive evidence of cities on all the continents, its residents must have discovered the other land mass and exploited it as well, perhaps multiple times. These circumstances meant the Terans would have to be cautious in drawing conclusions from direct comparisons between Sol c and Teran at selected points in time. The paths to those times and the processes involved would be as important as the conditions themselves. John knew that just because a correlation was found in the conditions of two systems at particular points in time, it did not mean that they had tracked or would continue to track along together. In the case of Teran and Sol c, it was most likely the conditions would not track. He would have to simulate developments on Sol c based on information from Sol c, and not rely heavily on inputs from comparable points in Teran development. The same general sequence of events might apply, though not necessarily at the same rate.

He further speculated that early societal development on Sol c took place as if the planet was comprised of two separate worlds. He confirmed via a series of simulations that one of the key factors determining the course of events during the period of agricultural maturation and preindustrial development on Teran was that all the major nations were in constant, relatively close physical contact by land from the beginning. This new planet was not the same. Development on Sol c would be strongly influenced by the large isolating distance by sea between the two halves.

John had come up to Caleb's cabin for one of his periodic visits. They were sitting at the breakfast table looking out the widow, drinking coffee.

"John, your simulation results are remarkable. Sol c is definitely on a faster development track than Teran at the same stage of sophistication. It seems to be accelerating, doesn't it?"

"Yes, it does," John answered. "Once a certain point is reached, it will become obvious. When they start developing widespread telecommunications, they should really take off. So far I've been concentrating on technology and descriptive data. The use of coal, the amount of city lighting, population estimates. I wish there was a way we could learn more on their social development."

"I'm afraid that will have to wait until they begin radio broadcasting, so we can start listening to them. Do you have a time frame for it that you are comfortable with?"

"It's far enough out, so there is a fair amount of uncertainty. It looks like ninety years or more, around 1940."

"The Main Ship will have passed them by then. Things ought to get quite interesting during the approach though, I expect your talents will be in high demand," Caleb said. "In the meantime maybe you can read ahead on Teran's social development."

"I already have, it's starting to get a little disturbing." John replied.

"When you get to the point where we begin off-planet colonization, let me know. You will find it to be more than a little disturbing." Caleb answered.

"That sounds pretty ominous, as much as I look forward to learning more about our past, I feel a little anxious over what is coming." They sat in silence for a minute, then John got up.

"I'd better head down to the shuttle station or I'll be late for dinner with Mom and Dad. I'll keep you posted on my progress, Uncle Caleb."

As John extended his readings on Teran social development, the content did indeed get more disturbing. The problems stemmed from over population. Eventually it exceeded fifteen billion, precipitating political turmoil, nuclear conflicts, resource depletion, pollution of air, water, and the ground, global warming, melting ice caps, and vast disparities in wealth. This last issue led to the initial space colonies. Those with sufficient financial resources got off the planet and stayed off as conditions got worse. They took with them the brightest people they could find to build self-contained habitats that were the forerunners of the vessels that became the starships. They also conducted programs in genetic engineering and medical research. The resulting discoveries allow them to lengthen their lifespans by many decades.

The space colonists shared the results among themselves, anyone who was able to get off the planet was welcome to join them. They tried to share their new knowledge with those back on the planet, but the dominant national governments resisted. The situation eventually became chaotic. Numerous conflicts broke out as different groups vied for diminishing resources. Widespread dislocations occurred as the climate warmed and sea levels rose to inundate the coastal lowlands. The left-behind Terans were unable to grow sufficient food; radiation and pollution rendered wide areas unfit for agriculture or habitation. Runaway use of harmful chemicals lead to genetic damage, cancer, and infectious diseases that wiped out large numbers. The entrenched authoritarian political elites that controlled the major countries, and the corrupt governments they ran, were incapable of dealing with these enormous problems.

Finally society collapsed back to nearly preindustrial levels as political structures crumbled. Anarchy broke out, the population declined to fewer than a billion survivors. At that point the space colonies were able to step in to begin the restoration project that would repair the damage and return the planet to a state that could be sustained.

Over the ensuing years, John kept up his readings and simulation work on Teran history. Henry and Caleb watched the data coming back from Sol c. Along with their team, they built up a large body of knowledge on the planet's history. John was drawn deeply into their work. He kept up a running dialogue with Caleb and continued to visit him at the cabin.

Their work was followed by much of the ship's crew. John's predictions had led many to conclude that being discovered by the residents of Sol c was inevitable. The decision not to stop at Sol had been the right one; they were going to fly by, continuing on to Epsilon Eridani. There would be no landers on any of Sol's planets, the satellites would be withdrawn from the inner planets as soon as they suspected that radar was close to being invented.

John wondered what it would be like to visit Sol c and meet its inhabitants. That could never happen, he knew, because of the consensus. Still, he thought often of visiting the planet's surface, but never mentioned it to anyone. Not even his parents or Caleb.

Chapter 20
The HUB
(1857)

HUB construction was begun in 1840. By 1857 it was sufficiently well along that its permanent population could be significantly increased. Henry and Lucy decided it was time to move there. John was going with them, at least temporarily. He had declared his intention to go with the Main Ship to Sol, although it would not be leaving for another twenty-six years.

The activities of his upbringing group, which were already at a subdued level, were winding down. They had decided that John would be ready for the responsibilities of full adult status with the next year or two. Some of the group were already at the HUB, separation from the rest would not be a problem for the young man. In fact, Henry ruefully wondered if John would notice. Once John left for good on the ship, continuity would be maintained by Caleb. He was going with the Main Ship and hoped to live long enough to see Sol c when they got there. It would take forty-nine years from departure. Caleb would have to make it past 230 years of age to do it.

The HUB habitat chamber frame and skin had been completed, the interior was being pressurized and fitted out with the beginnings of a planet-like surface. Now the onboard systems would be installed. This phase would require much closer supervision of the construction robots. Additional residents were needed, Henry's and Lucy's skills would be of great use.

Henry had enjoyed working on the Sol c investigations. It was important work, the right thing for him at the time, but he never felt it was an all-consuming passion as engineering had been. It was time to leave the ship and do his part in bringing the HUB and its deep-space communications systems online. The break from engineering had made him realize how important it was to him, he was looking forward to getting back to his first love.

It was also perfect for Lucy. She would have the opportunity to play a major part in the establishment of the agricultural facilities on the HUB. Though her parents' farm was now in the hands of her nephew, she had continued to maintain working contact with its operations. She was excited about the chance to start her own farm from scratch.

Like the Main Ship, the HUB was positioned in an orbit around Alpha Centauri A between the third planet and Alpha Centauri B which was located where a large outer gas giant planet would be. There were no further bodies of planetary size. The HUB's orbit was inclined by 30 degrees with respect to the plane of the two stars.

Its position between the double stars and orbital tilt would allow the continuous line of sight needed for communications back to Epsilon Indi and forward to the ship as it traveled to its next destination. They did not want to get either star in between, not even for a short period. This also allowed near approaches to the asteroids, which were their sources of raw materials.

The habitat part of the HUB would initially house fifty thousand of the Main Ship's population staying behind. The remaining fifty-five thousand would make the trip to Sol. The choice was ultimately up to each adult. Those staying at the HUB would conduct a wide variety of activities related to the investigation and eventual population of the Alpha Centauri system, as well as maintain and operate the communications apparatus.

Habitats were designed to hold a hundred thousand residents, the same as a Main Ship. It took twenty years to get one to the point where it had established ecosystems with a climate that could be regulated, hence there was a limit to how fast the population could grow.

The habitats got their power directly from the star. Eventually thousands of these vessels would be built and positioned around it. The planets would probably never be permanently settled. Outposts had been built for scientific work, visitors could enjoy the surface for brief periods, but the environment would be left alone to evolve on its own. The Terans would live in the HUB or habitat vessels. They would not interfere with the natural processes on any of the planets so long as life-generating evolutionary processes were in place.

Construction started with robots and crews from the Main Ship fabricating a construction complex. It produced the components of the HUB and habitat vessels, which would be ferried to their permanent orbital locations for assembly.

The ship would remain on station at Alpha Centauri for forty-five years; until construction on the HUB and initial habitat cylinder had gotten to the point where the outpost was self-sustaining. Routine maintenance and refitting of the ship would be done during that time.

Within five years of Main Ship departure, the communications beams would reach full power, allowing the ship to maintain continuous contact all the way to Sol. In addition, full HUB operation would significantly increase the amount of data sent between the ship and Epsilon Indi.

The Terans had gradually increased the population on the Main Ship in the last ten years of the journey to Alpha Centauri. It got a little crowded at the end, as soon as they arrived and completed some minimal HUB construction, conditions returned to normal. The notable exception was that the previous average age of 137 years was now much lower, many aboard the ship were busy with their learning activities. This period would last until the youngsters reached age thirty-five to forty, so they would not be contributing much early on. By the time the ship departed for Sol, however, enough of them would be ready to contribute sufficiently to allow both the HUB and the ship to be fully staffed.

The crew of the Main Ship lived and worked in extended groups of ten to over a hundred. The groups were not static, as people moved based on relationships with other individuals, changes in career, and moves between the HUB and ship. A large portion of the ship's inhabitants worked on careers in technical fields, these almost always overlapped with a facet of the ship's operation or were in a field that could contribute to its improvement. As a result it was difficult to tell where most people's careers ended and the day-to-day operational activities of the ship began. This was why so little fixed time in one's weekly schedule needed to be devoted to non-career-related functions. These functions were, of course, vital to their own survival, nearly everyone went about these duties diligently. Most enjoyed the opportunity to stay in touch with the state of the ship. Lack of diligence was infrequent. It was immediately detected and reported by the ship's systems. It was considered a serious breach of personal responsibility and dealt with swiftly by one's peers or extended family group. Persistent cases were rare. These were handled by the ship's judicial system.

The systems were practically foolproof, requiring only a few months' training to learn how to run one of them. The operations teams typically provided high-level supervision and error monitoring. They would also bootstrap the start-up of new systems or supervise repair procedures in the case of severe malfunctions. If necessary a part of the crew could work up to twenty-five or thirty hours a week for a short period while others received the requisite training. It had rarely been done, but it was considered an acceptable backup in case the mix of skills was slightly off. They had never had a problem with numbers, since only around fifty thousand people were actually needed in the early stages of the development of the HUB, or at the start of the next voyage of the Main Ship. They could easily correct any deficiencies by accelerating the population growth for a while. In a society that tightly controlled its population level, it was not difficult to find volunteers for the occasional growth spurt.

Henry, Lucy, and John crossed to the HUB on one of the regular shuttles. The trip took three weeks.

Conditions on the HUB when they arrived were much less refined than in the Main Ship. It was bare stone and metal. The habitat chamber was rock and sand with no atmosphere. Since Henry was involved in the construction of the HUB, they spent most of their time there, this meant living in the crew area within the hull. Residential quarters in the hull included only the essentials, there were few large interior spaces, none had any vegetation. They would be living indoors until they could move to the habitat. The HUB would be much more comfortable when it became functional in the next five years. Then they would spend as much time there as possible, where living and working would be the same as in the Main Ship.

Henry kept in contact with friends and family back on the ship, especially Caleb. He continued to work off and on with the Sol c group. He was pleased that John was doing so, as well. The ship was near enough that communications delays were just a few minutes, trips back and forth took a couple weeks on the regularly scheduled shuttles.

Once at the HUB, Henry took on full-time responsibility for construction of a component of the main internal communication systems. His time spent on Sol c matters dropped equally as fast. It wasn't that Sol c no longer inter-ested him, just that he had a new, more urgent task in front of him. Sol c was way out in the future, at most he would only be a spectator. He had a new job to do and, as was his nature, he went at it full bore. His team consisted of 125 members plus a thousand robots.

John's running was challenged by a lack of wide-open spaces. The main hallways of the HUB's housing levels were serviceable, but not scenic. He returned to the ship a couple times a year for scheduled marathons. He always placed high in these events and won once when his main nemesis was not entered.

Though John was not required or even expected to, he spent much of his time working with Henry's construction team when he was at the HUB. His analytical and organizational skills were immediately apparent, they were put to good use. John was still technically in his upbringing period, but no one in his upbringing group felt his spending a significant part of his time with the construction team was harmful. In fact, they felt it would help his socialization skills. His teammates quickly recognized his natural ability to accept responsibility. He dealt with difficult situations in a non-judgmental manner, the team soon began treating him as an equal member.

A year later, the maturity John demonstrated while working with the construction team, led to the formal recognition of what was already a reality. He was approved early for adult status by his upbringing group. He was granted full access to the HUB's and ship's systems, and gained exclusive control of his personal activities records. A formal ceremony marking this milestone took place when he turned thirty-five.

His new status meant he could go anywhere, do anything he chose. He could go back to the ship, stay at the HUB, or go to one of the habitat vessels being constructed in orbit. He decided to stay at the HUB, at least for the immediate future.

John's personal monitor data was now his own private property, he had sole access. Outsiders would be allowed entry if he tried to do something that could endanger others or the ship. Even then it would be only a few select individuals under strict controls.

John had decided to go on the crossing to Sol. First, however, he would go to Alpha Centauri A c—or Devon, as they had named it—to experience the surface of a planet firsthand. He dreamed about visiting Sol's planets. He wanted to be prepared for the possibility if they decided to stop there instead of flying by, although the third planet would be off-limits. Devon was the best available place to see a real world.

Chapter 21
Devon
(1863)

John's visit to the surface of Devon, Alpha Centauri A's third planet, was a revelation to him. He had spent his entire life in the protected confines of the Main Ship or the HUB and eagerly anticipated his ten-week visit to the planet.

Alpha Centauri A's inner planet was a charred cinder too hot and barren for life. The second planet was also quite warm, but could support life at the highest latitudes. It was only 0.6 the size of Teran, consequently its gravity field was relatively weak. There was little water vapor or oxygen in its atmosphere. Beyond Devon was an asteroid belt, after that came Alpha Centauri B, which also had three planets.

Like its companion, Alpha Centauri B's inner planet was hot and desolate. The second, at the inner edge of the habitable zone, was enveloped by a dense atmosphere of poisonous gases. The third planet was near the outer edge of the habitable zone. It was a little too cold, although the equatorial latitudes were moderate. There was a good deal of water locked up in its polar ice caps but little oxygen in the atmosphere, which was dominated by ammonia and methane. The planet was 1.05 the size of Teran, so the gravity was right. Unfortunately, it had a history of wide shifts in the inclination of its rotational axis. Currently it was inclined by 77 degrees to the plane of its orbit around Alpha

Centauri B, which caused extreme variations of temperature during the year across all latitudes, resulting in harsh weather conditions on the entire planet. The length of the cycle from minimum inclination of 13 degrees to maximum and back to minimum was 148,000 years. These rapidly shifting climatic regimes would be especially troublesome in the early stages of the evolution of life on the planet.

If, like the Terans' home planet or the third planet in the Solar system, there was a moon of even modest size, the rotational wobble that caused the wide shifts in inclination would have been significantly reduced. Often the influence of other large planets in a star system will help stabilize the rotational wobble of smaller inner planets, which was not the case, however, for Alpha Centauri B's third planet. It had been doubly unlucky.

Though Devon had biological inhabitants, the state of evolution on the planet was early in the progression to intelligent life. It would take several hundred million years, give or take a comet impact or two, before advanced land animals appeared. Right now the Terans were trying to learn as much as they could while getting the HUB completed.

With Devon's atmosphere containing close to 18 percent oxygen, the Terans could survive on the surface without respiration equipment. Re-engineered red corpuscles were needed to increase oxygen uptake efficiency to avoid exhaustion. This allowed several dozen manned outposts to be set up on the surface. Their main purpose was to support the scientific expeditions studying the planet's atmosphere, land, and oceanic depths. The outposts also provided accommodations for visitors, but were not plush vacation resorts. Visitors were expected to spend at least part of their time contributing to the technical activities taking place. Visiting did, however, give them a change of pace from the construction demands at the HUB, plus offered numerous chances to sightsee as the scientific teams ranged across the planet.

Devon's surface was much different from the environment on their home world. The land was devoid of life except for the low-lying coastal margins. There were extensive zones of temperate climate covered with rock, sand, and gravel. There was, however, some spectacular scenery; huge gorges filled with wild rivers, ranges of tall craggy mountains, and wide spread deserts.

Land vegetation was dominated by spore bearing plants, which were well established in wetlands near sea level. Modest encroachment beyond this had only recently started, most of the uplands and higher elevations were not vegetated, save for a few patches of lichen. This lack of vegetation made surface geological investigations and aerial surveying straightforward.

Animal life was equally as primitive, mostly amphibious types confined to the same areas as the dominant vegetation, plus a few early proto-reptilians that had begun to venture farther out. Then there were the insects, already highly evolved and profuse. They were the main difficulty when it came to conducting activities on foot in the coastal zone, and would continue to be a nuisance for hundreds of millions of years.

Life in the oceans had been flourishing much longer than on land, advancing to the point where it was dangerous for the Terans to put to sea in small vessels. The dominant chordates had evolved to enormous proportions and levels of potential violence. Only the largest research vessels were manned; most of the investigatory work was done remotely.

The Teran population on the planet, including a permanent staff of scientists and guides would probably never exceed ten thousand.

The residents of the habitats would come down to the planet for periodic visits of a month or two, but would spend the vast majority of their lives in the safety of their orbiting worlds. Because of the small size of the facilities and the unpredictable nature of the surface, the number of visitors allowed was limited. Priority had been given to those who would be departing with the ship.

The docking procedure with the high-orbit station had finished, John was standing at the exit waiting for the door to open. It had been a pleasant eighteen day trip from the HUB, now he was anxious to get started on the planet. He knew it was foolish to be so edgy; it would be another two weeks before he was cleared through decontamination. Only then would he be allowed to leave for the low-orbit transit station and finally go down to the surface.

Decontamination was a lengthy and necessary process designed to prevent the unplanned introduction of alien life forms to the planet's environment. The biggest nuisance was the billions upon billions of microbes everyone carried. During decontamination John would be infected with new microbes that were partly biological, partly biotechnologically engineered. Some would spread throughout the interior and exterior of his body, gobbling up any native microbes they encountered. They would remain in his system for ten days until everything was gone, then self-destruct. Others would replace vital microbes, such as those needed for digestion. All were engineered to reproduce no more than a few times before self-destructing. John would have to continuously ingest new ones while on the surface or his digestion would stop. He would also have to periodically ingest cleanup microbes to eliminate the few that had not self-destructed on time.

The process was well understood and tightly monitored, especially for first-timers like John. The right mix had to be tailored to each person's unique physiology. Digestive upset for a few days was the main risk until the correct combination of reengineered microbes was established. He settled in, completing the process in the typical ten days.

Next he had to go in isolation in the low-orbit station two hundred miles above the surface. At this altitude the planet dominated the view from the observing bubble in the main assembly area. John spent much of his time looking through one of the high-power telescopes, picking out details of the landforms between clouds. To him, Devon appeared to be an extraordinary place with mountains, canyons, hills, valleys, rivers, lakes, oceans, and deserts. He caught the next shuttle scheduled to depart for the surface.

John knew this would be the most exciting phase of the journey. The shuttles were essentially space planes; rocket powered above the densest parts of the atmosphere, jet powered at lower altitudes. Entering the atmosphere was where the real fireworks happened. Atmospheric entry friction caused the skin of the vehicle to heat up significantly, the resulting superheated gas trailing away produced a fiery show for the passengers. After the retro-rockets fired to begin the entry process, the engines would not be used unless the shuttle could not put down on its first pass at the landing strip. The process was nearly as old as spaceflight itself, and completely automated. John felt no concern. Once buckled in his seat, he sat back to enjoyed the ride.

The Terans had established a welcome center and base camp on an island continent in the northern ocean. The largest landmasses, however, were in the southern hemisphere of the planet. The Terans had selected the smaller one for its geologic stability and relative remoteness. This would be the only part of the planet they would inhabit permanently, even here it would be limited. John arrived on the surface in the middle of a thunderstorm. The shuttle landed before the worst of the storm, but they were forced to stay onboard until it passed. In the process they were exposed—treated, in his opinion—to a fifteen-minute lightning display, an event that none onboard had ever witnessed before.

After disembarking John located his quarters, dropped off his travel pack, and immediately set out for the colony headquarters, where he could meet with the work leaders and guides. There he would establish a schedule of activities. John had already read the scientific reports concerning the island as well as the rest of the planet. He was particularly interested in the geology, having read as much background information as he could find.

The planet was formed, along with the rest of this star system, five billion years ago. Life had developed following the classic route of anaerobic bacteria evolving in an ammonia-rich atmosphere. The bacteria slowly enriched the atmosphere with oxygen until photosynthetic plants and then oxygen-breathing animals evolved. Both the animal and plant life-forms were primitive. During this time the planet enjoyed warm, stable atmospheric conditions. In the past few million years, continental drift had begun to break the main landmass into smaller pieces. The Teran plan was to leave most of the planet untouched and observe what was going on.

The next ten weeks were a well-earned diversion for John. He wanted to relax while losing himself in exploring the wilds of this exotic place. He spent the first few days in orientation lectures and safety programs. The resident naturalists wanted to make sure visitors were fully aware of what they were confronting, since it was so different from living in a habitat or the HUB. They then made several short forays away from the settled zone under controlled conditions. Once they were sure a visitor appreciated the forces at work around them, they were free to start experiencing the planet. For most this meant traveling in an auto piloted hovercraft near the surface, following the pre-planned routes to sites of interest. Visitors also accompanied the naturalists and scientific professionals on their rounds, assisting with what they were doing. John preferred the hands-on approach, he immediately decided to join a group going on a geologic mapping trip to the mountains.

They met early the next morning to board the hovercraft. That was when he met Vanya. He was a little early in arriving, several of the permanent residents conducting the trip were standing around talking. He noticed her right away, admiring her tall, athletic appearance. She looked like she was in her mid-fifties, he knew right away he wanted to meet her. Two additional visitors along with the final resident and trip leader arrived, the eight of them boarded the craft. John deliberately sat near enough to Vanya to observe but not so close that he would have to strike up a conversation. Reserved by nature, he was especially shy with women he found attractive.

About ten minutes into the flight, the leader got up and introduced himself, the other residents did the same. Vanya explained that she was doing sedimentary geology and was interested in studying the depositional history of the local area's sand-shale sequences. The outcrops in the foothills of the mountains provided numerous prime rock exposures, which she was using to construct a model of a major portion of the geologic history of the region. She planned to combine her findings with remote sensing data from stress and electromagnetic waves along with studies of the gravitational and magnetic fields to develop a three-dimensional picture of the surface and subsurface structure. Her work at the outcrops would provide information on rock types and depositional processes that would lead to a dynamic explanation of how the current geologic configuration had occurred. Essentially the entire team, which included members not present on that day, was trying to reconstruct the geologic history of this part of the planet.

On the personal side, she had been on the planet for ten years, previously working in several areas on the main continent doing similar research. Vanya enjoyed being on the planet, not seeming to mind the conditions. She took full advantage of the enormous exploratory potential of the place, her interests were not entirely scientific. She spent much of her free time exploring the surrounding mountains from each site where they worked, climbing among the peaks, sleeping out under the stars. Her family group was located by Neutrontown in the Main Ship. John decided he was going to be a sedimentologist for the next few weeks.

Once the residents finished their introductions, it was the visitors' turn. When John's came, he explained that he had been working on the HUB's communications systems and was committed to leaving with the Main Ship. He added that his primary areas of interest were communications and simulation science, he left it at that. He was not in the habit of telling strangers that he actually considered himself a historian, that what he was trying to simulate was history. That information had gotten so many queer looks that he had stopped volunteering it. When people asked, he said his most recent simulations were of plasma flow in the ship's engine systems, which was true. As they became more familiar with his work, people usually learned that he was very good at it. He had found a way to appreciably improve the computational accuracy and performance of the plasma simulation that had led to a 0.23 percent efficiency increase of the ship's engines. Talking to John's friends and colleagues was the only way to discover this particular information. In closing, John stated, while looking directly at Vanya, that he thought it might be interesting to learn about sedimentary geology, especially since this might be the one time in his life he got to see sediments. Vanya noticed the attention but did not respond. Brad, the leader of the team, winked at her and smiled. This was not the first time a young male visitor had taken a sudden interest in sedimentology when Vanya was onboard.

Chapter 22
First Field Trip
(1863)

The transport's forward motion slowed as it settled down on the small landing pad in the middle of a recently made clearing, "John, this is our stop," Vanya called out as she and Brad got up to leave the craft. None of the other visitors made a move to rise; they were going along with the rest of the party who were involved in the surveying part of the project.

Surveying was popular with visitors because it always involved trips to high mountain peaks in the region. The views were terrific, they made for spectacular wall images that would impress their friends when they got back home. There was something spiritual about mountaintops. Reaching the pinnacle stirred people's imaginations, John was no exception. Before leaving, he wanted to stand atop one of the mountains that towered to the west.

He, Vanya, and Brad cleared the craft's entrance, they walked to the waiting robots as their colleagues headed westward in the shuttle. They would meet again in three days. In the interim the two groups would be in constant contact, as well as with the base camp back at the main settlement.

Brad began, "John, the robots have been at work for weeks in this area, running traverses from outcrop to outcrop from the hills here on the coastal plain up to the higher peaks of the main mountain range to the west." Their landing spot was on the edge of the plains that stretched eastward from the foothills to the ocean.

"Most of the best outcrops were located by aerial or satellite photos," Vanya added. "The robots used the locations to run traverses from one to another in long zigzag patterns. They examined the rocks at each outcrop testing for mineral composition and physical properties such as density, grain size, porosity, and permeability."

John tore his gaze away from Vanya to look at the immediate area.

The nearby vegetation was low, not much over two feet high, it covered most of the soil, which was thin and low in organic matter. Toward the east onto the coastal plain, it changed to widely dispersed treelike plants until it became a continuous forest of fern-trees. John's group would initially head to the forest, then circle around turning uphill away from the thickest vegetation.

The robots led the way as Vanya continued, "We will be running a traverse that goes along a series of outcrops that will give us a chance to examine the entirety of the sedimentary section that is exposed in this area."

They wore bodysuits made of a lightweight yet strong material that would repel insects, prevent scratches from the vegetation and penetration by small biting or stinging creatures. The robots would take care of any large insects that got too close.

Brad picked-up the discussion, "We won't be doing anything the robots can't do on their own. However, as you can appreciate, the need to see firsthand what one is studying and do at least a part of the hands-on work, no matter how small, is primal."

John felt that the adventure of being in the wilderness, the sense of independence it provided, no matter how well looked-after they were by the robots, served to heighten the pleasure of the work.

On the way to the first outcrop, Brad and Vanya introduced him to the general procedures of field geology. They ran through what they would do to determine the particular geometric and physical properties needed to map the local geology. With the aid of a display screen on the back of the robot leading the way, Brad helped John understand the markings and color codes on the geologic map that was in the process of being refined. "These symbols mark a series of locations in our traverse we will use to fill in vital parts of the puzzle of the local geologic structure."

He displayed a second map that showed a larger-scale view of the regional geology. With it Vanya reviewed what they knew of the history. "Essentially the tectonic plate we are on has been rifted from the large main continent to the south, it is slowly making its way northwestward. This area consists of the worn-down remnants of a once great mountain range that was created by a previous collision of the two continents. The highest peaks exceed thirteen thousand feet; at one time they could have been as high as twenty-five thousand.

"The rocks in the outcrops we will be visiting today and tomorrow are all sedimentary. One of our main objectives is to locate any evidence of fossils. These sediments were once below sea level, we want to establish how deep the water was when the deposition occurred, what the water temperature, salinity, and other physical conditions were. Examining fossils, especially microfossils, can help answer these questions. The robots will do much of this for us here in the field, while we search for macrofossils. Later, back at base camp, we will study the fossils in order to tie them into the geologic history.

"On our last day we will pass into a completely different type of geology. As we approach the high peaks, the inner core of the mountains will be exposed at the surface. The outcrops there will be metamorphic or igneous rocks. This is beyond the vegetated zone, we will be at altitudes above which the planet's primitive plants can survive. At that point we will effectively be on one continuous outcrop."

They arrived at the first location, and immediately set about their tasks. For the initial few stops, John mostly observed. Soon, however, he had picked up the essentials of operating the measurement equipment and began taking turns with the other two. This was a great help to Brad and Vanya, because it freed them to do more looking around than usual.

John also did a lot of casual observing, not just on the outcrops, but along the routes between them, where he observed the strange plants that lived there. The "natural" areas back on the ship were composed of mature forests containing seed-bearing trees, flowers, and grasses. Birds, insects, and small to medium-sized mammals dominated the ship's animal population. The environment was constructed to duplicate the temperate forests found on Teran.

Here on Devon the vegetated zone was much more open. There were tree-sized plants spaced ten to thirty feet apart, which grew to a maximum of twenty to thirty feet. They had leaves which grew directly from the main trunk; no branches were present. When the leaves—which were enormous—fell off, they produced a deep scar, which left the trunks looking like a cheese grater. The ground was covered with fallen trunks and deteriorating leaves, it was very damp. The air temperature was in the low 80s, the humidity was high, above 70 percent. He knew from his initial readings before arrival that these conditions were typical for spring weather. Later in the summer it would get much hotter, even in winter the air temperature would rarely go below 60 degrees. The dampness was necessary for the trees to propagate. They reproduced via spores, like ferns, the presence of water was necessary to get sperm and egg together. As a result of this, the forest ended when the water got scarce; in this case at higher elevations to the west. There was a notable lack of diversity. There were only three or four kinds of tree-sized species along with ten smaller ones forming the undergrowth.

The animal life also lacked diversity. There were plentiful insects of various sizes; some as large as a man's forearm, plus the occasional small amphibian. Other than that, there did not appear to be much in the way of medium to large land-based life forms. The oceans were a different story. They were teeming with fishes, a host of invertebrates, corals, and aquatic plants. John learned from his background readings that the swampy shoreline areas had the largest assortment of plant and animal life. It would be another fifty to seventy-five million years before evolution produced the type of life that could survive in the harsher environs of the uplands, high peaks, or the dry interior plains.

John's group proceeded from outcrop to outcrop as the day progressed, repeating the investigation procedures at each one. Vanya and Brad continually updated the maps while holding a running discussion on the local ramifications of the tectonic processes that had led to the present set of geologic conditions. John did his best to follow their conversation, even asking a few questions that turned out to be not at all dumb, but he felt like the outsider, tagalong that he was. At the lunch break the talk turned away from the purely scientific tasks at hand, mostly at John's instigation. He wanted to get to know his companions better, Vanya especially, so he began a small inquiry into their backgrounds.

From Brad's public records, John had learned that Brad had been doing geology for the past five years. Before that he had spent most of his time in agricultural genetics, first on the ship where he was born eighty-five years ago, then, for the twenty years prior to coming to the survey project, on the newly constructed HUB facilities. Brad was tall and fit-looking, he had always spent a good deal of time on physical pursuits. He had run the gamut from bicycling to running to mountaineering, which was his latest hot interest now that he was close to large peaks. The public records showed pictures of him with friends at scenic spots on the planet, as well as older shots of him going back to childhood, along with short narratives on people, places, and events.

Vanya's public data was not very revealing. She had started out in geology and stayed with it. Like John, she was born on the Main Ship during the trip to Alpha Centauri. No birthdate was given, there were only a few photos and little else.

John asked her how she had gotten interested in geology. "I was around age ten, I guess," she answered. "There was much about Devon and the rest of the Centauri system to learn. When I heard there would be an extensive period of exploration of the planet's surface, that geological examination would be one of the major parts of the effort, I decided that was what I wanted to do."

She had prepared herself for this work well. When the first teams were being formed, she had been among the earliest selected. As a result, she had already spent twenty years on the planet.

"What do you do you do in your free time?" John inquired.

"Well, like many of the planet-based crew, I spend my vacations on the HUB, the opposite of you."

He had hoped for a bit more elaboration so he changed course. "Do the mountains have the same draw for you as Brad?"

"She actually introduced them to me," Brad broke in.

"Yes, the bug bit me soon after I arrived. It must come with living so close to them," she replied.

And she's a very experienced mountaineer, John thought, judging by the familiarity she had with the peaks both in the local area and further afield. That was the end of personal conversation. They went back to work.

Before dinner John tried again to strike up a conversation. He reinitiated the discussion on mountaineering he had tried to begin at lunch. He wanted to know more about her, this seemed a sensible route. Also, he was starting to feel a little of the magnetic attraction of the peaks, himself. They had visited eight outcrops during the day, covering seven miles. In the process they had ascended from the plains at one hundred feet above sea level to three hundred feet at their present location.

"This camp gives a great panorama of the mountain ranges to the west. Did you pick it out?" John asked, looking toward Vanya, as the three of them walked up onto the sun deck where dinner would be served.

"Yes, you can see many of the big peaks." She proceeded to point out the prominent ones nearby. With some prodding by Brad, she provided short descriptions of the routes to their tops. This was followed by a couple stories of her climbing experiences. Brad figured prominently, having participated in a number of trips with her.

John was relieved that Brad joined in, that got her talking about something she obviously loved.

After dinner they moved to the work tent to check the day's progress on the mapping system and review the plan for tomorrow. The data collected from the day's exposures confirmed the presence of a large thrust fault in the region. They had crossed it between stops six and seven in the middle of the afternoon. They expected to cross another tomorrow, locating the actual fault in an outcrop they would reach at midday. The two geologists were excited about this impending event. John thought it was interesting, but he was much more excited about the mountains. He gradually got Vanya and Brad talking of them again after the map work had been completed. The discussion eventually got away from adventures to a favorite subject whenever mountaineers gathered, misadventures.

They recounted the events of several near disastrous trips to the peaks; a couple they had been involved in themselves. Though no one had been seriously injured, the possibility of dire consequences registered strongly with John. In every case the fact that they always maintained constant communications with the base meant that rescue and medical transport were dispatched immediately when needed. He was starting to develop a less romantic, more respectful picture in his mind of mountain travel.

They turned in for the night a little after 9:00 p.m. It had been a long day with the 5:00 a.m. departure from base, they wanted to be on their way to the first outcrop by 6:00 a.m.

The next two days sped by, John rapidly integrated into the team. He shared many of the routine field duties, although his lack of deep geological knowledge meant his contribution to the data interpretation was minimal. They found the second thrust fault as expected. On the third day, they crossed the unconformity that separated the sedimentary rock of the plains and foothills from the metamorphic rocks of the uplands. The evening conversations again centered on mountaineering, John became hooked on giving it a try. Both Vanya and Brad had warmed to him considerably. It became obvious to John that they had a close relationship, but its exact nature had not been revealed. They did sleep in separate tents, John didn't know whether this was typical or only to guard their privacy. As with most Terans they were withdrawn when it came to discussing with outsiders their deeper emotions.

On that third evening, they invited John to go with them on their next trek in the mountains. The next day they spent the morning consolidating their findings while waiting for the transport to arrive. By late afternoon they were back at base. After a rest day, they planned on going on a two-day trip to peak 542. It was medium sized at 11,560 feet, it would be a good introductory trip for John. He leaped at the opportunity, feigning surprise, at the same time realizing that Brad and Vanya had probably planned it specifically for him.

Chapter 23
A Visit to the Uplands
(1863)

John prepared for departure as the transport approached the drop-off point. They were being let off in a high valley ringed by peaks on three sides. The transport would then return to base. He started to feel a little nervousness as it finally hit him that they would be on their own for the next three days. No robots. No transport. Just themselves and what they carried on their backs. The one thing they did not have to bring was water. There was plenty of that coming down from the snow and ice fields above them, but there was no vegetation, the only shelter from the elements would be their gear. John knew the experience would test his character.

Their equipment was lightweight and strong, the food was loaded with carbohydrates and nutrients. Each of their packs included a tent, sleeping bag, extra clothes, food, cooking implements, water bottle, and survival gear. They weighed twenty-five pounds. They also carried long-range communications sets that had a rugged extra outer case. Even so, John could not help being a little apprehensive. He welcomed the new sensation of their small group being on its own; at the same time, he was wary of the dangers. He understood that nature and the mountains were unforgiving. For the first time in his life, he would be cutting the considerable umbilical cord that connected Terans with the protecting cocoon of their society.

It was not merely a symbolic connection. On the ship or in the habitats, everyone always wore communicators. They were integrated in their clothing. It provided an instant link with anybody else onboard and kept the ship's systems informed of each person's whereabouts. Most important, it monitored vital signs such as pulse and blood pressure. Assistance could be dispatched at the slightest indication of trouble, even if a person could not summon aid on his own or realized the need existed. Help was usually seconds away, since everyone had several personal robots and traveled with at least one all the time. The robots, tied to the ship's monitoring systems, were on hand as first responders.

The health and safety advantages were obvious. On the traverse of the previous week, the workers had robots with them, keeping a constant link to the base. A transport could be dispatched to arrive in minutes. Losing this protective umbrella gave John an eerie feeling. One device would be left on, set to transponder mode so they could at least provide an indication of their position to the base—a safety precaution the base staff insisted upon.

There were six in John's party. He watched them as they did final checks then hoisted their packs onto their backs. They wore a variety of clothing styles and colors, John thought it was a startling range of tastes for a group that held a common interest. It was almost as if they had decided ahead of time to each wear something completely different.

Vanya, as the most experienced mountaineer, was the leader. Brad would be second leader. Anne was the most experienced in first aid while Vijay was an expert rock climber. All except John had been trained in mountain rescue, two of them knew CPR. Introductions were done for John's benefit, since he was the nonresident. The group comprised two women and four men, with John the youngest. Troy was probably the oldest, John guessed he was around 160.

With input from Brad and Troy, Vanya had organized the trip, selecting the objective and route.

In nearly everything Terans did that involved a group, the selection of a leader, when it was thought one was necessary, was done by a simple vote by the group members. The sole exception was in education, where the teacher was in charge; even here, if the student's complaints were valid and numerous enough, the student had a voice. Once a Teran reached adulthood and got involved in a vocation, everything was strictly democratic. Work groups were self-selecting, the members decided who would be first among equals. They also determined what the role entailed. Sometimes it simply meant chairing meetings or acting as spokesperson. In other instances it involved significant decision making on behalf of the group. The process varied according to the preferences of the individuals involved and the nature of their work, it could change with time.

For their mountaineering expedition none of this applied. Vanya was in charge; she had put the trip together; she had selected the participants, or at least screened them for suitability and qualifications; she would be responsible for route finding, pace setting, and judging and acting on the conditions they encountered along the way. No one had elected her; everyone knew that this was the most sensible approach.

Recognizing this was when the seriousness of what they were about to undertake really sank in for John. That five Terans would without the slightest question turn over a major portion of their personal safety and autonomy to another for an extended period was extraordinary. However, that they would then go ahead and function as a group without this fact being evident, John did not find to be remarkable.

After the introductions Vanya began the trip orientation. "We will traverse the three peaks at the head of the valley in front of us. The climbing starts up the left flank of the valley shoulder a mile ahead. Once on the top of the valley wall, we ascend the ridge to the first summit. Next we descend to a saddle to spend the night in a protected area below on the far side. The second day we traverse the second and third peaks then descend the opposite side of the valley back to our starting point. We rendezvous with the transport at the original drop-off point for an early evening return to base."

The route totaled twenty miles and five thousand feet of ascent. It would not be a great challenge for most, although John thought Troy might feel the strain. John was used to doing twenty-mile runs as a part of his marathon training, hence the distance would not be a problem for him. The ascent coupled with the weight of the pack and spending a night on the ground at altitude might take a toll, but he felt ready. He was filled with excitement as they headed out in the early-morning mist.

Vijay and Vanya were carrying technical climbing tools. They told John that the route did not involve anything more challenging than a few short stretches on moderate rock slopes, most of the trek was simply a matter of walking.

John had been warned earlier by Brad that there was some exposure on the trail between the second and third peaks. "Exposure" meant sharp drops on one or both sides of a route that otherwise required no particular skills beyond enough balance to stand upright. There was no danger provided one stayed on the trail, although John sensed that maybe there was more to it than that. He decided to submerge his fears for the time being. Unfortunately, he soon found they would not stay completely buried, he began probing the other members of the group for descriptions of this segment of the trip. Their responses were uniformly reassuring, yet he never felt reassured.

The first phase of the trek was similar to his long runs, where it took around thirty minutes for his body to get used to the exercise. Once he warmed up from this initial effort, he felt much better. The rest of the day would be relaxing. The group worked their way up the valley slope in a diagonal fashion to avoid going directly up the steep hill.

It was already quite warm by midmorning. The sun was out with no clouds in sight, John was grateful for the mild breeze blowing from the west. Everyone removed all except the thinnest layer of clothing, they took frequent short water breaks. Vanya wanted to keep them moving. She had explained earlier that it would be best to reach the far side of the summit before noon because there always the possibility of afternoon thunderstorms this time of year.

Since the weather moved in from the west, behind the peak immediately in front of them, she wanted them to be well on their way down by late morning. Vanya had checked the weather satellite info before they started. The immediate area was clear, but thunderstorms could build up unexpectedly. Clear skies at 8:00 a.m. could be filled with rain and lightning five hours later. She would check the satellite data several times before they began the final phase of the ascent. Once they did there was no turning back.

They reached the summit a little after 10:00 a.m., pausing for a while to admire the views. The ascent was uneventful, the weather had held, although clouds were now coming in from the west. With teleglasses they could make out the outlines of the base, which was an island of white in a sea of green. Beyond was a bluish hint of the ocean. The high peaks in the west towered above the one they stood on. Several reached to nearly fourteen thousand feet and were covered in snow. Small glaciers ran down the valleys between several of the largest. They had been visited by transport, but no one had hiked the valleys or climbed the ridges to the peaks.

When John asked why not, Vanya answered that it was too dangerous. Some things were beyond the physical limits of their bodies and equipment. John wanted to give this additional thought.

After fifteen minutes on top, Vanya gave the signal to head down. Dark clouds were moving in. The weather map from the satellite showed a strong line of intense storm activity forming rapidly. They would need to descend to the safety of the saddle to wait out the weather. After the storms passed, the front should bring much clearer conditions.

The rain started when they were halfway down. It was light at first, blown in by the winds ahead of the storm. They could hear the rumble of thunder and see distant lightning flashes. A few minutes later, it began to hail, now they had to stop. The hail buildup on the rocks turned the footing treacherous. They couldn't risk a broken ankle, leg, or worse.

The mountain slope was fairly uniform, their best option was to find whatever protection they could in a small nearby depression. As the storm swept over them, they were pelted with pea-sized hailstones which stung as they hit. The interval between lighting flash and thunderclap kept shortening until the storm was on top of them, they were exposed to its full fury for ten minutes. Lightning twice struck a small promontory several hundred yards to their right—terrifying John. He was trembling when it ended, which he tried valiantly to control. Even though the others had been through thunderstorms before, their animated talk told him that this one was more intense than anything they had experienced in the past.

The rapid weather change amazed him. The storm had just passed yet already the sun was coming out. He was concerned they might have had to spend the night where they were because of the hail that had accumulated. In twenty minutes, however, they were back on the way down. The hail was melting rapidly, they wanted to establish camp before the next line of storms gathering in the distance moved in.

Late in the afternoon they arrived at the area Vanya had selected for that night's camp. They were two hundred feet down from the saddle on its eastern side in a bowl that provided protection on three sides. After a hearty dinner taken up by conversation of the day's events, they turned in for the night. Tomorrow would be even more strenuous than today.

The second line of storms rolled in just before midnight, a distant clap of thunder jolted John awake. Since he knew he couldn't sleep through it, he decided to go out to watch the show. He quickly dressed and walked westward climbing to the shoulder of the saddle. It was clear back to the east, one of the small moons shined brightly overhead. He could see the storm coming straight up the valley toward him. First the wind, then the rain. This time the few lightning strikes that occurred were far up in the clouds outlining the storm dramatically. He decided to stay to watch it pass. Ultimately, however, he had to abandon his perch because the wind got too strong. It was becoming difficult to stand up against it, he retreated to the protection of some nearby rocks. As he did, he met Vanya, who had been watching the storm as well.

"We landed in a lightning storm, now this. I never knew how powerful nature could be," John said.

"Yes. It can be quite a shock the first couple times," Vanya answered with a smile.

After a few moments of silence, she continued, "My first storm took me by surprise, too, I remember every second of it."

Vanya paused, then went on. "I was one of the earliest to arrive on the planet. I started going to the mountains almost immediately and feel I am only beginning to get to know them. Every time I visit there is something new, something different, more to see and learn. I guess that's why I keep coming back."

John looked out to the valley below watching the flashes of lightning for a moment. "Vanya, I came down to the planet to get a look at it before the ship left. I was planning to fly around, hit the high points, spend a week here or there, then head back to the HUB. After spending the three days on the traverse, I realize what I really want is to spend more time in the mountains so I can get to know them as much as possible."

"What made you decide to go with the ship?" Vanya asked.

"Oh, mostly my desire to see what's out there. It must be similar to how you feel when you are in the mountains; I know I felt it myself as we were setting out yesterday."

"My, how vague. Is there one thing in particular?" Vanya gave him a look.

"Well, yes, there is. It's Sol c. There's at least some sort of primitive civilization there. I want to get a close-up look at it."

"I'm not surprised. I've been following the work the Sol c teams have been doing, including your contributions. I actually knew who you were when we first met. I know you are very interested in history even though you did not mention it."

"You didn't say anything back then. Why not?"

"No, you deserved your privacy. But I'm glad we're sharing it now."

They both stood there for a while longer as the storm played itself out. The wind had died down, the rumble of thunder was becoming distant. Tomorrow would be a long day with another early wake-up. They started back to their tents, John turned the conversation over in his mind as he walked. They had talked before, but always in the presence of others. This was the first time they had been alone together. He smiled to himself at the irony that on such a large planet with so few people, it had taken him five days to spend a couple minutes alone with this woman. He realized he was developing strong feelings for Vanya and wasn't sure what to do.

Vanya thought about their meeting, too. She had been impressed by John's curiosity and intellect from the start. He was one of the few visitors she had met who came to a survey trip already informed on the planet's geology. Most of them knew what was going on, what to expect at a cursory level, but they spent most of their time doing menial tasks, observing the geologists, or sightseeing. John had arrived as well prepared as some of the new geologists and proceeded to share in their duties. He was not satisfied to be a spectator, she and the others liked him all the more because of it. Vanya was also starting to feel attracted to him. He was really still a young man, fresh out of his educational period. She was only fifteen years his senior—but fifteen years at this stage of life was a lot.

She had felt she knew him immediately. As time went by, she became aware of why. They were both much the same: quiet, reflective souls, not prone to rash decisions or pointless change yet ready to act decisively and with finality when they were certain of their course.

The next day dawned clear and bright, the air had a just-cleansed smell, the sky that crystalline quality it gets after a storm. The effect was magnified in the cool, thin air of the mountains, it felt wonderful to breathe. They reached the summit of the second peak before midmorning. It was the highest of the three mountains in their traverse, they were able to see their entire route from the top. The saddle where they had spent the previous night was twenty-five hundred feet below. The ridge to the final summit was below on the opposite side, this was what now caught John's attention. From where they stood, it looked razor thin. It was steep on both the downhill and uphill sides. He started to get an uneasy feeling in his stomach.

Vanya walked over to him to provide some quiet words of assurance, "It's not as bad as it looks. A real pussycat, actually."

John nodded. "Most pussycats don't look quite that scary," he said, wondering how she had known what he was thinking.

Brad approached as well volunteering that he had been nervous the first time he had seen the ridge. "My initial thought was to double back and meet everyone at the finish."

That didn't make John feel any better. He looked around to see if the others were coming to reassure him. They had not moved. If they had joined in as well, it would have been a really bad sign. Vanya and Brad had merely sensed his concern when they noticed him staring down at their next objective with a quizzical gaze.

"Let's go see what this ridge is like," Brad called out to the others. Vanya took a rope out of her pack and slung it on her shoulder. Vijay pulled out a collection of rock anchors and wedges from his pack, he clipped them to his belt. John eyed them suspiciously as they started down.

Once they got onto the ridge, the going was much easier. As he approached it, he began to realize that the viewing angle they'd had from the second peak made it look a lot more difficult than it was.

As they approached the narrowest part of the ridge, he saw that it was nearly flat. The descent and ascent on the opposite side were the steepest parts. John relaxed when he realized they would not have to deal with both a narrow ridge and steep rock at the same time. When they got to the narrowest part, he saw that the drop-off on both sides was precipitous, probably a thousand feet. The distance across was just over one hundred feet.

Vijay tied onto the rope while Anne set up a belay system. When he was ready, Vijay calmly stepped onto the ridge and walked across, where he anchored his end of the rope to form a fixed guide for the rest. Each person in turn clipped onto the rope and traverse the narrows. Before John's turn came, Brad gave him instructions on what to do. The important thing was to ignore the rope, walk normally. If he did slip, the rope would save him. If that happened, he should remain calm and try to climb back up onto the ridge. If he needed assistance, one of the others would come out.

John took the first couple of steps very tentatively. The rock was dry, the crossing was almost as wide as a sidewalk. After getting thirty feet out, he started to relax. He was conscious of the rope but did not rely on it. By the midpoint he was feeling confident enough to pause to take a look down both sides. He gulped hard as he contemplated the enormous drops. When he safely reached the other side, he felt an elation like nothing he had known before. The others understood what had taken place, because they had experienced it themselves. They congratulated him on making it across, he had become a real mountaineer.

They lunched for an hour on the top of the third peak, enjoying the view and watching the few small clouds go by. There would be no thunderstorms today. The afternoon was consumed by the descent followed by the walk back out to the rendezvous point, where they met the transport for the return to base. After cleaning up, they gathered for a group dinner to relive their adventure.

Chapter 24
Seaside and Glacier
(1863)

The following week Vanya's team would be spending their time at the base, finishing up the maps for the area they had surveyed, then preparing to begin mapping in the next sector to the north. John took this opportunity to go down to the coast to visit the sea. He also wanted to spend time reflecting on their climbing trip.

The transport dropped him off at the marine biological station up the hill from the oceanfront. As he headed down to the vacation huts at the water's edge, he thought of the week ahead, how he was looking forward to resting a little and doing some reading. In particular he wanted to dig back in ancient Teran history to learn about mountaineering on his home planet. Teran had many ranges of high mountains, a couple approaching thirty-three thousand feet, much higher than those he had recently visited, bigger than the tallest on this planet. People visited them, no one actually climbed them. They took transports to the observation decks. It wasn't that they were lazy; it was that climbing one of the big peaks with only what you could carry was deemed to be far too risky, practically suicidal. There had been a time, several thousand years before, when people had actually climbed those mountains. John wanted to find out how they did it, and why.

The marine bio-station was an active place with many crews coming and going to the reefs or destinations further offshore to study the ocean life. It was actually a far more interesting place than the land in that respect, since evolution had not had the time to diversify animal life much beyond the water. Under the sea, however, things had been well developed for a long time. During the week John would get around to taking a marine excursion and try sailing on one of the lakes. He had no real desire to take as intense a role with one of the other teams as he had with the geologists. Maybe he was a little tired, maybe he felt there was nothing out there that could top his recent experience, or maybe it was that there was no Vanya. He figured it was all three.

He had placed a request for mountaineering accounts in the high-peak regions of Teran, now they were starting to come in. Normally information requests from the archives were satisfied almost immediately, since the data was usually in the systems on the planet or on the HUB. What John was seeking could only be found back at the ship, hence the cause of much of the delay. Another contributing factor was that no one had accessed those particular files since the ship had left Teran. John immediately scanned them to see what he had, determining that though they were very limited, they would be adequate for his purposes. Apparently those who had supervised the initial loading of the archive did not feel it was necessary to include much beyond technical information on mountaineering. This would help anyone who happened to come upon a planet that had mountains and needed or wished to climb them. He was disappointed, however, that there were no personal accounts from those who had actually climbed high peaks. John sought such firsthand descriptions as much as the raw how-to information. Knowing a lot less of the realities of what to expect put more risk in what he was planning, but it would heighten the adventure aspect of the trip. He spent the next two days reading the files and using the local machine shop to construct equipment. He had one of the manufacturing robots make several complete sets of heavy-duty boots, clothing, tents, and sleeping bags. The next thing he had to do was test what had been made.

After examining maps of the higher mountains beyond where they had traveled the week before, John located an ideal place to do a trial. So far he had not talked to anyone about what he was up to; he was not ready to reveal his plans even to Vanya or Brad. He scheduled a transport for the next night and left Vanya a message that he was going on a brief overnight trip and would call the next morning.

The transport arrived at his quarters at 4:00 p.m., he loaded up his gear, set the course and was off. He had to file a flight plan with the control center at the base. They would know where the transport was at all times; filing the plan would prevent someone from coming out after him once they realized where he was going. He also had to say what he was planning to do. He told transport control that he was going to be drilling an ice core on one of the glaciers, he had to go overnight so work could begin at dawn. Never mind that he was not a glaciologist or that doing one ice core in an area that had already been cored extensively made much sense, or that the previous cores had all been done by the robots. Transport control would accept his explanation. Terans rarely lied or deceived one another; it was deeply ingrained in their upbringing, honestly was as much a part of them as their desire for safety and security.

Deception was practiced to spare someone's feelings, usually after much consideration. Now John was not only going to deceive, but to lie. He was going to the glacier to sleep outdoors using his newly made gear in the most inhospitable conditions he could find in the region. He had no intention of getting an ice core and would not come back with one. He was forsaking his safety, as well—a renegade combination in Teran society! John did not consider this aspect for more than a few minutes. He had had a taste of the independence, the solitude offered by the high peaks, now he wanted to try for as complete an experience of that as possible.

The transport arrived at the glacier at 5:00 p.m. It hovered while slowly moving up to its head at thirteen thousand feet. After surveying the glacier's surface, John moved down to its base and found a flat area on one shoulder that would make a good campsite. At eleven thousand feet, it was exposed to the weather from the north, luckily, there was a protected area downhill for the transport. The peak itself loomed another twenty-seven hundred feet above the sheer face of the cirque that had been carved above the top of the glacier. The walls were steep and free of snow, there was no avalanche danger. Rock fall was a potential problem. The face looked well frozen, he would be away in the morning before the sun hit it and started loosening small and not-so-small boulders such as the ones scattered on the surface of the glacier in the immediate vicinity.

He put on his protective clothing and set up the tent, putting the sleeping bag and cooking gear inside. He got back in the shuttle and directed it down to a protected location at the foot of the glacier, then did a final check on the weather conditions. The air temperature was 15 degrees, the wind was 8 miles per hour from the north. Light snow had begun to fall. The satellite data showed the predicted storm was moving in on schedule. He got out and closed the hatch; he left his communication pod onboard so the base would think he was in the shuttle. It would continue to relay the physical telemetry collected by his clothing sensors, unless he got really cold and someone noticed, he would not be bothered. He felt the altitude as he walked the five hundred feet uphill to the tent. In spite of his conditioning, going from sea level to eleven thousand feet without any intermediate acclimatization was difficult for him. He didn't have a headache, he just felt slightly out of breath. He got in the tent and started dinner.

After eating John lay inside his sleeping bag listening to the rising wind; the pitch was a low rush, although it had heightened noticeably since he arrived. Restless, he got up to check outside. It was starting to get dark, the sun was already hidden by the mass of the mountain to the southwest. The remaining light was leaking around the sides of the peak; in a few minutes it would be gone. He turned on his hand beacon and began walking up to the ridge, the wind buffeting him as he climbed toward the rocks above the edge of the glacier while light snow fell. He reached the rocks after twenty minutes, his altimeter showed 11,285 feet. From there to the summit the route appeared to be rock or gravel at a slope of 20 to 25 degrees, climbable without any special equipment. In the morning he would photograph it at close range from the transport before returning to base. If his study of the satellite photos of the peak was correct, this ridge would lead directly to the summit without much difficulty, except for the altitude and weather conditions. The top was 13,708 feet. Not the highest mountain in the range, but nearly so. He was interested in it because it was the tallest peak on the ocean side of the range, sitting slightly away from the central mass of its highest part. On three sides the peaks were two to four thousand feet lower, to the east, toward the sea, there were only overgrown foothills. The views would be spectacular.

The wind was growing stronger as the snow fall intensified. He lost the light entirely as he started back down the ridge to the tent. He reached it as the snow approached whiteout conditions. He was glad he had not waited any longer to return. Without his transponder he was on his own to navigate in this harsh, unfamiliar world.

The wind howled most of the night, gusting to 75 miles per hour at one point, the temperature dropped to 10 degrees below zero by morning. He slept fitfully because of the intensity of the noise and the cold that crept into the sleeping bag in spite of its thick insulation. The first rays of the sun penetrating the interior of the orange tent finally stirred him. He immediately got up to survey the landscape. The wind was down to almost nothing, the sky was a clear deep blue. There had been two feet of snowfall overnight, the tent was half buried. When he saw the drifts on the ridge, he was glad he had taken the advice of one of the references on building a snow-block wall along the upwind sides of the tent platform. It had probably kept the tent, and him along with it, on the mountain that night. He bundled up his gear, leaving the tent behind; it would have taken him hours to dig it out, he did not want to be nearby when the sun started loosening the rocks on the cliffs above. He half walked, half slid down to the transport and piled in for the return trip to the base.

It had been an uncomfortably noisy night; he was tired from lack of sleep, but he had determined that one could survive handily in the conditions of the high peaks. The transport maneuvered up the ridge to the summit. Views of the ridge showed that it was as free from technical difficulties as he suspected. He was now prepared to take the next step.

Brad and Vanya were not totally happy with John when he told them of his night on the glacier. They reminded him of the primary lessons for safety in the wild, chiefly the one on not traveling alone. He was unrepentant though, and glad he did not tell them about leaving his transponder on the transport. When he told them he wanted to go back to climb the peak, they were hesitant until he showed them the photos of the route. They decided it would be a challenging but not technically difficult climb, agreeing that the main problems would be weather and altitude. The gear John had made when combined with the transport's weather reporting systems would allow a margin of safety, if not a level of physical comfort they could deal with. They commended him on the thoroughness of his preparations.

Then he told them he wanted to hike in to the mountain expedition style, instead of simply climbing from where he camped for the night. The walk in would require three days. Including an equal amount coming out, plus a day to climb the peak from the head of the glacier, adding a day or two of cushion for bad weather, it came to at least an eight-day commitment. After much discussion with John, Brad and Vanya agreed to do the hike in, but not out. They would take the transport back. In addition they insisted on light packs for the hike; the transport would haul the bulkier equipment and meet them at their stopping points. John would see to making additional equipment, they would meet the following weekend to check their gear. Departure was set for the middle of the next week.

Chapter 25
An Expedition
(1863)

The group had grown to six by the time they started out. Anne and Vijay had been on the traverse from three weeks before. The newcomer was Dave Wellington, a gangly man with a scraggly beard. He seemed always to walk with his arms folded, often tugging or stroking his beard with one hand as if lost in thought; which, apparently, he often was. He was a noted theoretical physicist, down from the HUB for one of his periodic visits. Dave claimed that visiting the mountains always cleared his head, he was more productive for weeks afterward. When he was stuck on a particularly thorny problem, it helped him to get away for a while. During a trip or shortly after returning, he usually was able to solve the problem and move ahead. In the past ten years, he had spent as much time as anyone in the mountains, Brad and Vanya considered him immediately when they were filling out the group's complement. It was fortunate Dave was already on Devon for a getaway.

John quickly took a liking to Dave, despite their different personalities and appearances. A gaunt man with a gray-flecked beard that made him look old and wizened, Dave was quiet to the point of being taciturn, he did not reveal himself often or easily. Like John he was not an individual who dealt in triviality or the superficial, though compared to him John was outgoing. John did not meet new people easily, although once the ice had been broken and a common ground established, he could be disconcertingly open at times. He could at least tolerate people or situations he felt were tedious and lacked substance, whereas Dave shut them out, departing as quickly and quietly as possible. Nonetheless, the two men shared a singularity of purpose. In the future, at a point in life where most of their cohort would be starting their third career, John and Dave would still be on their first. Neither saw the need nor had the desire to do anything other than what they initially chose. John was fascinated with the past because he felt it could tell him what the future might hold. Dave was fascinated with the way the natural world worked, he wanted to know why things are the way they are.

Their jumping-off point was at the start of the low hills twenty-five miles from the foot of the glacier. The hike in was pleasant, they made good time, reaching the glacier midafternoon of the third day. The next day, they traveled up the glacier to the high campsite John had used the week before, finding the tent he had left behind. It was flattened and almost completely buried in snow. They summoned the transport, unloaded the overnight gear, and set up camp. They would climb to the summit the next day if the weather permitted. Unfortunately, the forecast was changing, showing a storm front moving in, their hopes were not high.

Dawn arrived with overcast skies and light snow. Conditions were predicted to deteriorate during the course of the day. They would be in for a bit of a wait. After breakfast the group took a short acclimatization hike up to the head of the glacier. This allowed them to get familiar with the beginning of the route up the left shoulder and ridge to the summit. The cloud ceiling was down to that level, so after a quick lunch they headed back to camp. John and Dave returned to the tents. He had hoped Vanya would too, but she went with the others back to the transport to pass the time inside its comfortable confines. Plus they had work they could do, friends and colleagues to keep in touch with. John and Dave had shared a tent the night before, they got back in when the heavy snow began a bit after 2:00 p.m. Their friends in the transport came out at 6:00 for dinner and to spend the night in the tents. Though not large, there was a comfortable amount of space in the camp, since the tents shared a common vestibule area. They talked for a while before falling asleep early.

The wind came up after midnight, just as during John's first trip. By 2:00 a.m. was howling at over 60 miles per hour. In the thin air at this altitude, the wind pressure was not what it would be at sea level, but it was strong enough to blast the tents and make it difficult to stand up outside. The remainder of the night passed with little sleep. In the morning the snow was still falling hard, the wind created blizzard conditions. The weather satellite images showed the storm to be large. It would take at least another day or two to clear. Again John and Dave's companions decided to pass the day in the transport. Limited in size as it was, they would rather brave the storm to get onboard than spend the day out of contact in the tents. Although he considered going to the transport as well, there would be no chance for him to get better acquainted with Vanya in there. John decided to stay put with Dave. They both had reading to do and actually enjoyed the tents. Since they had the three tents to themselves for the day, they moved the gear into one, stretching out alone in each of the other two. Because of the noise from the storm they were essentially isolated, unless one took the initiative to make contact.

At lunch Dave began to relate a few of his previous experiences in the mountains. The pair had spent the last three days traveling together, and three nights sharing a tent, this was the first time Dave had opened up. John had already talked a lot about his one previous trip plus a little of his personal interests. Dave had not done much more than listen attentively, responding with a short sentence or two.

"I enjoy the solitude of the mountains," he said now, "and the solitude within myself I can only truly find up here. This is why I prefer staying in the tents. It is my chance to get away from the technology, the manmade devices and systems we have created to help manage and protect our lives."

John nodded in agreement.

Dave continued. "Sure, we are confined to this tent, but it is a temporary physical confinement. In reality we are all confined within our own minds, but this is only confinement if you let it be. For me being in the mountains allows me to focus my full attention outward to escape completely any feelings of confinement that may have arisen since my last visit. Being holed up in the tent during this storm truly heightens the intensity of the effect."

John sat quietly for a few moments. He now knew why he had been so attracted to the mountains. A melancholy feeling came over him when he realized he would not be able to come back here many more times.

"Once I leave with the ship, I will likely never set foot on a mountain again," he said.

Then he realized Dave was really talking of a state of mind that one could carry anywhere. Dave had found that being in the mountains was a good way to renew it. There were other ways, such as running, or places, like the sea, where one could accomplish the same thing with the same state of mind.

The storm ended that afternoon, the sky was clear by evening. The rest of the group rejoined them for dinner once again and spent the night in the tents before the next day's climb to the summit. They awoke at 4:00 a.m. The air was fresh with a slight breeze. The temperature was in the 20s. After breakfast, they were quickly on the trail up onto the ridge before the day warmed up. The initial part of their route from the camp to the ridge was covered in snow; traveling through it before dawn was a bit of an ordeal. They made the ridge in time to see the sun rise over the lowlands to the east. The sky filled with evolving patterns of cinnabar, purple, red, rust, then finally bright orange and yellow before giving way to the glow of the planet's star. The wind from the storm had swept most of the loose fresh snow off the high ridge; it was now mainly hard-packed snow interspersed with patches of rock and gravel. The way to the summit looked clear of difficulties.

They passed above thirteen thousand feet at 9:00 a.m., with around seven hundred feet of ascent remaining. Brad and John turned out to be the strongest climbers, summiting at 10:00. The altitude slowed the entire group considerably. Dave and Vanya arrived thirty minutes later, followed closely by Anne and Vijay. They had been in good condition prior to the trip, but agreed that waiting for the storm had helped make the final ascent easier. The forced two-day wait in the camp at eleven thousand feet had given them an opportunity to acclimate to the altitude.

Vijay volunteered, as he and Anne arrived: "Summits are special places, the only way you can understand is to visit one. It doesn't have to be a major peak or even the highest point in the area; it just has to be far enough up to be able to get a good look at the surrounding territory.

"As a child I remember the tree fort I built. You could climb up to the top part of the huge maple it was in and see all around. This afforded a good view of most of my child's world, including the neighborhood I lived in, the town center in one direction, the fields outside of town in the other. Now, on the summit of this peak, I view in the same way much of my adult world. It brings back these memories with many of the same feelings."

Dave, in an unusual move, picked-up the train of thought.

"The exhilaration of accomplishment one gets upon arrival is incredible. This soon subsides, however, the mind begins to wander as you take in the spectacle surrounding you. You begin to feel as if you could float above the landscape, seeing in stark clarity what is below. This is the feeling one gets on the summit, what I have described is how I felt after first figuring out the Demming quantum noise equation. I had reached a summit of the mind. The experience was much like today's summit of topography."

Everyone understood and voiced agreement.

They spent an hour on top, lunching as they talked and admired the view. Too soon it was time to start down. They descended via the route of their upward journey. On the way down they stayed closer together than on the ascent, it was much easier to have a conversation since they were not so out of breath. John got the chance to talk one on one with Vanya. They walked together much of the way. As they went, their conversation turned away from the mountains and became personal. They each talked a lot about themselves, what they wanted from the future. The experience enhanced his growing feelings for her, he was beginning to feel she might be more than passingly interested in him as well. By the end of the day, John felt as if something was happening between him and Vanya.

After stopping at the glacier camp to offload gear to the transport, they hiked the last five miles down to the foot of the glacier. That night was spent in a comfortable camp where they could rest from the previous days' efforts.

The next morning all save John and Dave boarded the transport to return to the base station. The two would walk back out to their original starting point. Dave said he wouldn't feel complete if he did not do it this way. John concurred.

As John was repacking his backpack for the trip out, Vanya came over and sat down on the ground next to him.

"John, what are your plans after you get back to base? Brad and I were hoping you would rejoin us for a while longer on the surveys."

"I would enjoy that, too, I was going to ask if you wouldn't mind me hanging around for another week or two before I go back to the HUB. First, though, I want to see some of the rest of the Devon."

"Would you like a tour guide?"

John smiled. "Who do you have in mind?"

"Why me, of course." She poked him on the shoulder.

John smiled again as he got up to walk her to the transport.

Chapter 26
Sightseeing
(1863)

With Vanya as his guide, John visited many of the natural wonders of the magnificent world that was Devon. Canyons, rivers, high waterfalls, deserts, tropical islands, and, of course, the mountains, including volcanoes. It was just the two of them on a trip built for romance, which is exactly what developed.

The flora and fauna covered a restricted range of the land near sea level. Vanya led him in and through it. They were assaulted by insects, got stuck in bogs, were exhausted by the heat and humidity, endured storms, and saw a tornado from a distance. They spent evenings together discussing the day's activities and planning the next. After the planning, they were together at night, as well.

They went to sea on one of the research vessels where they helped capture and study enormous fishes, actually chordates—no bones, just cartilage—fifty- to one-hundred-foot-long sharks; the most devastating predators that would ever live in this or any other ocean. Dinosaurs were millions of years in the future for Devon. They would sometimes equal but not exceed the power and violence of these deep-sea giants.

John's visit was approaching its end as he rambled around the surface of the planet with Vanya or sometimes on his own. He spent more time on her geological field trips, as well as a couple mountaineering adventures with Dave and the others.

Finally his time was up. John had to go back to the HUB to allow someone else to come down to see Devon.

"John, it was a pleasure having you on the survey crew, even though you stole Vanya away from time to time," Brad stated as he shook John's hand.

"I've enjoyed everything about it, I wish I could stay longer, but my allotment is up."

"You could always come back as permanent staff, although I know you have work that can only be done back at the HUB or Main Ship. Perhaps Vanya can change your mind during the next three months." Vanya was taking time off to go back to the HUB with John. Afterward, she would return to Devon to continue her work.

"We'll see," answered Vanya, in her heart she knew it would not happen. She would not try. She could no sooner ask him to stay for good on Devon than he could ask her to come up to the HUB permanently. They had many years ahead of them before the ship departed. John would be able to return to Devon, she could go to the HUB any time she wished. They would have to accommodate each other's desires, spending time together when they could, or else part ways completely.

At the HUB Vanya met John's parents and he met hers. Then they took a trip out to the Main Ship so she could meet Caleb. He played tour guide for her this time as she renewed long-dormant memories of the ship. One stop in particular thrilled her: the viewing bubble where John had watched the probe launch.

As their relationship deepened, John still felt a sense of uncertainty. He was convinced his feelings for her were stronger than hers were for him. He was uneasy knowing she could attract any number of men while he would probably never attract someone like her again. This was not a lack of confidence on John's part, it was simple reality.

Initially he was sure it was a short-term fling. John did not think Vanya might dump him and move on to someone else. Rather, he thought her interest would wane with time. Committing to a relationship did not seem to be her style, many of her male colleagues had commented on how aloof she was. When their relationship became apparent, several of the men expressed genuine dismay, they wondered how he had done it. John didn't know, himself. He had been smitten from the start, he thought it probably showed despite his efforts to hide it. John was relatively young and inexperienced. By contrast, Vanya was mature and wise. She was also intelligent, charming, and beautiful. There was nothing he could do purposefully to gain her affection, he wouldn't have known where to begin. So he had done nothing, which perhaps had been the best thing to do.

It was after they had been together for several years that, in retrospect, he fully understood that she had simply picked him. That was all there was to it. If their relationship ended, it would be at a time of her choosing. As far as he was concerned, she was in charge. As time passed his feelings deepened, he was not confident enough with women to see that her feelings were deepening, too. She would not always go with him on his explorations of the planet or to the HUB, yet she was always there to meet him when he returned, the romance seemed not to skip a beat; it even intensified.

The Devon Geologic Survey put him on the visiting staff rotation so he could make regular trips down to the planet to work on the field crew. He and Vanya went on sightseeing trips or mountaineering expeditions in their spare time. He continued his simulation studies of the Sol c civilization and shared his results with her. When he went back to the HUB, Vanya often went with him. They enjoyed each other's company while they were together, lost themselves in their work when they were apart. Reunions were sweet, partings were sad.

The HUB was where the big computers were, John also needed to consult with colleagues in their group that had grown to over two dozen. As leader he had to do some things that could not be performed remotely. The history research moved ahead, John's knowledge of the Teran past grew substantially. By combining the satellite data with the simulation results, his team gradually put together a picture of the current state of the development of Sol c's civilization, plus an outline of its possible future path.

John traveled to the Main Ship once or twice a year to visit Caleb. Vanya often went on these visits; she loved seeing Uncle Caleb and spending time at the cabin. Caleb loved to see her too and flirted with her a good deal. They talked frequently of what had been learned, about their fears for the civilization on Sol c if contact was initiated too soon or if they were accidentally discovered.

John and Vanya's life together fell into a comfortable routine. They were never really apart that much. Neither of them thought much on the ship's inevitable departure. For the next twenty years, they traded visits making their long-distance relationship work.

PART 2

The Crossing to Sol

Chapter 27
Departure
(1883)

It was clear Sol c was developing faster than Teran had in the beginning stages of industrialization. In fact the pace of progress was running much faster. It was starting to look to the Terans as though the Main Ship might be detectable during its flyby if it came too close. It was possible their communications transmissions could become detectable before they exited the Solar System when the HUB beam would be turned away from it to follow the ship to Epsilon Eridani.

John frequently argued that they needed to know more of what was happening on the planet than what they were getting from the satellites. The simulations were only as good as the inputs, those from Sol c were not detailed or comprehensive enough. This conclusion was shared by the members of his group, Caleb and his Geezers agreed, but no one knew what could be done about it short of starting a discussion issue to reconsider the consensus on no landers going to the planet. Eventually this was done, with no success.

Since there was life on Sol c, they would not interfere with it, just observe. They would watch what happened as development worked its way. They would keep comparing their observations with what they knew of their home planet.

But the presence of a newly discovered civilization was more than John could resist. If Sol c had been any other kind of planet, he would not be going with the ship. It was not though, he was too tied to it intellectually and emotionally. He had to go. It was not only alive, it was inhabited by beings sophisticated enough to have at least the beginnings of an industrial society.

On his latest trip with Vanya to see Caleb, John's frustration boiled over.

"When I was a kid we were planning on stopping at Sol, I dreamed of visiting the surface of Sol c. Now we can't even get a lander there when the need is so critical. Maybe someone should just go anyway to operate the landers from orbit."

"Namely you?" Caleb interjected.

"Someone would be sent after you, wouldn't they?" said Vanya.

John said he did not care, that once he got away they could only follow, not catch up. If that happened they all might as well stay for a while and rejoin the ship as it passed by Sol.

That conversation had been five months ago. Now they were back on Devon. The future they had been ignoring for many years was fast approaching. Vanya felt a growing discontent over their pending separation. She could go with him. In recent years she had talked more and more about the possibility, but her attachment to Devon was as strong as the hold Sol c had on John.

He said he could adapt to living on the Devon, move to another field of interest. After all, geology and history were not that different, both dealt with the past. But, he was being inevitably pulled to Sol c, he knew that she realized it, too. They spent a final week together on Devon in the mountains talking frequently about his going to Sol c. He did not know how he would do it. He told her she would know it had happened when the time came.

They said their good-byes, and he departed to return to the HUB. She said she would follow for one last week together.

John was in a melancholy mood as he rode back up to the HUB for the last time. It was going to be enormously painful to part from his parents, other relatives, friends, upbringing group and work team members staying behind.

As the airlock door to the HUB reception center opened, John heard a shout as he spotted a group of around fifty people with his mom and dad at the front.

"Welcome home, John!" his mother said as they hugged. Henry stuck out a hand when they separated.

"I don't understand," John started. "I've only been gone a couple months."

"Now, John," Lucy replied, "this is not so much a welcome home as it is the start of your departure party. Until you leave us, we will be together celebrating. We have a month, we are going to make the most of it."

John hugged his mother and kissed her on the cheek.

They were soon headed down to take a shuttle partway along the circumference of the habitat chamber to their home.

True to Lucy's word, the celebration lasted the rest of John's stopover at the HUB. There was a steady ebb and flow of visitors, with many staying for days at a time. It was a period to both reminisce and look forward to the adventure that awaited him. It was a way to say good-bye slowly.

With three days to go, John went out for his last long run inside the habitat. He ran along dirt roads, paths through farm fields and across open grasslands. There were few homes, the trees he saw were not yet very tall. The HUB habitat chamber was now a few decades old, but its interior development was still in its early stages. It would take several more decades before large trees became common as the forests matured. There were relatively few people onboard at this point. The interior living space was seven thousand square miles with a population of less than fifty thousand. For now it was spacious.

John passed the familiar landmarks he used to measure off the miles. He waved at people he passed along the way and stopped to drink at local water fountains. At the halfway point, he stopped at a small general store for a snack.

"John, I hear you are leaving us soon," said Grif from behind the counter.

"Yes, I'm off in a couple of days. I'm afraid this is my last stop here. I'll really miss these rest breaks as well as our discussions on history."

Grif was one of the few people onboard the HUB who had been interested in history for as long as John. Many others had gotten hooked on it when John started posting his simulation results after the first probe sent back confirmation of civilization on Sol c, Grif had been there from the beginning. They both spent a lot of time on their wall screens searching the historical records, and often talked about their latest finds. Though Grif was not on John's team, he frequently contributed interesting insights.

As John finished his drink and headed for the door, Grif called out that he would see him at the departure.

As John re-started his run, he began to think of Vanya. She had not come up to the HUB. The sadness of their potential separation overcame him. Intellectually he had always known it would be difficult. He had accepted that it was inevitable, it would take a long time for the ache to fade. Perhaps he would never completely get over it, a part of him would always be with her on Devon. He sent her a tender farewell video note on the way. When he got home, she was at the door of his quarters. She had come up to the HUB on the latest shuttle.

"John," Vanya began, "I had to come to give you this."

She handed him a package. It was a DNA record attached to a cryocanister containing several dozen of her eggs. When the time came, she wanted to be the biomother of his child. It was the single most intimate and enduring commitment someone in their society could make. After they kissed and held each other for several minutes, he led her in the door. They walked across the room to a similar package sitting on a table. It was addressed to Vanya.

"I left this here for you. I was going to have it sent once the ship departed."

It was his DNA record and a cryocanister of his sperm.

He was having a difficult time resisting his longing to go back with her, but the third planet of Sol was pulling him away.

"We will have each other's activity recordings to keep our memories alive. I will always be your mate," she said, "I will be here waiting for you to come back."

Chapter 28
Arrival on the Main Ship
(1883)

John fidgeted in his seat, wishing the next few hours would go faster. His final trip out to the Main Ship from the HUB had taken three weeks, he spent much of that time preparing for his new life on the ship. He had been born on the Main Ship sixty years before, and was thirty-four when he left it with his parents for the HUB. He had been back often, mainly to see Caleb, now he was returning for good. He was anxious to get the journey to Sol under way. This was a big step, there was no turning back once the ship departed. Four months to wait, it seemed an eternity. John along with sixty thousand other souls were set to embark on a forty-eight-year odyssey to the next star.

The round-trip communications delay to Teran was approaching four hundred years. By the time they received reports from Teran, everything was ancient history. The home planet really only existed for them as something in the remote past to be recalled from time to time from the history logs. He had never been there, of course, nor had anyone he knew. They were autonomous out among the stars. Their connection to their home planet had become remote in time and space. It was no wonder Teran did not loom large in the minds of the ship's inhabitants.

John wondered what had made the first ones leave, to forsake the comfort and security of their home planet to spend a major portion of their lives in deep space. Seeking unknown worlds bespoke an intrepidness and yearning for adventure that did not seem part of the Teran psyche.

To John, outfitting a habitat with a propulsion system and launching it toward the closest star seemed a remarkable leap of faith for a society cautious by nature. Initially, he thought they had an unwavering faith in technology. The early starships were on their own for hundreds of years without the reassuring light and heat of a star. In the process of accelerating, they would exhaust most of their fuel, depending on scavenging stray particles from the near void of interstellar space. They did this not once but many times. At each destination they constructed new habitat worlds for themselves, then sent the ship on to the next star. There was no shortage of next stars to go to, there was no shortage of people wanting to go.

Why were they so willing? They were not fleeing oppression or seeking to get a start somewhere new where opportunity or anonymity was available. Large-scale migrations of the past were easily understood in these terms, not this one. They weren't running from, they were running to. They had decided to go see the galaxy for themselves.

They risked losing a life of freedom and comfort to find out if they were truly alone in the universe. They were taking a chance, at the same time they did not feel they were taking a risk because they had faith. Technology was part of the answer, but their faith was not in technology. Rather, it was faith in themselves. Faith in their ability to confront and overcome with the power of their minds whatever the void had in store.

So, John concluded, others had long ago decided to go to the stars for reasons similar to his own. Unlike the original crew, John had the reassurance of knowing the trip could be done. He was driven by anticipation of what they would find at the other end. Unlike previous crossings that went to worlds lacking intelligent life, this time they had direct evidence of a crude civilization.

As the previous voyages worked their way across this part of the galaxy, they constantly looked ahead at the stars and planets. Now they had found one that not only had the right physical characteristics, but also the unmistakable signs of a civilization. There were alien thinking beings out there. The Terans had spent many thousands of years wondering whether they existed, they had dedicated the past five thousand to actively searching for them. Having found them, John was not willing to miss the opportunity to see them up close at Sol c.

He got up to look out the port-side window. As usual, he had deliberately put off watching the ship during the approach. He didn't want to go through the tedious process of waiting for it to grow slowly in size from a speck. He always wanted his first look to be big enough to see its actual form. They were now closing in fast, it was time to take a peek. The ship took shape as it got larger, he remembered why everyone called it "can world." It was shaped like a can, cylindrical with the same height-to-width ratio as an ordinary storage drum. The ends, however, were hemispherical. The sides were littered with a jumble of projections. A gigantic collar-shaped screen ran around the circumference of the forward face. This was the base of the collector used to gather stray subatomic particles in deep space. They were channeled via conduits to the opposite end of the ship where they entered the fuel storage facilities. A portion of the particles would be used to power the light strip that provided illumination and heat to the main habitat chamber. Others were used to power the ship's systems. The rest were stored for later use.

The ship rotated at a rate that produced a centrifugal force equal to 1g at ground level, it felt perfectly normal walking around inside. When they were accelerating or decelerating, things got a little strange, however. With the ship's engines on one end, they had to travel with the main axis of the ship pointed toward their destination. This meant the added force during acceleration or deceleration shifted the direction of "down" by 2 percent. When the ship was stationary or coasting, down was perpendicular to the surface. While accelerating or decelerating, it was slightly off this line. Most of the time it was unnoticeable. On some occasions, such as at parties, it could be amusing when someone had had a bit too much to drink and lost their space legs.

A symmetrical pattern of cone-shaped nozzles was mounted on the aft end. These were the exhaust ports of the ship's engines. The engines consumed stored particles to produce thrust to nudge the ship gently on its way. The ship's acceleration never exceeded 0.02g; they could only encourage it to move forward. At this sedate rate of acceleration, they would reach 0.1c five years into their journey. After that they coasted.

The shuttle was now on final approach to the Main Ship, John snapped out of his daydream. "Well," he sighed to himself, "it really is basically a giant can. It would be nice if it had a dramatic shape." It was not until he put the size of the ship in perspective that he began again to be impressed. Now, still one hundred miles away with his nose pressed up against the window, John could barely take it in. The ship was absolutely enormous by any standard he knew.

It was the largest, most powerful vehicle ever created by Terans, and was one of many. By now there were several hundred in the fleet spread out in all directions from their home planet. The communications delays meant they did not learn of new vessels until long after they had been launched.

John spotted the viewing bubble, where he had watched the probe launch fifty-five years before, as the shuttle was nearing the docking port, the vessel would be inside shortly. Maneuvering a craft in space was not easy. Close to another one, it took strictly slow, small, easy thrusts to match speed and direction until the two vessels could mate. It was not the same as a surface-bound cart that could be started, stopped, or turned at will.

The ship's image filled the panes of the port-side observation lounge window. The walls contained enough corridors, passageways, and hidden recesses to satisfy the exploratory urges of any passenger. It would be his home for the next forty-eight years as they traveled to Sol, 4.4 light-years away. Sol had been designated destination 27-19: 27 because it was the twenty-seventh destination for the ship since it was launched, 19 because their ship was the nineteenth of its kind to be built.

He looked forward to the next weeks of intense activity that would see him settled-in to his new home. This would be followed by the departure of the ship itself. He hoped it would help him put aside his inner conflicts and any doubts he was harboring.

John passed out of the shuttle through the docking bay doors. He took the lift down to the interior surface of the cylinder, where he exited into the central reception area. Here he was welcomed by several of his parents' friends who had served as instructors, mentors, and general guides during the years of his upbringing.

Caleb came up to him immediately to give him a hearty hug.

"John, good to see you again. Welcome to the start of our new adventure!"

"Great to see you, too, Uncle Caleb. I can't wait to get going!"

"Same with me, although I may not live long enough to see Sol c with my own eyes. I want to get as close as I can, look at as much of the data as possible. Who knows? I might even surprise a few people and make it all the way there." Caleb replied.

The welcome was rather raucous, at least by Teran standards. Many other clans and kin were there meeting new arrivals.

After much hugging, hand shaking, back slapping, followed by a couple sips of champagne, the crowd slowly dispersed as people made their way to the transit tubes that would take them to their homes. John would be settling by his mother's relatives on the far side of the ship. He rode the lift up to the surface from the underground tube station, grabbed a bike from a nearby rack, put his small pack in the handlebar basket and headed for home.

Lucy's family compound was centered on a five-square-mile plot of rolling hills. It comprised barns, sheds, additional outbuildings, and six dwelling units arranged in a semicircle on the highest hilltop overlooking the surrounding countryside. The compound was a working farm run by his mother's nephew where they grew a variety of food grains and raised livestock. The bulk of the labor was done by robotic field machines. Most of the planning was automated with planting, harvesting, crop selection, and rotation cycles coordinated with the ship's climate control systems. The livestock was kept mainly for the sheer joy of it. Meat consumption by Terans was low, most of the menagerie consisted of draft animals, those prized for their coats, pets, plus a collection of exotica. It resembled a zoo more than a barnyard. The animals were typical of those found in the many farming compounds across the plain that circled the middle third of the inside of the ship.

John left his bike in the stand next to the gravel walkway that led up to the house on the far left of the semicircle. He walked slowly to the door and slipped inside. He was alone now. It seemed as though he was sneaking into a place he did not belong. It was his childhood home, but he felt like an intruder; he had rarely visited it on his previous trips to the Main Ship. His parents had built it right after they were married to be near his mother's parents and they had all lived there until they had moved to the HUB.

During the past year, John had designed and supervised a complete renovation of the interior plus an expansion of the upstairs. The renovations had been carried out by robots, the home was ready for him to occupy. His personal belongings had already arrived, everything was prepared the way he wanted it. He had it rebuilt expecting to live there for the duration of the crossing to Sol, he was anxious to settle in.

After a quick inspection tour, he went outside to admire the view of plains and highlands in the distance. Darkness was approaching as he leaned back in the deck chair, reflecting once again on the choices he had made.

He thrived on the information coming in from other star systems and immersed himself in the history of their travels and their home planet. He read of the new phenomena and technologies that were reported, most of all, he enjoyed learning about the personalities involved. For him history was an ever-unfolding story of people, their motivations, their ideas, how they connected. What led to what? What ideas sprung from which people coalesced around a particular mind-set at a certain time and place to create a particular breakthrough? Events of the past interested him in the same way that technology did. He wanted to find out how things fit together. How the pieces meshed, what was joined to what.

The HUB would have been an exciting place to live and work. The volume of communication traffic would increase steadily as it came fully on line. It was the reception point for data concerning new discoveries from other parts of the local area and beyond. It was the ideal location to study the latest technological developments. In many ways it would have been the perfect place for him. And he would be able to see Vanya often.

His main interest seemed odd to most. Activities during the years of the crossing would revolve around technical undertakings inside a gigantic machine. He had been one of the few historians on the HUB, he was now one of a few on the ship. His father originally was a propulsion expert, he had always pursued careers involving hardware or programming. Early in his life he was a champion distance runner. His mother was interested in astronomy and had previously undertaken careers in ionic propulsion systems, along with acting. John had acquired some of his interests from his parents. But he had found his main interest on his own, although Caleb quietly encouraged it. No one who knew John understood why he chose history, at the beginning they assumed it was a passing fancy. He would surely move on to something else soon enough, they said. For John, however, it was a consuming passion that would occupy him for the rest of his life.

He got up and went back inside. The formal living and dining rooms were on the left; the library and guestroom to the right; the kitchen and family room in the back. He climbed up the stairs to the second floor, where the family bedrooms were located. He continued up to the top floor that contained the office and study area. The large windows at the four sides of the completely open third floor looked out across the plain of the central zone of the habitat chamber. In the circumferential directions, grasslands interspersed with fields of grain stretched out completely around the ship.

Small communities mingled with larger towns. They were surrounded by gardens for fruits and vegetables, and fenced fields for livestock. He could see many miles until the curvature of the inner wall caused the view to be lost in the skyline.

Straight up through the skylight was the bright light of the linear sun that ran down the central axis of the cylinder providing light and heat to the interior. In the forward direction of the chamber, the fields gave way to the forest where Caleb lived.

He strode over to the COMM wall, a patchwork of windows that allowed video presentations, computer access, voice and video communications with anyone on the ship, and for the time being in the HUB. He placed a call to his parents back at the HUB.

After the 3 minute two-way time delay from the HUB he heard his father's voice. "We watched you get off the shuttle at the reception center," said Henry, "then saw you again at the transit station in Atomic Town. We figured you would be getting to the house about now. The changes you made look good."

"I hope you don't mind that the place is not that recognizable," John replied. "I wanted to have plenty of open space with a large work area. I didn't think I'd need the baby-care area, since I won't be scheduled for a child of my own for at least thirty years!"

"You should keep the designs," Lucy chimed in. "They have been well tested and worked marvelously for us. We will keep up with you in your daily activity recordings"

"I'll do the same." John replied.

They maintained their conversation as best as they could for a while longer given the time gap between replies, then signed off.

"They still think of me as a kid," John said to himself with some amusement. *I guess it's only natural. This is the first time I'll be away from them for more than a couple months, now I'll be gone for good.*

Lucy and Henry were considered middle-aged. She was 132, he was 140. As long as the development work on the HUB went well, they would have a chance for a second child. On the ship, he knew he would have to wait until near the end of the voyage before his turn came.

John wandered back outside onto the deck, he looked straight up to the fading light of early dusk. The opposite side of the ship was twenty-four miles away, he could not see it in daylight. At night, however, he could see the town lights and moving vehicles with a good pair of field glasses. Quantum City was directly across from them, on clear nights, he would enjoy lying on his back in the hammock staring up at its lights.

Clouds were moving in, a springtime rain was scheduled for that evening. John walked out into the field behind the house. Rain would be falling soon, he decided to keep walking. No need to worry about lightning, since it was prevented from happening. Large electrical discharges were disruptive to the ship's power and control systems. The weather systems were controlled carefully to avoid it. So carefully, in fact, that most of the ship's crew had never seen lightning. John, having seen it firsthand on Devon, understood the danger it presented.

Maybe John was starting to get to the heart of the matter. There was no catastrophic weather, no earthquakes or volcanoes, there was the occasional small fire in the forest, life in here was predictable, and extremely safe. The dangers could not be reduced to zero, but the Main Ship builders made it as close as possible.

As he turned back to the house, he thought that the ship was not such a bad place to live, although nothing could compare to the surface of a planet. His time with Vanya on Devon had been a revelation. She was probably already on her way back there. He went inside to send a message to her.

He was interrupted by someone at the front door. He could see through the window as he approached it that it was Vanya. She had followed him to the ship on a different shuttle.

"John, I'm coming with you," was all she got out before they fell into each other's arms.

"What changed your mind?" John asked after they parted.

"It was the DNA exchange. I want us together for our child's upbringing. Besides, there are two big stony planets and a bunch of moons at Sol waiting for a geologist to start looking them over."

Chapter 29
Alert
(1903)

John was leaning back to take a break from some late reading when the stage-one alert flashed on the screen. It passed quickly, right through stage two to three. The Scanning Correlating Monitor, or SCM, gave alerts every once in a while, occasionally they got to stage three, but John had never seen such a fast jump before.

The SCM's job was to monitor the electromagnetic recordings of radio waves relayed back by the satellites from Sol c for coherent signals. When one was suspected, a stage-one alert was issued. An analysis was done to determine the direction to its source and if the signal had any regularities that could indicate intelligent content. Additional checks were then conducted to ensure it was not something being generated from the satellite itself, one of its companions, or other known source. Sometimes stage three was reached when the checking process got behind the signal analysis, but the alert was always quickly canceled once it caught up. John was beginning to think that stage three had already persisted longer than normal when the alert jumped again, this time to stage five. This meant the signal had regular patterns of sufficient complexity to suggest a high probability of intelligent content and it was not coming from a known source. Vanya was now awake, she had come up to the third floor and sat next to him.

The COMM display screen was lit up with hundreds of messages, comments and questions. John had thought he was the only one looking at the SCM reports, given the late hour. It was after midnight. He knew that many people had the SCM on automatic wake-up, as he set the COMM message filter to his "A list." This way he would notice if Caleb, or one of his other close friends, tried to reach him.

He then requested a detailed display of the SCM output to see the details on what it had found. The data showed the radio portion of the electromagnetic spectrum, a distinct pattern in the amplitude modulations, with a source location in the northwest corner of the planet's biggest continent. If he knew his history, this had the characteristics of a typical radio telegraph transmission. Terans had not used that mode of communication for millennia; John immediately broadcast his conclusion. Jim Cuthbert, one of his team members, replied soon after, asking for a history file on radio communications. John connected him to the correct address then posted it on the bulletin board for others who might be interested. He got up for a hot drink while waiting for the COMM system to digest the flurry of messages.

Stage six came twenty minutes later, the consensus output from the COMM indicated that pretty much everyone on board was now awake. Opinion ranged from hoax, to an overlooked sub-probe or satellite, to the ultimate: radio communications by the nascent technical civilization on Sol c. Facts were limited at this point, one of the most difficult and important things had not yet been determined. What did the message say?

John sent a v-mail to George Constanza in communications engineering who responded immediately.

"Tell me, George, how long do you think it will take to detect a decipherable pattern in the signal? That's when my interest will really be piqued."

"Don't give up your day job," responded George. "It could take days, weeks, or even years. We have never gotten this far along in the alert sequence before. Come back when it hits stage eight. That's when we ought to be getting longer strings of message that could contain enough to begin analysis."

John took the advice. As he pushed back from the COMM console, he began sorting out his thoughts. The past thirty minutes had evaporated in a flurry of activity and excitement over the signal detection. It would now take at least several hours before anything further could be done, and then only if the signal didn't stop, which it promptly did.

"What happened?" Vanya asked.

"Don't know." John replied when suddenly the SCM window flashed, changing color from orange to green. Simultaneously, the status went back to normal with the message "Signal Termination" flashing in a little box. He requested details on what had been received: "Duration 27.23 minutes, of which 17.05 minutes contained coherent signal after level 5 signal processing. Longest continuous level 5 segment was 5.78 minutes, ending 3.67 minutes before termination."

John immediately went back to his history files to locate the Teran records on early radio broadcasting. Their first kilowatt-scale open-air broadcast had lasted fourteen minutes. The Teran tests had consisted of several unrelated transmissions consisting of long and short pulses interspersed with empty breaks, during which time engineering tests and adjustments were conducted. A series of such experiments had been conducted over the next several years as improvements were made to the hardware. Regular radio telegraph communications had not begun for another ten years.

John sent a message to George containing the gist of the history file plus his estimate that another signal could be intercepted in two or three days, then waited for him to call back. Ten minutes later he did.

"Thanks for the lead, John. The signal is pretty fuzzy. It barely stays above the reception threshold most of the time. There were no simple patterns in the longest piece of the record. Based on what you provided, we are working on the assumption that it is some sort of code. Maybe those years you spent doing history weren't wasted after all. Speaking of dead-end endeavors that are newly resuscitated, where is that part-time linguist friend of yours?"

He meant Jim, who studied languages in his spare time, which was quite eccentric given there was only one language used on the ship, there had been no others for going on three thousand years. A linguist was useful from time to time, however, since their onboard language drifted with time from that of the other ships with which they communicated. Most of the time the automatic translators did a good job with incoming messages, every once in a while they would get confused, Jim would step in to sort it out.

"Asleep," said John. "I'll see if his COMM will let me wake him," he added as he sent the request.

"Now what?" Jim's bleary-eyed face came back up in the window.

"Oh, nothing much. It's just that the ship may finally need the services of a full-time linguist for the first time in millennia. Being that you're the only one onboard, I thought you might be interested. Call George Constanza at communications, he'll fill you in."

Jim laughed and thanked him. He quickly sent a vmail to George.

John and George had originally met twenty years before at a seminar on new advances in simulation algorithms, George's curiosity was aroused when he discovered a historian in attendance at a conference put together by a bunch of engineers working on propulsion simulations. John was at the conference to listen to presentations on new simulation techniques and meet people who were experts in the field. He wanted to form a team to try out the ideas he had on such methods and use them in his analysis of data on the Teran past. George was intrigued by John's ideas, although he regarded them more with curiosity than professional interest. A lasting friendship grew out of this meeting that was rather one-sided with John constantly asking questions, probing George and his colleagues for information. The questions typically centered on various algorithms or simulation techniques and how they might be extended from engineering to other kinds of problems.

George was content to act as a source of technical assistance, only following John's efforts on a casual basis. When they got together he listened as John described the outcomes of his latest what-if games played using data from the history records. He found them entertaining, but until now he had given them no serious attention. Suddenly John's expertise seemed very valuable. George wanted to know more—a lot more—on what John could do and how he did it.

John reflected on those twenty years that George had alluded to. For him it had actually been closer to fifty. He had been a nut about history since childhood. It had certainly contributed heavily to the study of the civilization discovered on Sol c, but in the view of much of the crew it served no useful purpose in the ongoing operations of the ship. Until now, that is. It did have its entertainment value, this kept John as busy as he wanted to be. He was frequently asked to provide media presentations on one topic or another, becoming fairly well known as a result. What his ship mates did not know was the extraordinary lengths to which he had taken his research. As with the source of the signals, this would be revealed shortly.

It was now past 4:00 a.m., Vanya had long since gone back to sleep. He got dressed, left her a note, and went out to bike over to the local town center five miles away. When he got to the center, a lot of others were apparently up watching the COMM reports, since many of the living quarters had lights on inside.

Most of these people had no idea what the technical details of the reports meant; yet they had gotten up to watch for every fragment of information. What they did know was that the signal alert meant a possible identification of radio communications, once the alert went past stage five, it was probably not a false alarm. Why else would they have set their monitors to wake them no matter the time? Usually they did this only for very special information, such as deaths in the family. Obviously, most of his shipmates considered the possible existence of alien civilized beings to be quite important. It definitely was to him, he knew from his historical studies that it had been important to many others in the past. To see such a pervasive and dramatic demonstration of this made John feel good about the state of their civilization and the quality of its citizens.

He did not linger at the center. The signal had stopped, he figured it would be a few days at least before they got another. Additional news would be thin for the time being. John headed for the opposite side of town. Five minutes later he reached the town edge where he paused to look out on the fields as the light was beginning to come back up. A short period of rain had been scheduled for this area before dawn, it was letting up now. He decided to cycle the twenty-five miles to the town of Megaflop, where George lived. He got there in time for breakfast.

George's quarters were in a small high-rise complex next to one of the ship's four central computer installations. These were the nerve centers of the ship, consuming the interest of a majority of its inhabitants. They were surrounded by the largest towns. Megaflop housed fifteen thousand people, it teemed with activity. In contrast Starport, the town nearest John's home, had eighteen hundred occupants. It was only busy during the infrequent launches and landings of service shuttles. Of course, once the ship reached its destination, Starport and the surrounding towns associated with the docking facilities would become extremely busy. For the past seventeen years, since departure from Alpha Centauri A, Starport had been a sleepy community, which was what John wanted. His work consumed a lot of time on the computers, but could be done from anywhere on the ship. When he wanted a break, John came here to see George, or went to Graviton to see Jim.

He could smell the cereal cooking as he came in the entry. George, not surprised that he had come, escorted him to the kitchen where his family was already at the table. George liked togetherness, which explained why he lived with three generations in the small quarters of a high-rise.

They walked to the video wall where Caleb's and Jim's faces were smiling back.

"So you finally got up," John said to Caleb. "The alert has caused quite a stir. The COMM system was nearly overloaded with traffic."

"It was the same over here," Jim replied. "I checked the records, in the ten minutes after we jumped to stage five, the COMM was 50 percent busier than any period ever recorded. I'd say those folks on Sol c have gotten our attention."

"Do your history simulations tell you anything about what we should be looking for, John, if it is indeed a civilization in the early stages of experimenting with radio?" asked George.

"They tell me that it's probably not very civil," John began. "At least not according to what we've become accustomed to the past five thousand years. Back when we invented radio broadcasting, we were a pretty rough lot. In fact the driving force behind its invention was warfare. This was during the time when we had sovereign nation states with standing armies and their own individual types of government. There were constant conflicts, if you remember your childhood lessons."

"John, you're asking me to recall things I haven't pondered for 140 years," George replied.

"Now, go easy on him," Caleb chimed in. "What I would like to know is, assuming it really is a nascent technological civilization, what should we be looking for in the way of confirming evidence? What characteristics might these signals have if they *are* early radio tests?"

"I don't know what else I can add beyond what I told you a few hours ago," John replied. "I expect we will get more broadcasts of longer and longer duration as time goes by. Eventually they will become continuous. The content might be entirely coded. No spoken language. After another twenty years, we can expect to get voice transmissions. By then we will be within ten years of arrival, things could get very interesting."

John and George joined the rest of George's family at the breakfast table, the conversation soon returned to the signal. George's wife, Joan, addressing no one in particular, asked a series of questions on how the beings that sent the signal might look. There were the expected quips about numbers of heads and limbs, although they already knew from the high resolution satellite images that they were probably much like themselves.

"We seem to have already accepted the notion that we have encountered an alien technological civilization," said George. "Perhaps we're going a bit too fast. We should probably not take this seriously until we have gotten more signal, or found something specific in this one that is conclusive."

"George is right," said John. "We just assume the ship's systems have done a complete job of checking for false alerts, since none were detected and we got to stage nine, it must be real."

"There is always the chance something can slip up," said George. "That's why we rate stage nine at 90 percent probability. That still leaves a significant margin for error. We already have several teams going over the logs to double check, but the job will take months. If John's right, we will get another signal in a few days. That might tell us more."

"I wonder if we will be the first," Joan offered.

John and George gave her a puzzled look.

"You know, will we be the first Terans to register a true encounter?" she continued. "With the time delays communicating with other ships, someone else could have already made an encounter, we may not have gotten the word yet."

"We are over two hundred light-years from Teran, another two hundred from the ships heading out in the opposite direction," George offered, "We will never know for sure in our lifetimes. Stage five and higher SCM alerts are automatically sent back in the normal communications traffic to the HUB at Alpha Centauri, our claim has already been registered. They'll have it at the Epsilon Indi HUB in ten years. Since it went to stage nine, it will be automatically relayed back along the line to Teran and outward on the entire net."

John walked to the window. From the fifth floor he could see across the plain back toward Starport. The talk about communications time delays had made him think of where they were. He was not actually in an apartment in a high-rise looking out on the countryside. He was in a starship traveling at one-tenth the speed of light. They were almost two hundred light-years from their home planet, which none onboard had seen, they were headed for a star they knew was surrounded by at least eight planets and numerous smaller bodies. A few hours ago, they had learned that one of those planets might be inhabited by a technological civilization capable of radio transmission. It was not often that he thought of their cosmic circumstance, the significance of the radio signal, what it might portend was now hitting him.

"It will be slow for a few years as this thing builds," he commented, "although I suspect as we draw nearer to our destination, events will happen faster and faster. I hope we can prepare ourselves sufficiently to deal with them, no matter how bizarre."

"Uncle John, what kind of bizarre events?" inquired Joan's eight-year-old daughter, Sarah. "You sound a little scary."

"Oh, I don't mean to be, it's just that this represents something completely unknown for us. We've been looking forward to this day for so long, now that it appears to be at hand, it's a little disconcerting. Let's wait and see if we get a second signal before we get too caught up, okay?"

Then, turning to George as they walked together onto the outside deck, he said, "George, the second signal will come. Our lives have been permanently changed."

Chapter 30
Messages
(1908)

The COMM alert band on his wrist was vibrating again as John rolled over to look at the clock. It was 2:44 a.m., it took him a minute to realize what was happening. He had reset the alert system to wake him if there was a significant change in the pattern of the signals coming in from Sol. He got up quietly so as not to disturb Vanya and went upstairs to the COMM. He looked at the window containing the analysis output.

Another window was opening, Jim was already talking. "John, they have finally started what appears to be regular message transmissions. We can't decode it yet, but the larger flow of messages combined with higher transmit power should give us what we need to crack it. If we can get a couple hundred total hours recorded, I think we stand a good chance of starting to decipher their language."

John pondered the ceiling a moment and replied, "Good luck with that. So far the longest recording we have is a few minutes, it may be months before we can begin to understand what they are saying. By the way, how is your team doing?"

After they had encountered the initial signal, Jim had gathered a team to translate any spoken language that might be received. He was the sole dedicated linguist on the ship, but there were several others who had studied language a bit.

They, along with a few signal-processing specialists, mathematicians, and all-around puzzle solvers, had come together in the past five years. Now they would have something to work on.

"We have eleven on the team now," Jim answered, "as you might imagine, we are very eager to start work. Mary Kowalchek, a cellist with extensive knowledge of music theory, is the latest to have joined. We figured she might come in handy, since the history files you guided us to indicate that recorded music was invented on Teran at roughly the same time as radio. It was one of the earliest things regularly transmitted."

John said good night and went back to bed. Until there was actually some translated text to examine, there was no sense in missing out on the remainder of a good night's sleep.

Five months went by, Jim was starting to despair at ever being able to decipher the language in the transmissions. Early on they had concluded that the short (dots) and long (dashes) pulses were code for the written language. The unique long and short pulse combinations were few enough in number, they had to represent letters, numbers, and a few special symbols. They were not higher components of language such as syllables or words. The team had to assume that the basic structure of the language was not something radically different from their own. They were able to decipher a number of short parts at the beginning and end of several messages, these were invariably simple, containing little meaningful content. They appeared to be standard greetings or closings.

Then came the first reception of voice transmissions from continuous-wave broadcasting. It appeared to be a prepared text by a single speaker followed by a musical composition. The broadcast was repeated a week later. The technologists of Sol c had jumped from radio telegraph to voice in only a couple of years. It should have taken a couple decades. Increasing voice transmission followed along with a greatly increased volume of telegraphic transmissions.

The Terans were having a great deal of difficulty getting consistent results when using several messages in combination to beef up the volume of information for the translation algorithms. Mary was the one who hit upon the problem. She realized they might be receiving messages in different languages. She had spent a lot of time listening to the output, which had been cleaned up considerably by the signal processing analysts. Mary's trained musical ear allowed her to recognize that parts of the messages sounded different from others, they could be divided into distinct styles. It had simply not occurred to the group that everyone on Sol c would not speak a common language as they did.

Soon they were able to translate large portions of the messages. The ones from years earlier seemed to be reports on a boat race, the weather, and the king's knee. There were at least three languages used by the people doing the transmitting. It became apparent based on the content of the signals that the speakers were not always carrying on a conversation. Much of the recent content appeared to be news reports.

John closed the bulletin board window for the translation reports and initiated another one of his history simulation routines. This was a low-level probability generator developed many years ago. Based on a set of input conditions, it would estimate the probability of the existence of certain broad societal conditions. He back-tested it extensively on Teran history, he knew it could guide him in his thinking on what might be happening on the planet.

There were several sets of transmission sources in different languages located in the northwest corner of the main landmass plus other sources in the northeast part of the large north-south continent. Much of the content was in monologue or prepared text. He wanted to know the probability that multiple separate nation-states were involved. The results were 65 percent probable, which did not surprise him.

He then asked for the probability that the states involved were hostile to one another. The result was inconclusive. There was not enough information to establish a sufficient level of confidence. John sensed, however, that he already knew the answer. They needed more time to monitor the signals to expand the scope of the content.

George pointed out the next issue they would have to deal with. "John, the probe transmissions up and down the chain to Sol are also going to the planet. What is the possibility of inadvertent contact?"

John thought a moment then replied, "The engineers think it unlikely that their counterparts on Sol c will be able to detect the probe signals anytime soon, let alone realize they're from intelligent beings. Remember, we need to maintain contact with the probes that have passed Sol and are heading to Epsilon Eridani. The Main Ship flyby depends on those signals for navigation. However, there is the HUB signal, which is much stronger."

Soon enough, arguments began to rage on the bulletin board. One group wanted to signal the HUB to cease transmitting to the ship because those signals were on a direct line to Sol c. At its current strength, the HUB signal would not be detectable so there was no risk right away. When it boosted its power level to full strength over the next few years, there could be a slight chance of detection.

The engineers concluded that at the lowest levels needed to maintain contact, the HUB signal at the planet would show up as a low-level background hiss across a wide band of the electromagnetic spectrum. Because of the encoding methods used to pack as much information into the signal as possible, it would appear to be random noise to the scientists of Sol c, if they could detect it. The engineers felt that the mathematical capabilities of the beings on Sol c would not be sophisticated enough for them to suspect any intelligent content in the signal, or that it was a deliberately transmitted signal. What they might notice would be a sudden change in the power level of the transmissions.

Once the Main Ship completed its flyby of Sol and began the crossing to Epsilon Eridani, the HUB beam would slowly move away from Sol c as it followed the Main Ship. What the Terans did not know was whether this would happen before the population of Sol c noticed their signal or were capable of noticing its absence.

Discussion on the COMM boards mounted dramatically after the first voice translations had been posted. The opinion tracker indicated a large contingent in favor of sending radio signals to the target planet, hoping for return contact.

Another significant minority, contrary to one of their main directives, wanted to stop to announce themselves personally. They argued that the ship should extend an invitation to join in the construction and operation of a HUB at Sol c. Many others, however, urged caution. A rapidly developing society would not necessarily be stable. There was a lot of evidence indicating progress was concentrated in just a few areas, indeed most of the planet was probably not very advanced. The shock of arriving aliens might be too great for the planet's inhabitants. The Terans should wait until the Sol c civilization commenced star travel, as per the original directive.

Although John was in favor of establishing contact, he didn't think it was a good idea to do so this early. He was able to find the point in Teran's history that matched well with the newly detected society. Unfortunately, there were not enough signals to determine more than a few basic cultural conditions on the planet, John found a fairly good match based on technology levels. He was convinced that if this new society was developing along lines similar to their own past, it would be better to wait before deciding to make contact.

At the equivalent point in Teran's past, the planet was organized as a large number of relatively independent nation-states with a handful being in dominant positions. Violence and war were common, the threat of military action was used to further national goals. During this period technological improvements in machinery, communications, manufacturing, and many other areas began to greatly improve the level of prosperity in several of the major nations, an extended time of relative peace had set in.

This period of quiet lasted for seventy-five years as prosperity slowly spread. Technological advances eventually led to nuclear power, and, unfortunately, nuclear weapons. Even though much of the planet was achieving a relatively comfortable standard of living, none of the military establishments had been dismantled. Instead they were fortified as new, increasingly violent weapons were created. The reasoning was the state had to protect what it had now that it was prosperous, it had to be strong in order to maintain trade relations with foreign nations.

John recognized through a series of simulations that one of the key factors that determined the course of events in this period on Teran was that the major nations were on the same landmass. Relatively close physical contact could be maintained. This new planet was not the same. If both major landmasses on Sol c were fully inhabited, as surely they must be by this time, he reasoned, then these critical geographical influences would be completely different. John had no idea, however, what those influences would be. He did not have enough information to do any detailed simulations of the new civilization's development, he would have to wait for the broadcasts to increase and be translated. That's why he felt they should wait before initiating contact. It looked like they were encountering Sol c's society at a pivotal point in its development. The shock of receiving a message from an alien society could have unpredictable consequences. John began to post the Teran history texts, along with his interpretations and opinions on the bulletin boards.

Once again the conservative approach prevailed. The consensus was to wait at least until sometime after the civilization on Sol c began space travel. Once this happened, the Terans could decide when to begin radio broadcasting to Sol c. The Main Ship's crew agreed that it had to be apparent that the messages were from an alien civilization, with the content pointing to Alpha Centauri A as the source and providing a way to confirm the message's origin. Once the inhabitants of Sol c began star travel, the Terans would initiate physical contact.

Chapter 31
Taking a Break
(September 1908)

Backpack in hand, John stood up as the shuttle pulled into North End Station. After ascending the steps to the surface, he headed to the cabin he had scheduled. It was four miles away near Caleb's. He would have a chance to visit with him while at the same time having his solitude. Vanya had stayed back home for the time being, she would come up later for a visit with Caleb. It was a cool afternoon, he wanted to enjoy the fall weather by walking in. His robot followed a hundred feet behind.

John found the path, he was quickly enveloped by trees as he began walking. They were tall and the forest floor was unobstructed, having reached climax status centuries ago. The muted light and fresh scent from the pines lent an ancient, mystical quality to the area. It was the one place on the ship where he could forget he was living in an artificial world. He had come here to get away from the day-to-day activity going on with the signals. He wanted a break from his simulation work and the shipboard discussions on contact and communications beams.

He had to clear his mind of the short-term issues that dominated his days to look at the larger picture of what contact meant to them, what it would mean to those on Sol c when it came. That time had not been decided. They had put it off to the indefinite future. The consensus was that at some point they would recognize that circumstances were right. Then they would act, but no one had figured out how. Many assumed the ship would send a radio message at the appropriate time, John didn't think it was going to be that simple.

He walked along the trail enjoying the sounds and smells of the forest eventually coming to a small clearing half a mile from the cabin. He sat down, being in no hurry, leaned back and closed his eyes. He awoke after what he figured was a few minutes to the sight of an old bearded man with a cane sitting on a rock a few yards away.

"Been asleep for half an hour or so," the old man commented as John opened his eyes and slowly sat up. "You flatlanders lead such frenzied lives. This happens a lot when you first get up here. Don't realize how worn out you are until you lie down. The air and the trees do the rest. Feelin' refreshed now?"

John didn't know what to make of him, until he remembered there was a caretaker up here who looked after the thirty-odd cabins scattered over this part of the woods. Not that a caretaker was needed, since the small vacation homes were self-sufficient. The man simply liked being a caretaker and living in the woods. John had seen him occasionally on his visits with Vanya to see Caleb, but did not know him well. Quentin kept to himself, even Caleb rarely saw him. John thought this encounter was unusual, he wondered what had triggered it.

"You must be Quentin, and yes, I do feel much better," John replied.

"Quentin Pierce it is. I'm at your service, for what it's worth. Come on, I'll walk you the rest of the way to your place. I've been getting it ready for you."

They walked along in silence until John felt compelled to ask how and when Quentin had known he was coming, since he hadn't told anyone his intent.

"Saw the house open its windows this morning, the robot was doing some extra cleaning," Quentin answered. After a few steps he added, "I messaged Caleb to find out who was coming. He told me you were headed up for a while."

The pair reached the cabin and paused at the steps to the sun porch. John turned but before he could say anything, Quentin spoke.

"Well, you want your peace and quiet, so I'll be on my way. Anything you need, give a yell. I'm always around the area." Then with a quick wave, he departed.

John went inside, puzzling over this seemingly chance meeting. He wanted something to drink, then planned to sit in the rocker on the porch to while away the late afternoon. He was going to bed early and wanted to sleep late the next morning. The only plans he had were lots of naps interspersed with walks. Eventually, he would start to consider what should be done next, he would be here at least three weeks, there was no rush.

The days were bright, clear, and warm, the nights cool, the way it ought to be in September. It was, of course, no accident. The ship's weather systems were programmed for a long stretch of nice weather every year at this time. It was convenient to have exact knowledge of the weather far in advance, but John wished they had allowed for a few surprises once in a while. That's not what most of the residents wanted, so he made his own surprises by not checking the weather plans. This time he had, that was to make sure his stay did not exactly match the annual fall fair-weather spell. He wanted a few rainy days, therefore he deliberately came to the cabin when the weather would change.

He put on his hiking boots every morning after breakfast and took off in a different direction. He went without a positioning device so he would not know exactly where he was going. He wanted to lose himself for a few hours to enjoy the forest. Actually getting lost was difficult, anyway. As long as he was fit enough to walk eight miles, he could align himself with the sun and walk out to the forest edge. It was downhill, as well. If he got in any physical difficulty, robots would come to the rescue. John usually left his personal robot at home, he knew there were always others out there. They kept track of anyone within range and would respond immediately if needed. As long as he was wearing clothes, the robots would be reading his vital signs. Since he didn't feel like walking around naked, he knew they would always be on the lookout for him.

On the fifth morning, John ran into Caleb as he was heading out. Caleb had a sack in his hand, he appeared to be bringing some groceries. Apples, he thought. John called out as Caleb approached the clearing in front of the cabin.

"Caleb, what a nice surprise. Would you care to join me for a walk?"

Caleb got to the porch and shook his head.

"You probably go too far for this old man. I brought you a few things Quentin thought you might like." Inside the bag were a shirt, pants, underwear, socks, a hat, and a pair of walking shoes.

John was a little puzzled since he was already fully equipped, but expressed his thanks with a smile.

"I know you brought everything you need," said Caleb, "these are handmade with natural materials. Not a single sensor in them."

John looked back and grinned. Quentin and Caleb seemed to know what he wanted before he knew himself. He took the gifts inside to change. Now he could get lost in the woods without any robots knowing where he was. It would be a truly liberating feeling.

By the time he had spent a week at the cabin, he had started to develop a plan. He was bothered by doubts concerning how contact with Sol c should work, how they could be sure of the right time. They did not want to be premature. Much of the decision relied on his simulations and comparisons done with their own past. John knew the simulations were estimates at best, he had nothing more than a limited profile of Sol c to go on. They were mainly receiving radio telegraph with a few voice transmissions. Although they could translate them, it only gave him a small window into their civilization. The problem was they were two light-years away. It would take twenty years to reach Sol c, then they would zip through the Solar System in less than a day on the way to Epsilon Eridani. There would be no time to explore the system in person. John thought they needed more time in the immediate neighborhood, he was working on a way to do it without changing the ship's schedule or course.

The next morning while on one of his hikes, he came across a small apple orchard. He heard someone working among the trees, it turned out to be Quentin.

"So you are an orchard man, too," John called out as he approached.

"Been doin' it fer years," Quentin answered. "I'm pickin' the last of the crop from these young trees. I've got a few bushels in the next row if you'd like some. How are you enjoyin' your retreat?"

"Funny you should call it a retreat, I guess that's what it is. In a military retreat you're temporarily going backward in hopes of eventually starting to move ahead again. I prefer to think I'm stepping aside to mull things over before jumping back into the fray. Either way, I don't think headway will be made anytime soon."

Aside from their earlier encounter, he had not spent any time with Quentin, this seemed a good time to get to know him a better.

He lingered while Quentin said, "I've been here doing the caretaker thing and generally living in the woods for most of the past eighty years. I grow most of my own food and make my own clothes. For the things I can't do, I barter with a few others who are doing the same thing."

"That means you must have come up here when my dad was onboard, before we left the ship for the HUB," said John. "Did you know him?"

"Yes, indeed. I knew your dad back then, even saw you a few times when you were a youngster."

"I guess everyone gets to meet everyone else on the ship eventually."

"Oh, yes. Sooner or later you run across most of them. But I can't recall more than a few hundred without resorting to the archives. Your dad was someone I remember very well."

"How did you know my father?" asked John, intrigued by the connection. "Was it through his team? Did you work in propulsion at one time?"

"No, I was never a scientist or an engineer. Never had much interest in math or physics. I was your dad's coach. He was one of the most gifted athletes I ever saw. A natural runner. Could do most anything with his body he wanted without thinking about it, I heard some of that rubbed off on you."

"Yeah, I did okay when I was younger. I was not as fast as he was, but I had endurance. I did well in the marathon and other long distances. I also bike raced. As you've seen, I still do a lot of walking. I just wish there were a couple big mountains in this thing," John finished wistfully. An image of Vanya on the top of one of the peaks they had climbed came to mind momentarily before he snapped back to the conversation at hand.

Quentin got down from the short ladder he had been picking from and walked slowly toward John. He looked directly at him and asked point-blank, "Are you going? Have you made up your mind for sure?"

John was silent for a few seconds then stammered, "Huh, how did you know what I was planning? I haven't discussed it with anyone except Vanya—not even Caleb knows"

"I didn't mean to startle you with my bluntness," said Quentin. "It was an educated guess. It's what I would do if I were in your shoes. Caleb thinks so, too. He came to the same conclusion a while back. Hell, I'd go with you if I could. Unfortunately, I'm afraid I'll be dead before you are partway into it."

They sat in silence before curiosity got the better of John. "How did you figure it out?"

"As I said, I knew your father a long time ago, you are much like him. When you came onboard before the ship's departure, he asked me to keep an eye on your progress, be available if I thought you might need someone to talk to. He would have loved to be doing it himself, but he had already spent over a hundred years on the ship. He was ready to stay put near a planet for the first time in his life.

"We've kept up a steady communication through the years, although with the two-year time delay now, he doesn't know about these most recent events yet. Anyway, given what you are doing, how little you have been able to piece together, how much more there is to find out, it occurred to me that the best way to proceed would be to get as close to Sol c as quickly as possible to monitor the planet firsthand."

"Those were my thoughts exactly," replied John. "More importantly, I think someone needs to be there to handle the question of direct contact when the time comes. It's clear that industrial and technological development is moving ahead faster than at the same stage on Teran. If it continues, as I believe it will, we should be prepared for much earlier contact than we currently anticipate. In fact, if their development begins to accelerate, they may find us before we realize they're capable of it.

"My plan is to arrange for contact to occur as a direct result of their technological march to space exploration. This would be a lot better than us waiting around trying to guess the best time to send them a radio message. Our message should be a physically tangible thing, and be placed where they can find it once they are capable of space travel in their own planetary system. I think some sort of marker placed on or near one of the outer planets is best. Once they're capable of manned travel that far from Sol c, if they are anything like us, they'll begin to think seriously about sending unmanned probes out to the stars. This method of contact can only be done by someone in proximity to their planetary system. Given the ship's flight-plan, that means a mission in another vessel."

"Are you going to do it?" Quentin asked.

"Yes, I believe I will," John stated, suddenly sure.

After his encounter with Quentin, John walked on to Caleb's cabin. Caleb met him at the top of the steps as he came up onto the front porch.

"Welcome, I'm glad you decided to come for lunch."

"Good to see you, Uncle Caleb. Thanks for the invite, your timing was good. I haven't been avoiding you, just spending time by myself, thinking and planning. I need to run something by you to get your reaction."

"Well, I've been thinking, too, let's sit down and hear what you are up to."

They walked over to the pair of deck chairs. For the next twenty minutes, John ran through his thoughts on going to

Sol c. When he finished Caleb sat still for a few minutes then spoke. "I was at the point where I was going to post an opinion to do much what you propose, although your ideas are more developed. I didn't do it because I was afraid it would be turned down, which I feel would be a major mistake. I was trying to come up with a strong enough argument to avoid that, now I think we have one."

He hesitated then asked, "Would you care for a traveling companion?"

"Yes I would, I'm sure Vanya would not mind as well, she's going too by the way. What do we do if we *are* turned down?"

They were not turned down, that was the problem. John's plan was morphed into a major expedition with a crew of one hundred in a fleet of four shuttles. John, Caleb, and the Geezers were sure this was absolutely the wrong way to go about first hand investigation of Sol c, but a large number supported the plan. Nothing had yet been decided, though.

The Geezers called on John in person unexpectedly at his cabin a few days later.

"Let's go for a walk, John," Caleb said as John greeted them with a quizzical look. "Put on those hiking clothes I gave you a while back—you look good in them.

After they had gone a half mile or so into the woods, they stopped at a stream to rest. The water was rushing across the rocks, providing a fresh smell to the air.

"This is a good place to talk," Caleb began. "The splashing of the stream combined with our sensor-less clothes will keep the robots and the ship from hearing us."

"I see you are wearing some of Quentin's creations," John said. "This must be important."

"It is." Caleb then spoke directly to the issue. "What if we just go? We get in a shuttle, leave, and keep on going."

"If you were caught, there would be a pretty big commotion onboard," one of the Geezers replied, "so you have to not get caught. That is why we took precautions to meet like this."

"The ship cannot hear us, because of the circumstances, it should not be particularly aroused. We are simply up in the woods for a hike, not messing around by something important. It does not even seem to be bothering to try to read our lips. We know because we have already done a test out here, it is safe to meet here occasionally.

"It does know that our vital signs are not available because of the lack of clothing sensors, it is used to us doing this, and it keeps the robots at a respectful distance. Since it can see us, anything unusual such as one of us falling down, would result in a quick visit by one of them, however.

"We know the ship will not interfere directly in domestic affairs unless someone is physically threatened. If one of us went to a shuttle right now, got in and started to move away from the ship, it would not react in any way. The problem is our actions would trigger a whole bunch of alerts to those in charge of the shuttles, questions would quickly be asked. The solution here is to schedule the shuttle ahead of time and set a sensible itinerary."

"You seem to have it all figured out for me," John interrupted.

"Well, not exactly. We have to keep them from recalling the shuttle. This would require a reverse thrust of the shuttle engines to slow it back down to less than the Main Ship's speed. They could then wait to overtake you. Their problem is that at some point you will not have enough fuel left to do that, they will never catch you. Once you get far enough away and to high enough speed, it will be difficult for them to justify issuing a recall of the shuttle. Your fuel supply would be too low and could not be replenished until you got close to Sol. They would never drain your fuel supply down below the safety level, no matter what."

"Why won't they come after us?" John asked.

"It would not make much sense to come after you because even if they catch-up to you, they can't bring you back. They would be in the same fuel situation as you. They would have to keep going on along with you.

"One answer is to accelerate as hard and fast as you can tolerate to drain the fuel down as quickly as possible to prevent the recall. At 5g it could be done in ten days, but it is doubtful you or the shuttle would survive that amount of acceleration for as much as an hour. We have to figure out a way to block the signal for a while to create a delay in their taking action."

Chapter 32
Departure, Again
(December 1908)

Once again, the conservative nature of their companions exerted itself, they began backpedaling on the plan to send a small fleet of shuttles ahead to Sol. John, Vanya and Caleb decided not to wait for a final decision, they would leave as soon as possible.

One of the Geezers worked part-time with the particle collector screen team. He was able to organize a survey trip to the outer screens. A trusted member of the screen maintenance team was let in on the plan and would accompany them. The others would return to the ship in emergency pods before the trio accelerated on their way to Sol.

Using the emergency pods would draw a lot of attention, but also create confusion over what had happened. They expected that to give them enough time to put the second part of the plan in place.

They checked out the available shuttles stored in the ship's docking bays, and found one that was fully fueled, well stocked, and up to date on maintenance. It was medium sized, a thousand feet long and six hundred feet in diameter. Normally there would be two to five hundred passengers; because of its many smaller utility craft, it was used frequently for exterior inspections of the ship. It was also used for occasional parties and other functions. There were thirty others like it, it would hardly be missed. It was the most recently used, hence most recently provisioned and inspected. They scheduled it for the survey.

There was little they had to take with them. The shuttle contained everything in the way of necessities. Between onboard provisions and the recycling systems, a hundred people could easily live on it for five years without reprovisioning. The three of them should have no problem for the fifty to sixty years they planned to be gone. If they broke out the seed supply to grow live plants, they could last almost indefinitely.

John went through his data files, noting the ones he wanted to take with him. He would download them right after he took off. The others would always be available, past a certain point though, the time delay would be such that they would not be worth waiting for. That point would be at around one light-year, which meant any request would take two years to be filled.

They would have continuous direct, two-way communications with the Main Ship until it got out of range of the shuttle's transmitters. After half a light-year's distance, they would have trouble detecting the weakening signal, at that point they would have to piggyback off the communications chain formed by the probes.

The shuttle was capable of reaching a speed of 0.14c without gravitational assistance. When added to the ship's current speed of 0.10c, it would reach 0.24c, the remaining two-plus light-years to Sol c would take ten years, they would arrive thirteen years before the Main Ship.

After breakfast the next day, John and Vanya shouldered their travel packs and walked to the underground station. They took a tube car to the forward end of the ship then rode an elevator up the end cap face for what would probably be the last time for them. John thought about the first ride he had done with his father to watch the probe launch many years before. It took forty-five minutes to get to the shuttle bay. Caleb was already there waiting. The rest of the group showed up over the next half hour.

Once everyone was on board, they set a slow route to the outer screens, making several stops along the way to do inspections, like an actual survey team would.

Next they set course for one of the most distant array telescopes. They added this to the itinerary at the suggestion of Hal, one of their screen team insiders. The telescope needed maintenance, a couple of robots were on site preparing for the overhaul. It was not unusual for survey crews to go for a look at such activities, so no one would think anything of it.

As they approached the telescope, Vanya, Hal and the geezers got in the emergency escape pods. Before exiting the shuttle, John had emptied the contents of his travel pack and attached several thin metal foil sheets to the graspers of Vanya's pod. Once outside the shuttle in her escape pod, she proceeded to use the graspers to cover the shuttle's external communications dishes with the sheets, effectively blocking recall or any other signals from arriving or being sent.

She placed a small transmitter inside the foil sheet on the receiver nearest the shuttle entry. Vanya returned to the shuttle in her pod while the others hovered outside. The planted transmitter was programmed to emit a signal to the shuttle, changing the flight plan. It would look like it was sent from the Main Ship, the shuttle would dutifully execute it. Once Vanya was safely back inside, the shuttle oriented itself on the path to Sol and began accelerating.

It would take three months at 1g with periodic bursts of acceleration to 2g's to get up to maximum speed. During that time they would be confined to the flat area at the aft of the craft. Once the acceleration phase was completed, the shuttle would begin spinning along its central axis like the Main Ship does to produce an inertial gravity field. This would allow them to roam around at will on the inside of the cylinder walls.

In the meantime Hal and the Geezers began putting out the cover story as they headed away in their escape pods. The shuttle had lost power, they had temporarily abandoned it. John and Caleb decided to stay onboard to see if they could do anything to get it restored. Vanya had gone back to be with John. This bit of detail was necessary because there were only five life signs being detected in the pods by the Main Ship's sensors, they knew that eight had been onboard. With no communications ability with the shuttle, the ship's crew had to take their word for it.

"We called the robots over from the telescope maintenance party," Hal added. "They will get here in fifteen minutes."

"Thanks," responded the communications chief. "We signaled them, too. Once they get to the shuttle, we should be able to restore at least minimal communications."

"I don't know about that," answered Hal. "We've already tried the low-power, short-range transceivers and got nothing. The power failure must be complete." He added, "We are going to head on in since we don't have forever to hang around in these pods."

They had already used an hour of life support, it would take six more to get back to the ship. The pods were good for ten hours, max.

When the robots got to the location the shuttle had been in when it had its so-called power failure, they found nothing there. John, Vanya and Caleb were long gone, accelerating toward Sol.

Even though communications were down, the crew guessed that the three who had stayed on the shuttle might have been able to restore propulsion, they might be heading slowly back to the Main Ship. The work robots were sent back to their maintenance job, it was decided that they would have to wait for the shuttle to get back to find out what had happened. They were not particularly worried about John, Vanya and Caleb, since they could survive on the shuttle for at least a week with low or no power. If it got too risky, they could always manually launch in the emergency pods.

Shuttle operations leaders met Hal and the Geezers as they exited the pods in the Main Ship docking bay.

"It was quite peculiar," Hal began. "A rolling power failure that took systems out one by one over ten minutes. We got out while it was happening. When it was done, the shuttle was dead silent." After a pause he asked coyly, "Any word from them?"

"Nothing. We are searching the area of the shuttle's last position, plus the path back in with the optical and infrared telescopes, but have not seen anything. This does not mean a lot, though, since the shuttle doesn't have much of an optical signature. If it is as dead as you say it is, it will be cooling off quickly and won't have a large heat signature, either," replied the operations chief. "We sent another shuttle out on the direct path to them, let's wait for them to meet."

Five hours later the rescue shuttle arrived at the missing shuttle's last recorded location. It failed to find the craft.

"Nothing out here," reported the rescue shuttle leader. "We did continuous radar sweeps in all directions the whole trip out but did not see a thing. We will stay out here and keep looking, this is one giant mystery."

As the days and weeks passed, the mystery deepened. There was a lot of concern for John, Vanya and Caleb, which slowly turned to resignation that they had been lost for good in a rare, incomprehensible event. It was very difficult to come up with rational explanations of what had happened, many were becoming worried that there might be hidden flaws in the shuttle systems. A complete review of their design was ordered, extensive tests were run. None of the proposed failure scenarios proved out, no problems were discovered.

After two months they were well on their way. The shuttle was traveling at .2c and they were still accelerating. They had expended enough fuel to make a recall unlikely.

John went out to remove the foil covers from the dishes. He received a message immediately. It was from Hal, who had been transmitting periodically since they left. They had agreed ahead of time to come clean at the two-month mark. John sent back a reply that they were okay.

"How's the weather out there?" Hal asked in his gravelly voice.

"Clear, infinite ceiling, visibility ten parsecs," came John's triumphant reply three days later.

He also send a message to his parents. His personal activities log had been interrupted during the communication black-out, he wanted to make sure they got the whole story directly from him. Before coming out to join him on the ship, Vanya had told his parents not to be alarmed if something unusual happened, hence he was not concerned that they thought he could be dead.

They had gotten away without arousing any suspicion about what they had done, most important, without any pursuers—although their accomplices would now catch heat for their role in the deception.

John, Vanya and Caleb were on their own for the indefinite future. The prospect did not disturb them; they had all the modern conveniences. They could visit with friends when they wanted via the COMM, at least until the time delays became unwieldy. After that they could maintain contact via personal activities reports.

John knew he would miss the fields of the central plains and the forests in the north end. Right now, however, they had taken on a task he knew was more important than comfort or well-being.

Chapter 33
Eros to Lagrange Point 4
(1918 - 1919)

John parked the shuttle behind Eros on January 5, 1918. Eros was the perfect vantage point for them. They planned to sit in front of the asteroid while monitoring radio signals from the planet that they now knew its inhabits called Earth. This asteroid, an oblong rock twenty-five miles long and half as wide at the middle, traveled around Sol in an elliptical orbit mostly outside the Earth's own, but periodically passed inside Earth's orbit. A close approach was coming up in a few months.

They could receive data relayed from probe satellites orbiting Earth, although these would be removed to be sent to the outer planets at some point. Earth technology would eventually get to the stage where the satellites' signals could be detected, since they used common radio band transmission to send data to the larger sub-probes in the outer Solar System.

The asteroid would serve as a hiding place when they periodically sent their own messages out to the probe chain trailing back to the Main Ship. They would orbit to the backside and use the radio band transmitters. With their transmission beams pointed away from Earth toward the probes, they would be largely masked by the bulk of the asteroid. Later, when Earth engineering arrived at the point where they could detect these reduced levels of electromagnetic emissions, they would switch to the optical transmitters. Since these required a much greater aiming precision, it would require them to spend greater amounts of time on the back side of the asteroid, out of contact with transmissions from Earth.

Much had happened from the time the first signals were received at the Main Ship in 1903 until their subsequent departure for Earth on the shuttle. Up to that point, the Main Ship had received only sporadic signals, chiefly radio telegraph messages. Shortly before they left, voice transmission had started; now there was a continuous stream of voice communications. The original ones had been infrequent and generally short. The Terans had been barely able to figure out the languages involved, ultimately identifying three that were known by their speakers as: English, French, and Spanish. The use of radio had grown steadily from short range tests to transoceanic transmissions to the first voice broadcasts in 1907. Transmission power levels increased dramatically, signal bandwidth narrowed significantly, indicating a steady advance of technology. It was during this time that they discovered that the inhabitants of Sol c referred to their planet as Earth.

Since the early messages were short on technical data, it was difficult to gain much information on the senders or their societies. John and his shipmates had to rely on data coming from the orbiting satellites instead.

From them they got a tremendous amount of weather data along with information on crop distribution and population density. They constructed a complete, detailed set of maps of Earth's surface down to individual buildings. They were able to deduce a certain amount regarding Earth's cultures from its buildings, they inferred the presence of certain athletic and entertainment facilities. But this was not the same as being among the population.

They did not send the large exploratory landers because, in order to avoid detection, the landers would have to be put in remote locations. This would not help them find out more on Earth's residents. The landers could provide things not obtainable from orbit, such as soil and rock samples, a limited collection of vegetation and small animals; that could wait. If Earth's technological development maintained its current pace, John knew his people would be able to learn everything they wanted from television broadcasts within a few decades. As an alternative to sending landers, they did several high-altitude fly-throughs of the atmosphere to collect dust and pollen samples.

Counter to the wishes of those back on the Main Ship, John planned to visit the planet in person, but he did not intend to reveal himself or otherwise make contact. Before attempting a visit he needed a lot of preparation. It started with learning as much as possible of conditions on the surface, the people, culture, languages; a complete understanding of the hazards was needed. To avoid detection, he would have to be inconspicuous. This meant looking and acting like a native.

As proof of how little they had learned from radio traffic, they almost missed the start of a world war. At the time, radio telegraph used for military communications was in its infancy. Through the course of the war, it increased steadily. In August 1914, on the eastern front where the first large-scale hostilities began, the Russians had few radios. The Germans had more, but the range of the instruments on both sides was limited. No messages that would have tipped them off about what was taking place on the ground were detected. It was only later in 1915, when it became obvious from news reports that were a part of the regular broadcasts begun that year, that they recognized a major conflict was going on involving many of the nation-states of the northern hemisphere.

Analysis of satellite photo images revealed movement of large numbers of people and vehicles. In hindsight it should have been obvious to them what was going on. They had noted the activity but could not come up with an explanation. The leading hypothesis was mass migration due to a natural disaster. When the same types of activities were seen in Western Europe, they added the possibility of a large-scale military conflict. Then radio traffic began to pick up dramatically, dominated initially by longer range military communications. They quickly became convinced a war had started.

John knew war would dominate the direction of technological development on the planet if it was anything like Teran at this stage of its growth. Since war had not been a part of their society for thousands of years, it was difficult initially to accept it as the probable explanation for what they were seeing.

With the voice transmissions, John now knew how Earth people sounded, he quickly learned to speak English and

French. However, he did have much insight on their facial appearance. Satellite photos did not have the right viewpoint to determine appearance. All they saw was the tops of heads. The only times the Earth people seem to lie down outdoors was along the edges of bodies of water, even then they were nearly fully clothed. At least John could tell they were bipedal, could estimate their heights and a general sense of their body form. Their general form was enough like Terans to make him believe he could blend in un-noticed if his face was not too different. He also needed to hear how they sounded, moved, and used their limbs. The solution was to send in one of the smallest sub-probes to place video and audio monitoring devices. He would make sure they were located out of reach and be extremely difficult to spot.

Caleb scanned through the satellite files until he found a town in the upper Midwest of the United States that had little nighttime traffic and no streetlights. The sub-probe would go in under cover of darkness and mount the devices on the side of a few buildings in the downtown area. They would not need more than a few hours of recording, the sensors would be retrieved the next night.

Biological information was important as well. Chances were the Terans' biological makeup was so different from the inhabitants of Earth that there was little need to worry about cross-infection. They did need to identify any substances that might be dangerous, consequently, they sent other small sub-probes in to collect water, insect, plant and animal samples. It would not be possible to do an exhaustive study because that would take large teams of robots and people on the surface for many decades. They would, however, be able to get a good idea of the major things to look out for in the areas he would be traveling. The work was done at night in remote locations.

The next close approach of Eros would give them a chance to transfer to one of the planet's Lagrange points. These were locations where the gravity of the Earth and its moon balanced each other allowing stationary parking in orbit. Little fuel was needed to maintain location. They selected the fourth Lagrange point, L4. This was where the communications relay sub-probe for the low-orbit satellites was located.

From L4 John could take a lander down to the surface in a day. Caleb and Vanya would stay behind in the shuttle. John would carry a low power, high frequency radio transmitter, completely undetectable with current Earth technology, for biodata transmission plus voice and video so they could communicate with him and see what he was seeing. Back on the shuttle, they would be able to monitor the satellite data to keep John up to date on local weather and news. Vanya and Caleb would maintain communications back to the Main Ship.

John was most interested in visiting the United States, a country that spanned a continent in the northern part of the large north-south landmass. This nation was much younger than those of the northwestern part of the larger landmass, yet it had developed rapidly, playing a decisive role in the recent global conflict. Economically it appeared to be poised for rapid growth. Technologically, it was already a world leader. At the same time, it could be a wild uncivilized place, especially in its western areas. This was the kind of dynamic rough-edged society he wanted to experience.

At the same time, Vanya had been analyzing the satellite imagery for landing sites with easily accessible, useful resources. She settled on one in the central part of a place called Nevada. The area was uninhabited, the mountain ranges were interspersed with isolated smooth-floored valleys that would provide good landing conditions. Vanya had found that the local geology was advantageous for mineral deposits, she had spotted the evidence of surface mining operations. John would need a source of income, and gold or silver should be able to supply it.

Chapter 34
First Landing
(August 1919)

It was late evening on August 26, 1919, the craft glided in for a silent landing. A robot unloaded the mining and camp equipment along with John's personal gear: a rucksack with food, bedroll, and foul-weather clothing. Then it set-up their small mining operation in a nearby dry wash. With Vanya's remote assistance, by the next afternoon they had produced ten pounds of gold nuggets. Just after dawn the following morning John would be ready to start out.

He hoped he looked like a westerner. His physical appearance was human enough, even a physician would have to see him unclothed to notice any differences. He had grown a beard and purposely dirtied his outfit. At thirty miles from the nearest settlement, he wanted to appear as though he had been out there a while in case he stumbled upon anyone.

He retested his transponders. One was in his belt buckle, another was built into the rucksack. A third was sewn in the lining of his coat. These would provide him with continuous contact with the shuttle and allow the lander to monitor his location. They would be used to set up the rendezvous when he was ready to leave. If anything happened to him, the shipboard systems would not automatically respond. Any action would be under Vanya's and Caleb's supervision. For the most part, John was on his own. If he got sick, he would have to treat himself, although the likelihood of this was minute. They had done extensive tests on Earth's microbes from the high-atmosphere flybys and the small robotic landers. He had been immunized against the few that might be dangerous to him.

The microbes he normally carried were a greater issue. His physiology was different enough from humans so that he could not infect them, but as for planetary landings like his at Devon, no foreign biological agents would be carried to the surface of the planet. That is, except the traveler, who would leave eventually.

These microbes were not harmful to life on Earth, but they might be able to survive there. It would not be desirable for a future biologist to find some of them triggering an investigating of their DNA. In order to avoid this, he went through the same decontamination procedures used for his trips to Devon, and he carried the same engineered replacement microbes needed to maintain vital body functions.

This way if any got loose, they would die out quickly. In order to protect himself, John would have to periodically ingest fresh bacteria to replace the ones that had died. That was why he brought along his own salt, and body powder doctored with engineered bacteria. In addition, bacteria, even engineered ones, had a habit of mutating, hence the twelve hour time limit which kept the number of cell divisions and the accumulation of mutations low. As an added precaution, he would sterilize his wastes and wash with antibiotic soap. The lander was also completely sterilized.

The lander's doors closed behind the robot after it had stowed the mining equipment. The engines began to whine. It lifted off vertically, banked slightly, climbing rapidly. Take-off was unavoidably noisier due to the jet engines used to get back to high altitude. They were highly efficient, however, emitting a low whine with a bit of a hiss. The surrounding hills would shield most of the sound, which would only last for a few minutes. It would move into low Earth orbit to provide a relay point for communications with the shuttle at L4, and be handy to return to the ground when needed.

Two minutes later, he was alone in the quiet darkness. It was 10:45 p.m. local time. John turned on his lantern and got ready to spend the night on the ground.

He woke at daybreak to a brilliant red-orange sunrise. The sky was absolutely clear, the air a mild 73 degrees. In late August the temperature in this area would rise steadily until it peaked around 100 degrees. John got an early start in order to cover as much distance as possible before the extreme heat arrived. Breakfast was freeze-dried rations heated over an open fire. He would consume these until he was able to get something native. They had established that local sugars and carbohydrates were compatible enough with his gastro-intestinal system for him to get sufficient nutrition to survive. Proteins and enzymes were a different story, he would have to supplement his diet with the freeze-dried rations he brought with him. He set out shortly after breakfast heading north. The nearest town with a rail station was thirty miles away, he figured it would take him three days to get there. Vanya and the robotic lander had located several springs along the way, so water would not be a problem.

The first two days passed uneventfully. There was abundant wildlife to watch as he walked—pronghorn antelope, rabbits, hawks, mule deer, a lone coyote—plus lots of insects and small reptiles when he looked closely.

In the late morning of the third day, John came across a dirt wagon track heading down from a low pass to the east. It curved to the northwest in the direction he was headed. The map generated by the surveillance satellite showed a track at the twenty-five-mile point in his trek that went to Fallon, his intended destination. This was most likely the right road, he followed it.

After stopping for lunch in the shelter of a large rock, he decided to rest during the heat of the day. A little after 2:00 p.m., he noticed a plume of dust off in the distance to the east, the way he had come. It appeared to be moving along the road. He watched for a bit, thinking it could be wagons. He began to prepare himself mentally to move off the road to wait for them to pass. He wanted to be less vulnerable in his first human encounter. He then realized that whatever was creating the dust was moving faster than wagons pulled by animals plodding along in the middle of the day. Perhaps it was several riders on horseback. A few minutes later he saw that it was vehicles. He moved off to the side of the road, positioning himself behind his lunch rock that would hide him while at the same time allowing a clear view of the approaching strangers. From a couple hundred yards away, he spotted a string of ten vehicles of various shapes and sizes. As they got closer he realized they were operated by men in uniform. He realized what the group was. The story of the transcontinental convoy had been in the media intercepts recently.

He stood up and walked toward the road. The lead driver saw him right away, the man seated next to him signaled the driver to stop. A young officer hopped out and strode rapidly toward him. He was in Army field dress.

"Good afternoon, old-timer. I'm Colonel Dwight Eisenhower, United States Army. This is a long way from anywhere to be on foot. Been traveling long?"

"You don't know the half of it," John answered wryly.

He was relieved to understand what the man said. He had been studying English for a long time, this was his first conversation with a native. For a second he was taken aback by being called an old-timer, he quickly realized that physically he appeared to be in his sixties. With the addition of the beard and his rugged clothing, he looked old to them. At seventy-seven, however, John thought of himself as a young man.

"Been up in the hills banging around for a bit," he went on. "I'm headed back to town. My mule died last week, so I'm on foot."

"We're headed for Fallon," Eisenhower stated. "It's not military policy to pick up hitchhikers, but considering the circumstances, would you care for a lift?"

John smiled, he replied with a quick, "Sure enough, seein' hows I'm part owner of your vehicle." A lie, but he thought it was a nice touch.

Eisenhower grinned back and winked. "Ah, a victim of the new income tax. You must be doing pretty well, banging around in those hills. Your treasure is safe with us."

John realized he had gone a bit too far. Eisenhower was sharp. He understood that only the wealthy paid income tax. He probably concluded John was carrying gold or silver with him, which John would rather have kept secret.

The ride to town was bumpy and dusty, it took nearly an hour. The soldiers commented that it was the best road they had been on since leaving Salt Lake City, which John remembered was in a state called Utah. Initially, John thought he should have walked to Fallon, but riding with the men gave him a chance to practice his English and start learning his way around their society. At least this was less chaotic than a town.

There was a welcoming committee of well-wishers waiting for them as they approached Fallon just before 4:00 p.m. A couple of the convoy's scout vehicles were already there, Eisenhower's group was the first sizable contingent to arrive. The rest were strung out along the road for many miles. They would be arriving through-out the evening and into the night. Eisenhower shook hands with the mayor and sheriff then said a few words about their trip. In the middle of the commotion, John sneaked off to find the assay office.

When he walked out, he was shaking his head in amazement. Twenty dollars an ounce for gold! Based on prices he had seen locally, he figured he would need at least

$50,000 to travel and support himself comfortably without depleting his reserves too rapidly. That was twenty-five hundred ounces, or somewhat over two hundred pounds. Coming up with the gold was not a problem; it had taken less than half a day to extract the ten pounds he carried with him. He could not, however, deposit that much gold at one time, especially in a small town. It would arouse suspicion, could even set off a gold rush. Gold fever was not near as intense as it had been decades ago, but the potential was still there. John had to be careful. He exchanged a few ounces for gold coins, which immediately gave him an idea. Why not make his own coins?

He went down to the stables at the end of town to buy a mule. Then he stopped at a store to pick up tools and provisions. He didn't really need them, but he had to act the part. He set off the way he had come to meet the lander at his starting point and set up his mint.

Six weeks later John climbed aboard the westbound train. Wearing a new suit, he took a seat in the first-class passenger car. In preparation for his journey, John realized he was going to need a last name. He had noted the fact early on that people introduced themselves giving two or sometimes three names. He always elusively responded that he was John. For hotel registers and the banks he was going to need a last name. His family name translated to English as *fisherman*, he had decided to use John Fisher when a full name was needed. As it turned out, it was a fortunate choice.

He had wired ahead $5,000 to a bank in San Francisco, California, from the gold coins he had deposited in Carson

City, Nevada. The rest was back in the baggage car in four seventy-five-pound boxes along with the freeze-dried rations, his special salt, soap and body powder, plus electronic surveillance equipment. The boxes were large, though most of their insides were empty. Very heavy small boxes would be too obvious, given where he was coming from. Labeled "Dry Goods" they looked, felt, and smelled like wood. They were not wood, however. The boxes were absolutely impregnable to anyone else on the planet.

Once he settled in San Francisco, he slowly made the rounds of various banks, opening accounts and depositing his gold coins. He spread his deposits around, eventually transferred the funds to J. P. Morgan and Company in New York. In between bank visits, he toured the city, took a side trip to Monterey to see the famous coastline, and practiced his accent. He was trying to figure out how he wanted to sound.

In spite of the lack of an electronic financial network, he learned that in a place such as San Francisco the bankers all knew one another and talked among themselves. If he spread his transactions out over time, made them small enough, he would not arouse suspicions. He could not avoid depositing the gold coins, even though his activities could ultimately catch someone's interest. He planned to be on his way to New York before that happened, if it ever did.

John traveled the country working his way eastward, taking in as much as possible for the next several months. He boated across the Golden Gate strait to Marin County and traveled up the coast to see the giant redwoods. San Francisco had been completely rebuilt in the thirteen years since the earthquake in 1906, he marveled at the industry and ingenuity of its people. Next he turned east. He watched a ball game in Chicago. The Cubs lost that day, eventually finishing third in the league for the season. They would not win a World Series until well after he had left the Solar System.

He was in New York by Thanksgiving of 1919. Downtown Manhattan was intimidating. The population density was overwhelming, unlike anything he had experienced on the Main Ship. The experience was energizing, he quickly got into the spirit and pace of life in one of the planet's most dynamic cities. He even invested a part of his money in the stock market, doing well enough to skip the rendezvous he had planned to replenish his gold supply. He did not get a job, although he considered it. In the end he found the idea too restrictive. He made the New York area his home base from which he traveled around the eastern United States.

He felt he had gotten to Earth at the perfect time. Transportation systems, especially the railroads, were developed enough to let him travel widely. Powered air flight was in its infancy. Yet technology was not to the point where his arrival or departure from the planet could be detected.

Chapter 35
Repeat Visits
(1921 -1937)

John returned to the shuttle periodically, never spending more than six months on Earth during any one visit. While he was on Earth Vanya spent her time studying satellite imagery from Sol's planets and many of the larger moons doing remote geology. In between visits to Earth, the three of them made several trips to Mars, Jupiter and Saturn in the shuttle. They spend time on the surface of Mars, being careful not to leave any evidence of their presence, and toured the major moons of the two largest gas giants.

While on Earth, John spent much of his time in the New York Public Library with Caleb and Vanya literally looking over his shoulder via the video portion of their communication link. They read, thought about, and absorbed as much as they could on human society and its development. They wanted to know how this civilization had progressed, especially how it had happened so rapidly. They had already been surprised by the quick development of radio. Now they had to be on the lookout for indications of further extension into radar, radio astronomy, and rocketry.

Radio broadcasting was rapidly expanding. Radar would follow, once it became widely available, the risk of detection would be too great to consider landing any more. In fact John would have to instruct the satellites to move to higher orbits, then leave the vicinity of the planet altogether. Eventually they would have to move from L4 back to Eros. With the asteroid as a shield, they could remain there in the shuttle at least until space travel commenced.

Right now he could visit the planet as he pleased. Later he would have to be more careful. His craft was small and quiet. If he chose remote landing spots, came and went at night, he would not be detected. The craft was not, however, invisible to radar. Making it undetectable was certainly within the Terans' means, but they used radar themselves for tracking. They could have altered the lander or shuttle to have a much smaller radar signature before they had left the Main Ship, but it had not occurred to them; given their mode of departure, it would not have been possible, anyway. At the time it had appeared it would take humans a hundred years to get to radar.

Another key technology they had to consider was radio astronomy. It had not yet been invented, once it was, it would only be a matter of time before Earth's scientists stumbled across the Teran communication beam. The Terans could do little about this. The beam was out there, it was impossible to hide. The same physics the Terans had used to detect Sol and the civilization on its third planet allowed detection of their beams and ultimately them, as well. As long as the Main Ship was headed for the Solar System, the beam from the Alpha Centauri HUB would be pointed directly at it.

Finally there was rocketry. Here John was anticipating satellites being put in orbit around the planet. Once humans could do that, they would be able to track any object in the sky. They would have to leave Earth's neighborhood for good before that happened.

An extraordinary thing occurred in 1924. A loosely organized effort to convince the major broadcasters, including governments, to turn off their equipment for a brief period to permit uncontaminated recording of the ambient radio noise coming from outer space took place. The goal of the experiment was to determine if there were coherent signals containing evidence of an intelligent source not on Earth. The popular hope was that they might detect communications from Mars, which many people believed to be inhabited. The test was a failure, since no coherent signals from a source off the Earth were detected.

This startling event prompted them to remove the satellites from near-Earth orbit, this caused a stir back on the Main Ship. In addition a major ship wide COMM issue concerning the HUB beam from Alpha Centauri resulted in the decision to request that the HUB point a second transmission beam at Sol that would remain fixed there. The original beam would follow the Main Ship to Epsilon Eridani. The second beam would be set up and blended in slowly to cover the fact that the first one was fading away. This would keep the background noise level at Sol the same. With the time delay to Alpha Centauri for the request plus the delay back to Sol for the second beam, they had acted with just enough time before the ship was due to pass by Sol on its way to Epsilon Eridani.

Then in 1932, after the Main Ship passed Sol, Karl Jansky, an employee of a major telecommunications company, detected extraterrestrial signals—in this instance, powerful radio waves coming from a natural source in the center of the Milky Way. Radio astronomy was born with this event. The search for extraterrestrial intelligence, or SETI, would not be long in coming. These developments came as a shock to John. He had not expected them for decades. His studies of the Teran archives combined with simulated scenarios of Earth development indicated that radio astronomy and SETI would not begin until the 1980s.

A few years later, in one of his New York Library sessions, with Caleb and Vanya looking on as usual, John ran across an article on pulse radar ranging in a technical journal. This was an important breakthrough, they knew it would eventually lead to successful large-scale, long-distance radar. They had to keep an even closer watch on developments to determine how long this would take.

In 1935 the British began installation of a coastal radar system for defense. It was completed in 1938, covering the island from the northeast down the east coast and around to the southwest. There were increasing political tensions in Europe, this action was clearly a prelude to military activities. Once they began, John and Caleb realized that radar would be extended over large areas of the continents along with ships at sea, as it had been back home.

Soon after regular radio broadcasts started, John realized how different America was from the other societies on the planet. He recognized how different it was from societies on his home world during the same period of development as well. America was a wealthy nation organized unlike any other prosperous society. It was chaotic, almost anarchic at times. Local autonomy pervaded its political and business structures. It was not really run, yet it ran well, and very fast in a thousand different directions at once. This was especially true in the cities.

Teran development had been much more orderly, slower paced. It was largely guided from above. Based on Teran history, they had expected Earth to reach certain developmental milestones on a particular schedule. Each milestone on Earth was met earlier, often much earlier, than anticipated. Nearly every time, it was the Americans who rapidly exploited new technology, no matter where it had actually been invented.

Broadcast radio had started right after the World War I and blossomed quickly. The medium was discovered by an Italian twenty-five years before, the British were the first to take it seriously. The Americans, however, led the way in commercial expansion. Altogether, the time from the introduction of the radio telegraph to voice broadcasting was a tenth of what the Terans had expected. The expansion of sound, that is, voice and music broadcasting, was running several times more rapidly than anticipated; the introduction of private commercial broadcast operations caught them completely by surprise. In fact it took the Terans a while to figure out what was going on. Teran never had commercial radio or TV during the centuries they used these media, only government sanctioned outlets. The activity level and energy of this society astounded John. He grew more eager than ever to see as much as he could firsthand before it was too late to avoid detection.

Chapter 36
Tuxedo Park
(1939 - 1940)

During his frequent stays in New York, John attended public lectures in engineering and physics at Columbia University. They gave him an opportunity to assess development of the theoretical basis and the future pace of technological progress.

After one particularly interesting program on radio broadcasting, he spoke directly with the lecturer. They were soon engaged in a lively discussion on AM versus FM transmission. John was careful not to reveal anything that was not yet known, at the same time he tried to draw out as much as he could concerning the details of the lecturer's work in the field. The lecturer was apparently impressed with John's expertise, when he asked about his background, John simply replied he read a lot (at which he heard Caleb chuckling in his ear). This was better than making up a story, it was an acceptable answer in America at the time. The self-made man was an icon, Thomas Edison had died just a few years before. As they parted, the speaker invited John to stop by his office the next day.

Up to this point John had been careful to avoid developing personal relationships, he wanted to avoid anything that would draw attention. Making the news would not sit well with his former companions, some of whom were probably listening in back on the Main Ship.

The gentleman he was on his way to see was a leading expert in radio and the technology that would eventually lead to radar. John felt it was worth taking a chance on getting to know someone more closely if in return he could better understand when the risk of detection would become real. If one person had the requisite knowledge, then others probably did, as well. Before radar was implemented on a large scale, the three of them would have to be well clear of Earth.

John's meeting was supposed to last a half hour, it was scheduled for the end of the day at 4:30 p.m. They talked for more than an hour, at which point his host interrupted to say he had a dinner engagement and needed to be downstairs in a few minutes. He asked John if he would care to come along, he thought the folks he was dining with would be interested in meeting him. Not averse to a little adventure, John readily accepted, thinking they were going to a restaurant downtown.

"Be careful there, cowboy," Caleb whispered in his ear. Caleb had been referring to John as "cowboy" since his visit to the stockyards in Kansas City, Missouri. "Don't get into something you can't easily extract yourself from." Caleb did not normally talk to him when others were close by, but this was an extraordinary situation.

"Don't worry, I can always say the voices in my head have returned," John whispered as his host walked ahead down the hall. "That will surely end the evening immediately." He heard Vanya laugh in the background.

At the end of the hall by the stairwell, John's host stuck his head in one of the offices and called out, "Niels, ready to go?"

"I'll be along in a minute, meet you out front," came a heavily accented, disembodied reply.

It didn't take long for John to realize the outing would be a little less ordinary than he initially thought. The limousine tipped him off. Next it was the unseen man from the office. He recognized him immediately as the physicist Niels Bohr.

"Let me introduce you. Niels, this is John Fisher. John, please meet Niels Bohr." They shook hands and got in the back of the limo.

"John, I hope you don't mind a bit of a drive," said his host, "you may be getting back fairly late."

This gave John the chance to back out, for an instant he was tempted. He feared he might have been discovered, that he was being abducted and taken somewhere to be examined. The feeling passed quickly, as he realized there was no possible way his host could know who or what he was.

"I look forward to continuing our conversation," said John. "A night out might do me good."

The drive lasted an hour and took them a considerable distance out of the city to the northwest. They arrived at a gate with a guardhouse that displayed the words "Tuxedo Park" prominently. Once inside they were greeted by their host who requested they sign the guest register. John was loath to leave a permanent record of his presence, but he had no choice.

They were treated to a lavish dinner in the company of a selection of the country's leading scientists and engineers. He enjoyed it immensely. When he learned the background of their host, Alfred Loomis, he was particularly impressed. To be a leading financier as well as a scientist was unusual. To finance the activities of the latter from the efforts of the former was unprecedented. John had come face to face with the power and dynamism of the society he was living in. He grasped at once what it meant. The rapidly advancing technology that was outpacing his people's early development with embarrassing ease was not a short-term thing.

John enjoyed the company and wide-ranging discussions. When asked if he would be interested in staying at Tuxedo Park for a while to collaborate on some research, he declined, citing the need to attend to his mining interests out west. His host sympathized with him feeling that he had a kindred spirit in the elderly gentleman with a knack for spotting errors in math and physics arguments. For John's part his excuse was not a lie. His cash was running low in spite of his past stock market successes. He needed to get back to Nevada to replenish his gold supply. His abilities were impressive to his host, although John was no prodigy. He was simply pointing out mistakes he himself had made while learning the same material as a youngster.

In the process he learned that microwave research was progressing rapidly and was being applied to radio ranging, later to be called radar. The significance of pulsed waves had not yet been realized, at least not by this group. The British were keeping what they had done a secret. How long that might last, he could not know; John suspected not long, given the talent in the room.

"At least come by often to see what we are doing," Loomis offered as John was departing.

"I would be delighted," he replied.

After returning to the city, he used the lander to get back to Nevada. He knew he would need it anyway to do a little sightseeing. To get to the rendezvous point, he took a train up to the Mountain House in the Catskills. On a clear, cool October evening, he hiked in the light of a full moon west ten miles to a secluded clearing in the woods. The lander met him there to convey him to Nevada. In a week the robots dug up another three hundred pounds of small nuggets that were made into coins. John transported the gold back to his pickup point where he stashed it for further use. Then he went on to being a tourist.

John's itinerary included Angel Falls in Venezuela, the Seychelles islands in the Indian Ocean, the Karakorum Mountain Range in Pakistan, China and India; each one a spectacular locale where he could visit unnoticed.

Back in New York, he found a letter from Loomis waiting at his apartment. Loomis thanked him for the pleasure of his company at the recent diner and reiterated the offer that John visit when he had the chance. John wondered how Loomis had obtained his address. He had given it out only when necessary to banks or the required governmental authorities.

What John did not know was that he had been investigated. Loomis had done this partly because of the sensitive nature of his research work, partly to satisfy his curiosity.

Self-made millionaires who could hold their own in a conversation on microwave radiation with him and nuclear physics with Niels Bohr were not common. The investigation turned up John's bank account in New York with J. P. Morgan and Company right away, along with several additional accounts in San Francisco. Though they were not large by Loomis's standards, John appeared to have more than enough income to live on. However, no mining companies or claims anywhere out west could be found in his name. He was not registered with the IRS. These two facts when combined led Loomis to conclude John was using shell companies to shelter himself from the income tax—a practice common in some circles. There were plenty of John Fishers in New York in the 1930 census; so many, in fact, that he did not try to connect any of the entries to John. Loomis decided to take a chance, to go with his gut feeling that John was okay and sent the formal invitation letter to the address he had gotten from his friend, J. P. Morgan, Jr.

John took Loomis up on his offer to visit the lab periodically. He asked about everything that was going on, including of course, radar. It was the perfect way to keep tabs on its development.

In 1940 Loomis's pursuit of radar took on a whole new level of urgency with the German invasion of France in May. This led to the formation of the radiation lab at MIT and the shuttering of the Tuxedo Park lab, effectively cutting John off from further access. The MIT lab required significant background checks to get clearance, something he was not willing to submit to even if he had been asked to visit or join, which he was not.

In the years leading up to and through the war, John and Caleb watched as radar was perfected. By 1943 they knew the time for John's last trip down to Earth was drawing near.

"Mathematics is the language of physics," said John. "Together they are astonishing, mysterious. They are immutable, universal. What more could you want for the word of God?"

John paused. Although he had not meant to get testy, certain theological issues had been on his mind ever since he began reading various religious writings, he had already formed very firm convictions.

Father O'Mahoney was the latest in a series of religious leaders John had sought out to learn what humans believed, how those beliefs guided their lives.

The Father took a breath. "My son, you are at once wise and naive. We should discuss these matters at length another time. Now, however, I have to prepare for tomorrow's service."

With that, John bid him good-bye and left the cathedral. He would not be back.

John walked across the street and down a block to the plaza. He leaned against the railing while watching the skaters below, he thought back to his own upbringing, to the philosophical discussions with his parents. They'd had regular, wide-ranging talks during those years. They started small and simple then built up to include the deepest under-pinnings of how they perceived the universe and their place in it. The Terans had worked out a lot over the millennia, they felt secure in what they knew. They accepted the fact that they did not know everything, they would not and most likely could not ever completely grasp the full truth of existence. It was a state they arrived at through the course of much time and effort, it was not an accommodation. They still kept seeking answers.

The people of Earth were clearly in a phase of dynamic development of their own ideas on such matters. They had only begun to work things out, it was a time of religious turmoil. John knew there would be much more searching and turmoil to come.

There was a good deal of political and economic turmoil as well. John was a scientist at heart. All his people were. They knew that from science came technology, from technology came wealth. Technology and wealth were two sides of the same coin. One could not exist without the other, together they were the engines that drove progress. Loomis, John knew, understood this.

Alfred Loomis was an interesting man living in two worlds. John viewed him as an example of what others should aspire to. Loomis was a trained physicist, an expert engineer, as well as a businessman who understood economics well. To him the purpose of the financial system was to develop and implement technology, which in turn would lead to the growth of wealth and improved living conditions for all. Wealth in turn would provide greater financial resources for more technological development, keeping the cycle going. To John it was not the money; what mattered most was the freedom that resulted. Freedom from hunger and disease, freedom from work and worry, time to philosophize.

To John even the exceedingly wealthy Loomis was poor by the standards of his companions on their starship. They had the wealth to provide for their needs, satisfy all their wants. They no longer needed money because everything was free. Reaching this state had been liberating. No one any longer felt the need to acquire a lot of possessions, to strive for positions of power, or to fill their lives with constant activity.

Chapter 37
Back to Eros
(1946)

By the end of the Second World War, radar systems were sweeping out from the coasts of Europe and North America, whole-sky tracking was being done. The world was quickly becoming covered by ships and planes with radar scopes. It was time for John to leave Earth for good.

On a cold, clear January night in 1946, he met the lander on a frozen lake in northern Vermont. At 2:15 a.m. he left Earth for the last time. The rocket boosters kicked in at sixty thousand feet, a day and a half later he was docking with the shuttle at L4 that would take the three of them back to Eros. They would remain at L4 for a few weeks until the orbital trajectories allowed an efficient transit.

The Main Ship had passed through the Solar System fifteen years before, it was now more than a light-year from Earth on its way to Epsilon Eridani. They took it upon themselves to recall the remaining satellites around Earth, following up with a message to the ship on what they had done and why. The main restriction they set for themselves was to avoid detection. The goal was to initiate first contact at a time and place under their control. It would happen when they felt Earth was ready to handle it. Given this, they felt they had to act. If they waited for a return message to get guidance from the Main Ship, there was no guarantee the satellites would not be detected in the interim.

The existence of a large, un-regulated, democratic society, the influence of its popular culture and mass media were something John had not anticipated. On Teran such a society at this point in their political and technological development had not yet arisen, nor would it for several centuries. Teran at the comparable time in its history was dominated by three major powers; characterized by authoritarian, central bureaucracies with entrenched leadership classes. Development happened in episodic fashion with long intervals of stagnation. It was not driven by internal forces like the society of Alfred Loomis, instead it was permitted by the leadership every once in a while as external needs arose or their attention was diverted elsewhere. In the case of the 1924 experiment, the influence of popular culture and the media had almost as much to do with obtaining the necessary cooperation as a primary interest in science.

Popular interest had been stirred up by reports of astronomical observations that revealed the apparent presence of canals on Mars. The media kept interest alive. The scientists themselves, or at least their employers, were not above using the public's passions to promote funding of their work. John thought this a curiously inefficient way to fuel basic research and technological development. It was, of course, not the only force of change involved. Many times over the decades of his visits to Earth John, and Caleb and Vanya remotely, saw it at work, often driving some of the largest projects ever undertaken. The most significant would be the initiation of space travel in the 1960s, decades before one would have expected it based on comparisons with Teran.

Time passed at Eros station as the trio monitored radio traffic, listening to and then watching as much news from Earth as possible. The translators provided data in five major languages and a dozen minor ones. They surveyed the aftermath of the second great global conflict with utter despair. The dropping of atomic bombs on Nagasaki and Hiroshima in Japan marked a watershed. Teran had gone through nuclear conflict, as well. They hoped two bombs would be enough of a wake-up call. Back home, it had taken twenty.

Development was accelerating as a result of the war, a host of new technologies appeared. One was the radar that forced the Terans to remove their satellites. Another was the rocket. On Teran it had taken a hundred years to go from military rockets with a range of a couple hundred miles to manned spaceflight. Progress had been slow because it was extremely expensive. Once accomplished, however, expansion to permanently manned orbiting stations, then to colonies on their moons followed by trips to nearby planets, had been continuous and inexorable. John had a feeling things would be different for Earth.

In between monitoring newscasts, they busied themselves with plans for the marker that would be left behind. Early on Vanya had discovered and they had agreed on the site. The Saturnine moon Mimas had an enormous impact crater on it—a quarter of the diameter of the body itself. From a distance the crater with its central mound looked like a giant bull's-eye. The marker would be placed right at the top of the central mound. It could take several hundred years before Earth's inhabitants made their way out that far and eventually stumbled onto it. By then the Main Ship would be beyond Epsilon Eridani, its HUB would be up and running and communicating with the HUB at Centauri. The information in the marker would tell the Earthlings how to detect the HUBs' transmissions.

In 1963 Caleb found what they were going to use for the marker: a Gemini program space capsule. They would replicate one and leave it on Mimas. Having a sense of humor, Caleb figured it would make the humans think it was a hoax at first, then once they had figured out the signal codes and began listening to one of the HUBs, they would realize what the marker was.

They fabricated the capsule and readied it for the trip to Saturn. They needed to include instructions on how to read the HUB transmissions and the exact coordinates to point toward. In addition, they wanted to leave a record of themselves, their people, and John's travels on Earth. Unfortunately, current recording equipment on Earth was too primitive, the media were not reliable enough. Something that would last for perhaps a hundred years and hold a lot of information was needed. They, or at least one of them, would have to wait for Earth's scientists to invent it. Once this occurred the media and data formats could be duplicated to provide something familiar to the finders. Then the capsule would be placed on Mimas.

As they sat down for dinner after the final touches were completed on the capsule, Caleb brought up the tender subject of the end of their mission.

"John, you and Vanya should leave, head back to Alpha Centauri. The two of you could have gone years ago when you came back from your last visit to Earth. If you had you would be back there by now. Or you could have gone out to meet the Main Ship as it passed by, still you stayed on."

"Caleb, you could have gone out to meet the ship, too, but you didn't. We wanted to see things through to the end. Besides, the ship is heading in the wrong direction." Vanya answered.

"My life is nearing the end—I'm already on borrowed time. The ship held no future for me. Let me hang on here to place the capsule. That way you two can get back to Devon. You have done everything you set out to do."

They were reluctant to leave Caleb, but knew he was right.

John and Vanya would be able to keep up with the stream of data from Earth coming along the circulating probe chain. They would also keep up a running conversation with Caleb as they started the crossing. After that they would have each other's daily activity recordings. It would be a long journey by themselves in the shuttle. It was plenty big enough so they would not feel shut-in. There were exercise and entertainment facilities, a lab with sufficient computer power and archives to allow John to continue his history work and Vanya to work on the geology of Earth and Mars. They would maintain the garden, their numerous daily logs would allow them to keep track of friends and loved ones.

In January of 1964, John and Vanya left on the shuttle. Their trajectory took them to Jupiter then Saturn, where they used each planet's gravitational well to boost their velocity. A month later Caleb got to kid them about missing The Beatles live on *The Ed Sullivan Show*.

At the Sun the shuttle once again accelerated and finally turned toward his destination. The gravitational boosts when combined with the ship's engines would bring them up to a top speed of 0.16c. It would take twenty-eight years to get back to Alpha Centauri.

Chapter 38
En Route
(1968)

John pushed away from the viewer console in the control room. As he leaned back in his swivel chair, he raised his arms and clasped his hands behind his head, then he heard a feminine voice. "Hello, John."

Even though it was not Vanya, he wasn't startled. He would sometimes get messages unexpectedly. In fact, his father and especially Caleb had left a batch of recordings that would pop up and start playing at random times. He was puzzled, since he did not recognize the voice.

"John, my name is Clarise; I will appear on your viewer in a few seconds."

An unfamiliar face appeared on the screen. Its basic features were different enough from his own to arouse suspicions that it was not someone from the Main Ship.

"John, the next view you will see is of my ship. It is parked two hundred feet off your port side." By this time Vanya had come into the control room.

The image that appeared was of a slate-gray cylinder similar in size to his own craft. He immediately got up to look out the nearest port-side window. He didn't fully expect to see anything. He assumed this was Caleb having fun with him. What he instead saw was the same ship that was on the viewer.

"John and Vanya I hope I am not frightening you," Clarise said. "I mean you no harm. I have come to meet you. I too am a visitor to this planetary system. We have an outpost in the asteroid belt and have been monitoring Earth for quite some time. We have also been monitoring your activities."

"Where exactly are you from, how long is 'quite some time'?" John replied. He was having a conversation in real time, it was not a joke. What he saw out the portal was very real.

"We are from a planet whose star is located a third of the way around the galaxy from here. We have been on station at Sol for over three million years."

"You personally have been here for three million years?" Vanya uttered in astonishment.

"No. I have only been here twenty-five thousand years. Let's continue this face to face. I will come over to your ship to visit for a while."

John and Vanya were wary about their visitor's intentions but realized they probably had no choice in the matter. The shuttle's instruments were not indicating any physical objects by their ship, yet there it was in plain view. It had simply appeared. The visitor's technical superiority was apparent.

Finally curiosity overcame caution, John replied, "Of course. Please come across as soon as you can."

The air lock outer door opened and closed, then the inner one. In front of them stood a bipedal being nearly their own height. Clarise looked different enough for them to know she, at least that is what they assume because of the feminine name and voice, was an outsider. She was not so different, however, that they thought they were with someone totally alien.

"You can read about us later," Clarise said. "I downloaded a file with the history of my race. Don't wait too long, it will erase without a trace in ten days, it cannot be copied or forwarded. Right now I need to fill you in on my mission. As I said, we have been monitoring you since you arrived in this star system."

"Are you going to prevent Caleb from leaving the marker?" Vanya asked.

"No. We would not have allowed you to get close to Earth, let alone place the marker, if we did not condone your activities," answered Clarise. "We have been protecting both you and the inhabitants of Earth. Our directive, like yours, is to observe, not interfere. The observing must be closely controlled. First contact is never to be accidental, it should not be initiated abruptly."

"This seems to be first contact to me, and it was a bit abrupt," John replied somewhat testily.

"Once I leave, you will find that there will be no record of my visit or your interaction with me in your ship's records," Clarise said. "Furthermore, we have interacted several times already without your knowledge. This is not going to be first contact. That will come on your people's initiative. Just as the people of Earth will eventually reach a level of technological sophistication sufficient to discover you, so your people will eventually discover us. That day is well in the future, this is a little teaser to keep you looking, not unlike the marker."

"Then why this visit?"

"You are the earliest of your people to encounter another civilization," said Clarise. "We had to ensure the encounter went well. That is, that no harm came to you or those on Earth, that there were no unintended consequences.

"We started by tracking your probes, sub-probes, and satellites that visited the planets and their moons to make sure nothing happened to them. We made sure no artifacts got left behind. We also did an on-site inspection of your decontamination procedures. This has been done in the past for similar facilities including the one you both passed through numerous times on the way to Devon. In the case of Earth, we had to be doubly certain that you were not going to release any alien viruses, bacteria, or other biomaterials that could possibly contaminate the humans."

"A site visit? You have already been onboard our ship?" John interjected.

"None of us personally, but a couple of our small robots paid a visit."

"What if our procedures had not measured up?"

"You would have encountered technical problems just serious enough to prevent you from going to Earth," Clarise answered, "Not so serious as to endanger you, nor would we have prevented you from doing remote observations. John, most importantly we had to assure that no harm came to you. You were closely watched the whole time you were on the planet. As you know, it is a dangerous place, you were without your robotic guardians. In addition, you were often a fair distance from your lander. We were prepared to rescue you if it was needed. We wanted to make sure, if the worst did happen, that there was no body left behind for autopsy."

"Well, I am grateful. But how would you have rescued me from the streets of Manhattan if I had been hit by a bus?"

"As I said, we have been monitoring Earth for several million years and are not the first to be stationed here. We are merely the latest in a long line going back 750 million years. Suffice it to say that our technology allows us to remain completely hidden from the natives of Earth while coming and going as we please."

"The latest in a long line," John said, his voice trailing off. "There are many civilizations as advanced as yours?"

"There are several thousand, we are relative newcomers. Your people will probably be our replacements here."

"When will that happen?" Vanya queried.

"When you achieve light-speed transport. Though you'd better hurry up! From what we have seen of Earth, they may find you first."

"They are developing swiftly. What does the future hold for them?"

"It is still too early to tell. Right now they are poised at a point where they could eventually descend to the same kind of chaos your society experienced before moving off-planet. There is the possibility that, given wise leadership and the right choices, they could avoid that phase. We have seen both before. Time will tell.

"We can continue this in another conversation. Once you have viewed the file I left, we will talk again. Now why don't you put on your enviro-suits, we can go see my ship before I leave."

It was then that John realized Clarise had come across without any visible protection from the vacuum of space. He had to ask. "What I am looking at right now is not the real you, is it? You must be using some kind of protective suit."

"Well, you are right and wrong. I am not wearing a protective suit. I am perfectly able to tolerate space as I am. This is not, however, the real or, more precisely, the original me. Like you, we are born as biological entities and spend an initial few hundred years that way. We have achieved practical immortality by bioengineering durable, long-lasting bodies that we essentially grow into once we need to. You, too, are heading in the same direction and will eventually duplicate what we have done."

With that, John and Vanya got in their enviro-suits, they floated across to get a look at a light-speed starship.

When John and Vanya got back to their own ship, John immediately went to the files Clarise had left. At the same time her image appeared on the screen.

"I hope you enjoyed your visit to my ship."

"We did, very much. Will we see you again?" Vanya asked.

"Yes, I will drop by from time to time. By the way, Caleb says 'hi.'"

John opened his mouth to respond, but she cut in immediately.

"Yes, I visited him too, he knows everything you know, and he knows you know. I would ask you to refrain from discussing our encounter with him so as not to leave a record in your systems. We would prefer not to have to monitor your activities for the rest of your lives or meddle with your archives."

John nodded in agreement. They were practiced by now at keeping secrets, even whoppers like this, especially since Caleb was one of the few people they would consider telling and he already knew.

The file was basically a short history of galactic civilizations. The original one that made it out to the stars was about four billion years ago, not long after the Sun and its planetary system, along with Teran's star and planetary system, were formed. The Sun and John's home star were third generation. That is, they were composed of the stuff of other stars that in turn were composed of material from the first generation of stars after the big bang thirteen billion years ago.

The first generation of stars consisted almost entirely of hydrogen and helium, they had burned out quickly or supernovaed, producing the first generation of heavy elements. These heavy elements were needed to make rocky metalliferous planets such as Earth and Teran.

Even second-generation star systems did not have enough elements heavier than helium to produce the right kind of conditions for life. Only third-generation systems could succeed at this. They started showing up three to four billion years after the big bang. It took another four to five billion years for planetary environments to settle down and life to begin, then evolve to the point where a planet's inhabitants could venture out to the stars.

This happened around 9.5 billion years after the big bang or roughly 4.0 billion years ago. The initial group took several million years to fully explore the galaxy. Along the way they encountered a number of failed civilizations, a few due to asteroid impacts that wiped them out, a number from mishandling or lack of sufficient resources to support a large civilization long enough to make it to interstellar flight. None had destroyed themselves via nuclear holocaust, although some had tried. In one of the ironies of nature, it seemed that if a civilization could build enough nuclear weapons to kill itself off, it inhabited a planet rich enough in resources to be able to reach interstellar flight.

The earliest star-flight civilizations located many third-generation stars that were younger than their own, these including Sol and Teran's star. They waited and watched. Once life appeared on a planet and became established, they began visiting regularly. This began 750 million years ago on Earth and Teran. Before that, life had already arisen on other planets of third-generation stars. These, too, were watched. As civilizations emerged they were closely scrutinized. Eventually the new civilizations reached a level of sophistication that made it impossible for the watchers to hide any longer. Contact occurred, the newcomers were welcomed and told the history of those who had come before. Not everything was revealed to them, however. Non-contact was their prime directive—an idea Gene Roddenberry had gotten right in 1966 with his *Star Trek* television series, and that the entire galaxy already knew about. The second directive was allowing the newcomers to make their own discoveries, to progress at their own pace. The established civilizations were always there for conversation and friendship, but they did not give newcomers all the answers.

Among the secrets were supra-light-speed travel and communications that had taken millions of years of the combined efforts of a number of the early star-traveling civilizations to achieve. The combination allowed them to venture outside the galaxy. They contacted, then visited the neighboring galaxies and found the situation elsewhere was much the same. Some galaxies, however, were found to have hostile environments, they were devoid of life.

Clarise's records contained detailed accounts of Earth and Teran. They were a curious pair in that they had developed at nearly the same time and very close to one another. For the first time, the possibility of two nascent civilizations encountering each other had arisen. In the past, such contact had always been well after the achievement of star travel, it was always the new civilization that encountered one of the well-established ones. In the case of Earth and Teran, one recently emergent star-traveling civilization and another that had barely achieved space flight were on an inevitable course of contact. It was already clear that the Terans would not force the encounter. It was also clear that the Earthlings were developing rapidly, they would soon find the Terans no matter what anyone else did.

This was why Clarise had contacted them, John realized. Her people would not be revealing themselves to the Terans, just to John, Vanya and Caleb, and in such a way that they would be unable to prove Clarise's existence. They were permitting the Mimas marker because they would not interfere even though they were indirectly breaking their own directive by placing it there. The situation was difficult and unprecedented. Clarise's people would monitor the situation closely, especially the reactions of the Earthlings.

There would be additional visits from Clarise during the years it took John and Vanya to finish the crossing back to Alpha Centaurus. No record of her presence, however, would appear in the shuttle's databank.

On July 12, 1975, Caleb departed from his station at Eros bound for Saturn. The Earthlings had sent a number of unmanned missions to the inner and now outer planets in recent years. Most dangerous was their horde of amateur astronomers. Low-cost modern optics enabled a sizable group of them to scan the night sky for objects in the inner Solar System; in the coming decades, computerized control would greatly multiple their capabilities. Many comets and asteroids had been discovered by this group. In addition, government-sponsored programs to seek out the same sorts of bodies were growing ever more successful.

It seemed they were worried about possible impacts of these bodies with Earth. Caleb thought the worry was silly, even though it could happen. Indeed such collisions, a number of them sizable, had occurred in the past few million years. The humans, however, were powerless at the present to prevent one, if by chance they detected a threatening body in time. He felt it must have something to do with mass psychosis stemming from the openness of their society, and the unusual power of the media. But what did he know? He wasn't a psychologist.

In any event, if he was going to leave before the risk of being spotted got uncomfortably high, he would have to go now. He set course for Saturn in one of the landers. The other followed carrying the Gemini capsule.

Chapter 39
Back Home
(June 1992)

The final retro firing was completed, the craft that had taken John, Vanya and Caleb to Sol eighty-eight years before was securely positioned for docking at the Alpha Centauri HUB. In a few minutes John and Vanya would be inside. They were coming back to Devon to stay. He was 173, she 188. They would live out the rest of their lives together exploring the surface of the immense world that even Vanya had not gotten to know well in all its complexity before she left.

Later that same year, Caleb felt confident that the device needed for the recordings was available. He constructed a compact disc writer, copied the files they had prepared and put them in their carrying case. He placed the case inside the capsule for the trip down to the surface of Mimas. He felt a great relief at having completed the last task of his journey. He was amazed at himself for having lived long enough to do it. At 293 he had not set a record, though it was much longer than a normal Teran life span.

Caleb felt his body start to fail a few weeks later. There was nothing he could do to prevent or delay his ultimate end which would come quickly now. He climbed in one of the escape pods. The two small landers executed the program he had left to be activated upon his demise, they set out on the most direct course out of the Solar System. The escape pod headed toward the rings of Saturn where he intended his remains to circle the giant planet in the debris of the A ring for a long, long time.

John and Vanya settled on Devon. They built a small home much like the cabin in the woods on the Main Ship they both had loved visiting many years before. It was on the edge of the research compound where they first met. Four and a half years later, they watched as Caleb placed the marker capsule on Mimas. It sat right at the top of the central peak of the massive crater that dominated the moon's face. The marker was distinctive, it would be easily noticed by its intended audience.

Three weeks later John started to feel uneasy, slightly depressed but could not figure out why. His fear was that something had happened to someone close to him. His mother was still alive, though she was not in good health. John could not sleep that night, so he got up and went out on the porch to watch the stars and enjoy the cool night air. As he was sitting there, he heard a voice call his name. Someone came up the stairs. He could not tell who it was in the dark.

"Hi, John, don't you recognize me?" said the voice with a smile in its tone.

At first John thought it was Clarise. She had been true to her word about looking in on them from time to time, this was a good place for a visit since there were no outdoor sensors in the area and he could easily turn off the ones inside his house if needed. As the visitor got closer, it looked a lot like her, but the voice was different and strangely familiar.

"John, it's Caleb."

"What? How?" John gasped. Then he realized what was going on. "Oh, you are full of surprises, you had someone rig up a robot to look like Clarise with your synthesized voice."

"No, John, no tricks this time. It is really me, although this body was rigged up by Clarise's people," Caleb said.

"When—how?" was all John could sputter.

"They got to me just before my old body gave out, three weeks after I placed the capsule, and processed me into one of theirs. It took a while to get used to it. It is a lot stronger and healthier than my old one, especially given it had almost three hundred years on it. Sleeping and eating are optional, I still do it some, they said I would eventually grow out of those habits."

"Why didn't you let us know right away?"

"Well, they were not sure how well it would work, especially since I was much older, more worn-out than they are when they do the transition. They took me to the Pleiades to one of their centers for most of the job. It was a while before they got everything working properly. Then I went back to Earth to see it on the ground for myself. We left the Solar System yesterday, I came straight here."

"In that case, you better come in, we'll wake Vanya and let her in on your transformation. She'll be happy to see you, we have a lot to catch up on," John said.

"Yes, we do, and I want to see that daughter of yours," Caleb replied as they walked in the front door.

PART 3

Discovery

Chapter 40
Colorful Noise
(1994–2011)

Jesus DeNova was born in 1973 in the town of Los Teques in the mountainous region south of Caracas, Venezuela. The town was well known for the presence of the research and development laboratories of the national oil company, PDVSA. Jesus started working there as a summer hire in 1994 while he was in college. He eventually earned a Ph.D. in Mathematics from the National Autonomous University of Mexico. After college he returned to begin a career in the application of mathematics to digital signal processing, specializing in the fields of data compression, encryption, and decryption. His company dealt with enormous volumes of scientific data, they worked continuously to reduce the size of the data sets. At the same time, they had to maintain their extremely valuable information content intact. Successful data compression methods reduced the amount of memory, disk and tape storage. The data compression methods Jesus helped develop saved the company hundreds of thousands of bolivars each year.

Jesus had shown an aptitude for math at a very early age. His father was a custodian at the PDVSA lab, Jesus would come up after school to meet him at the end of his workday. Sometimes they would walk up into the hills above the facility to admire the views and the beauty of the large, bright-blue butterflies that inhabited the surrounding forest. Other times they would kick a football around on one of the laboratory's fields. On rainy days his dad could get him inside, they would walk the halls and peek in some of the offices to see what was written on the blackboards. It looked like gibberish to him, he thought he would never be able to understand any of it. As the years went by, he learned algebra then geometry and trigonometry. Parts of it started to make sense to him. However, he only saw the mathematics. He wanted to know the problems and the physics that lay behind the math.

One day a researcher on a break noticed him waiting outside and struck up a conversation. He was immediately impressed by the young man's knowledge. He spent an hour with Jesus reviewing basic physics and going over his calculus workbook with him. Jesus returned a few days later with a notebook full of equations he had worked through using math texts from the lab library. After that the meetings became weekly lessons. Years later when Jesus was on the staff, he and the researcher kept meeting regularly.

The lab scientist was Jorge Grenada, a grandfatherly man in his early sixties who had been with PDVSA for thirty years. He originally worked for the predecessor company before nationalization, earning a Ph.D. in Geophysics along the way. Jorge was one of the most senior and respected scientists in the company. He also had two hobbies. One was solving puzzles; word puzzles of all kinds, especially crosswords and cryptograms. The other was a deep interest in space exploration and the search for extraterrestrial intelligence.

Jorge followed technical developments in this field and participated, as did many thousands of individuals around the world, in SETI activities using his home computer to analyze signals downloaded from the World Wide Web. He saved the data to do analyses of his own design along with radio telescope data obtained from public sources. He introduced Jesus to these topics, as well. Jesus became immediately fascinated with SETI data, soon he was working on his own analysis techniques. Eventually, as their working relationship grew, the two developed and applied dozens of algorithms to this data, nothing even remotely resembling a coherent signal ever turned up.

Jesus became a supporting sponsor of the SETI Institute and The Planetary Society and like his mentor regularly downloaded files from the SETI Web site to process on his PCs.

An opportunity he had long dreamed of arose in 2006. The Allen Telescope Array, a radio telescope in northern California run by the University of California, Berkeley built with funds provided by Microsoft co-founder Paul Allen, advertised for experts to join them in processing the large amounts of data coming in from the newly commissioned instrument. Its mission was to look for intelligent signals from extraterrestrial societies along with standard astronomical observing. The search would entail unprecedented amounts of data processing and signal analysis. Jesus was one of the first hired.

He began by writing programs to sort through the data to single out suspicious signals for further analysis. There were numerous hits but none stood up to additional inspection.

Jesus believed the problem was that they were concentrating on individual narrow frequency bands independent of one another. He was certain that something akin to frequency-division multiplexing, used in current communications systems to divide a frequency band into subunits that carry separate signals, would be employed by any spacefaring civilization for long range space communications. He knew also that such signals would be difficult to detect, since they would appear to be part of the background noise that pervades space.

Jesus began to experiment with a number of algorithms he had used in previous work at PDVSA to analyze and classify the signal content of noisy data that had weak coherent signals in it. He started with a few data channels, building up to greater numbers of channels as time and computer power allowed. The techniques were computationally demanding, he often bumped up against the limitations of the machines he could get his hands on. Then all he could do was wait until someone in the organization got a newer, faster computer. He would immediately go beg for time on it. His progress was encouraging because he was getting indications of non-random content. At the same time, it was frustrating because he knew he did not have the needed information to extract a message. The algorithms assumed the sender employed a key; that is, information coded into the signal across many data channels in a specific manner selected by the sender. He did not have the key or any hope of obtaining it. It was unlikely anyone could crack the code, so far he had found no indication that a key was being provided by the sender. Jesus could not even be sure there was a sender. At this point his findings had been limited to slightly coherent or "colored noise," signal that was barely noticeable within the random or "white" background noise.

Jesus worked diligently at his regular duties and continued with his pet analysis methods. He wrote a number of scientific papers on his special projects and was frequently called upon to make presentations at meetings and symposia. He became the leader of a small contingent of investigators pursuing similar methods at a number of radio astronomy observatories and universities. They exchanged results and ideas and met from time to time to collaborate on new projects. Success seemed tantalizingly close at times, frustratingly, conclusive results always eluded them.

Chapter 41
The Summer Intern
(2012)

Jesus was not supposed to have a summer intern in 2012. It had been three years since he'd had a full summer at the Allen array to work uninterrupted, he was looking forward to it. At the last minute, however, he was asked to supervise a student from Cornell University who was studying astronomy—a favor to a colleague who had been called away to serve as a temporary adviser to the new director of the National Radio Astronomy Observatory. Jesus usually had one or two students each summer, they were always engineering, or computer science majors. An astrophysicist would be different and challenging. He was not sure how he was going to connect with this young woman, which was the primary challenge in providing a fulfilling experience for an intern.

When Shantel arrived Jesus was even less certain. She was a twenty-three-year-old, inner-city African-American woman from Brooklyn, with top grades through high school and an undergraduate degree in physics from New York University. She had earned an M.S. in Mathematics from the Courant Institute. Both her degrees were with honors. She was headed to Cornell in the fall to begin work on a Ph.D. in Astrophysics. It turned out that her background was a much better match with his interests than he expected.

Jesus found her plenty bright. She wore tight jeans and tube tops and was constantly on her iPad. He was a staid South American of Italian and Native American descent who spoke with a heavy accent, he wore pressed slacks and collared shirts. His flip-style cell phone was strictly for emergency roadside assistance.

Dave Brubaker, in charge of the summer student program, brought Shantel by early Monday morning.

The first words out of her mouth after the initial hellos were exchanged were, "Doctor DeNova, what's the deal with these SETI signals? There probably ain't nobody out there that wants anything to do with us."

Shantel had worked on cooling off her inner-city accent a bit, but only a bit, for the old foreign dude. She was not his worst nightmare, though she came close. Instead of taking the bait, Jesus thought he would try to see where she was coming from.

"We don't really have signals, Shantel, just hints, whispers of possibilities. But you make a good point. I am not sure why anyone would want to contact us, either. Do you think we are wasting our time?"

"I guess what I'm sayin' is that I remember a thing called the prime directive from *Star Trek*. No contact with civilizations that don't have warp drive. That would definitely be us. In the middle of all that fictional science, I think they had a good point. We won't find anyone till they want us to."

"Do you think there are others out there?" Jesus asked.

"Sure. There has to be. There's too much there out there, so much time has passed since the big bang. It'd be totally arrogant and statistically foolish to think we are the sole intelligent beings in the galaxy."

"You are familiar with the Drake Equation, then?" he asked.

"Yeah, but it only goes so far. It's a good collection of factors to consider when tryin' to figure the probability there are alien civilizations in the galaxy. The probability of Sun-like stars times the probability of Earth-like planets and so on. Half the probabilities are mostly guesses, the result is whatever you want it to be."

"Yes, I agree. Then what is the source of your conviction that others are out there?"

"There are roughly a hundred billion stars in the Milky Way. Let's say you plug your favorite numbers into the Drake Equation, you come up with one in a million having a habitable planet such as Earth that will go on to produce life, evolution, and civilization. That means there are a hundred thousand such planets in the galaxy.

"Now look at us. In a few thousand years, we went from wandering the savanna to space flight. Another few thousand, we'll likely be out among the stars, if we survive the next hundred or two. Take those one hundred thousand habitable planets that will produce civilizations, spread their appearance out evenly over, say, five billion years; the age of the Sun. This means these civilizations arise roughly every fifty thousand years. If they destroy themselves in the first two or three thousand, what do you have? No overlap in time, each one is completely alone for the short time they are around. If some do survive and given the galaxy is thirty thousand light-years across with habitable planets largely in the spiral arms, not the central core—too much sterilizing gamma radiation from nearby supernovae—even if two of them happened at the same time, they would likely be thousands of light-years apart.

"Say two of the hundred thousand don't destroy themselves and make it to star flight. We, of course, are one of the two. If the other happened before us, they most likely would have filled the galaxy by now."

"Keep going," Jesus said. He wanted her to stay on this line of thought; one which he had traveled many times.

"Look at North and South America. Starting with a few bands of wandering Siberian nomads, they filled both continents in a couple thousand years. Ten thousand miles north to south in two thousand years is five miles a year. Hell, I can walk five miles in a bit over an hour! At one one-hundredth the speed of light, or $0.01c$, you can get to Alpha Centauri in four hundred years, across the galaxy in six million. If you take a time window of five billion years either side of today and consider that six million years is nothing compared to that amount of time, if there were one other habitable planet that produces a civilization that survived to star travel, it's fifty-fifty that the galaxy is full today. If there were two others, it would be a 75 percent probability. A few more, it becomes a near certainty."

"So where are they, or are they all extinct?" Jesus asked.

"Any civilization capable of filling the galaxy and finding us would be capable of keeping themselves hidden until they want to be seen. They *are* out there."

"I agree completely with both your analysis and conclusion. By the way, why $0.01c$?"

"Oh, I extrapolated from recent progress. In 1900 trains could go fifty miles an hour. In 2000, rockets could go twenty-five thousand miles an hour. That's a factor of five hundred in one hundred years. 0.01c is around 7.5 million miles an hour, another factor of three hundred. Seems like that would be doable in couple of centuries. They're out there, they're talkin' among themselves, they're deliberately avoidin' us until they're sure we won't blow ourselves up."

Jesus had been sitting calmly while he listened. When she finished he smiled and eased back in his chair. The young lady had stunned him by her recitation.

During the past twenty minutes Shantel had reviewed many of the prime motivations behind Jesus's work. He didn't think anyone out there was directly trying to contact Earth, either. This notion, however, was in conflict with the main work of most SETI searches, which was to scan the sky for beacons—alien broadcasts deliberately constructed to be obvious and directed to stars that seemed to be likely candidates to harbor intelligent life. It was assumed that the sender would be much more advanced technologically than Earth. The Allen Telescope Array itself could serve as the same sort of beacon. Humans had been capable of radio broadcasting for little more than a hundred years, consequently signals from Earth had only moved out beyond the nearest stars.

An alien civilization broadcasting with beacons would therefore be at least as old as we are, Jesus thought, *likely much older*. Even a few thousand years would make a big difference. The aliens would not be trying to initiate contact with anyone they already knew; just new, emerging technological civilizations like Earth's. After thirty years of listening without so much as a peep, Jesus thought there was reason to be skeptical. He felt they would be better off concentrating on trying to identify chance transmissions not intended for Earthling ears. This required highly sophisticated data processing and analysis, it would be orders of magnitude harder than listening for beacons. He liked a good challenge, this was a whopper.

"If they are talking among themselves, Shantel, how would you go about listening in?"

"I don't think we can. I mean, they are bound to be usin' large arrays with very narrow beams, sendin' multiplexed messages as you described numerous times in your papers. You're dependin' on the Earth wanderin' across the path of one of their transmissions so you can pick it up. Doesn't that require a lot of luck?"

Jesus thought for a moment then said, "You are well-informed for someone fresh on the scene."

"I spent a few hours online lookin' over your papers and presentations, doing some research on line"

Indeed she must have, thought Jesus, *but she would have had to find and study at least a dozen papers and presentations, then synthesize them into the coherent recitation she had just made.*

"Have you tried to calculate how much luck would be needed?

I don't think I know what you mean by calculatin' the luck." She replied.

"Well, then, let me explain it," Jesus started in. "We can detect and separate out a coherent signal at a single narrow frequency channel sent from out to a thousand light-years. At that distance the beam size from a transmission beacon the size of Arecibo—the thousand-foot-diameter dish in Puerto Rico—would be roughly the size of the Solar System. It would take us fifty years, at minimum, longer if we did not traverse perpendicularly across it, to pass through such a signal beam. We would have that amount of time to detect it. We use the Allen Array to listen to very small parts of the sky in succession at a rapid rate. Or we can widen our field of view to listen to large parts of the sky at once. This second approach allows us to stand a chance at intercepting casual transmissions. If we encountered a beam, we would have enough time to detect it. If, as you say, they are out there all around us signaling to one another, there may be several beams crisscrossing the Solar System. If we assume the beams go at least from star to star, of which there are several thousand in the neighborhood, it turns out the odds are fairly good we are in one right now."

"So why haven't they been found?" Shantel asked.

"Because until recently our radio telescopes were tuned to half dozen relatively narrow bands surrounding the main frequencies of particularly interesting natural transmission lines, those for the lower-state transitions of molecular hydrogen, carbon monoxide, and several other molecules for example. These are the strongest, the most useful for science."

"If you are trying to do high information content communications, they would be the frequencies you would want to avoid because of the interference those strong lines cause," Shantel interjected.

"Precisely. In the past, our radio telescopes were set for the wrong frequencies if you wanted to intercept communications at microwave or radio-wave lengths. Today they have wide band receivers, but that doesn't matter because they are correlating instruments. They average the signal over long periods of time to reinforce the coherent spectral lines of interest thereby suppressing random background noise. Any communications, where the information being send would be modulated on the carrier's amplitude or frequency, would be averaged out to nearly nothing unless the signal is extremely strong, which means close by.

"When we are doing SETI observations, the Allen Array also does time averaging to gain sensitivity, which increases our chances of detecting a carrier signal, at the same time it reduces our opportunity to read whatever message is superimposed on it. The solution is a larger array with more antennas and more sensitive detectors. ALMA or EVLA signals before correlation would improve our capabilities, but as you know time on those instruments is highly competitive and very expensive."

Jesus suppressed a sigh in front of his student. The Atacama Large Millimeter/Submillimeter Array (ALMA) in Chile and the Expanded Very Large Array (EVLA) in New Mexico had superior powers to the Allen Array, he longed to have access to them. He finished, "I am particularly interested in ALMA because it is in the southern sky where the most interesting target stars are located."

"You mean like Alpha Centauri, Epsilon Indi, and Tau Ceti?" asked Shantel.

"Yes, those are the ones Drake originally looked at back in the 1960s, they are the most sensible if you want to be able to eavesdrop and keep an eye on us."

"ALMA and EVLA have wide, overlapping receiver bands across the radio spectrum. We can now look at a large number of frequency components."

"By the way, why radio frequencies?" Jesus asked.

"Dust, atmospheric and space," Shantel replied.

"That's right. There are two competing desires that are in conflict. For maximum transfer of information, you want to use as many frequencies as possible and go as high as you can. On the other hand, low frequencies are less disturbed by dust. The best compromise is probably the upper end of the radio band into the infrared.

"Now, they probably don't have to worry about the atmosphere because I'm sure their arrays are in space. This complicates matters for us because we will have extra interference to deal with. That's not the worst of it. We have to consider how you would construct a message using multiple frequencies. I would distribute it across a number of frequencies, that is, one bit at one frequency, the next bit at the next frequency, and so on for a few hundred or a thousand frequencies. Then I would go back to the first frequency and repeat the sequence until the message is done. I would also repeat the whole message multiple times at other frequencies, maybe interleave the frequencies of the copies to maximize the chance of having the entire message received correctly. In the end you send something out that looks very much like noise unless you know how the message is constructed. Our problem is we don't have the message construction key."

Shantel asked, "No way to do it without the key?"

"No one knows of a way yet, you have the entire summer," he quipped.

Jesus then took her downstairs to the bullpen to show her to her assigned cubicle and get her set up on the site email and the administrative system. After introducing Shantel to the other students who had arrived the week before, he left them on their own to get acquainted.

It was typical to give students a few days to get their feet on the ground, get to know the other students, the staff, and the facilities. First, there were obligatory onboarding activities such as safety training and a site visit to the array. In a few days, after these preliminaries were concluded, he would sit down with Shantel to discuss her interests and then propose topics that might make for a good summer project. He never got the chance. She was back in his office by the end of the morning.

"Doctor DeNova, I want to jump ahead, look at how we might decode a message if we got one. I want to see if I can figure out how to discover the key."

Jesus had not had time to completely swivel around in his chair to face her before she finished talking. He stared at her for moment then replied, "Well, what you are speaking of is a type of decryption which is an old, established discipline, I don't know that anyone has thought about it in the context of the kind of message we are interested in. I sure haven't! It's been all I can do to figure out how to deal with detecting something."

"I know nobody has, least ways I didn't get any Google hits from the different queries I made. I want to figure it out as my project."

"How would you go about it?" he asked.

"Simultaneous processing," she answered. He recognized immediately that it was a very good answer.

She went on: "Assumin' the message is replicated a number of times, we actually have multiple decryptions to do on the same content. This should be easier than normal decryption, where you just have one copy of the content. If we try to decrypt the copies together, we might be able to find correlations or patterns that can lead us to the answer."

"Okay. Write up a short proposal, I'll take a look at it."

She got it to him the next day, he reviewed and approved it that afternoon. Shantel would present it in the Thursday seminar then start to work. The plan was to begin with a hypothetical message created synthetically by computer. The message would be multiplexed and replicated across a wide band of frequencies, random noise would be added in to make it look as realistic as possible. Shantel would build a computer program to examine the many frequencies searching for smaller blocks of frequencies that looked similar. If some were found, a second program would then attempt to decrypt the content of the message using multiple blocks simultaneously.

She proposed to look at a synthetically generated, nearly random, colored-noise signal that represented what might be received by the Allen Telescope Array. At minimum she hoped to determine that there actually was coherent signal in the data. Positive results were not assured, who knew what would turn up? That was research, she would be getting a good taste of it in the real world of science.

Shantel dove into her work, rarely coming up for air. Jesus expected this, he scheduled more-frequent meetings with her than he had done with past students in the summer program. He did this not because he thought she needed the extra supervision. Quite the contrary. He did it to give her regular breaks so she would not burn out. Actually, they did not talk much about her project, aside from the fact that she was frustrated and not making much headway. To get her mind off her work, he steered the meetings to other subjects. He tried getting her to talk about herself, her background, where she wanted to go in her career.

Jesus broke the ice by telling the story of his poor childhood, the poverty of rural Venezuela, his parents, his father's custodial job.

"My dad was a janitor, too," Shantel began, "at the local grammar school. My mom worked as a clerk for the Triborough Bridge and Tunnel Authority. Neither finished high school because they had to go to work to help support their families. Dad managed to stay out of the gangs in Harlem where he grew up, he made sure it was easier for me and my brothers in Brooklyn. He did have one weakness: the horses. Mom didn't approve, but considerin' all the temptations available, she didn't say much. Besides, he was good at it, always at least broke even. Sometimes he did pretty well. He usually worked on the racing forms at the kitchen table. My two brothers were not much interested. As early as I can remember, I liked numbers an' was good at math. By the time I was ten, we were workin' the horses together and started makin' good money regularly. So much so that he stopped usin' local bookies. If anyone had found out how much money we were makin', we would be robbed for sure. He spread the bets around going to various OTB parlors and the track on weekends when they were in season. Between what he saved and scholarships, it paid for college for the three of us."

"You used the resources at hand," said Jesus, "the same as my father. I found out years later that it was no accident I ended up being tutored by the scientists at PDVSA. Like you, it was obvious I was interested in and good at math from an early age. The local schools did not have much in the way of advanced courses, but the teachers were aware of my abilities. They helped as much as they could. There were better private schools in Caracas, but the tuition was way out of our reach, and they were not an option. My parents came up with an alternative plan. Once a week, my mother would get us kids together to walk up the hill to meet my father at the lab at the end of the day. We were usually not allowed to go in, Dad would tell us what went on inside and point out the scientists as they were leaving. Some would wave or say hello. It seems everyone knew the man who swept the floors and emptied the trash baskets.

"Once I got old enough to make the walk by myself, I started meeting my father most work days. I would show up a half hour early, especially on rainy days, thinking that maybe I would get a chance to go inside. I wanted desperately to see what they were doing. Eventually, it worked. One of the scientists who came out for a smoke recognized me. He asked me how old I was, what grade I was in. I said I was thirteen and in the eighth grade. I told him I was studying calculus. He laughed at me and said they don't teach that in the local schools. I then reached in my backpack and pulled out the book my teachers had gotten me. I showed him my notes on the problems I was working on. He said I had gotten almost all of them correct, my teachers must be proud. I told him they don't know calculus, were unaware of my progress, I was doing it on my own. I did not realize it at the time, my life changed forever that day. He put his arm around me and escorted me in past the guards. He told them I was his new intern.

"Later Mom and Dad told me they had conspired to get me up there with the walks. They could not put me in a private school, instead they did the next best thing. They put me in a position to have a chance, then they trusted that fate would guide events."

Shantel took a moment to absorb Jesus's story. This was not the way she normally interacted with her professors.

"I think my dad did the same thing in a way," she offered. "Our apartment wasn't large, the kitchen table was pretty much it for work space. Dad could have waited till later in the evening, but he always made a deal of his 'racin' studies,' as he called them. He got his stuff out right after dinner. My brothers were usually out the door if their homework was done, but as I said, I got hooked early on. He had graphs and charts, lots of hand-built spreadsheets. He had loads of paper files of past performance data on everything from horses to jockeys, trainers, and you name it. I don't know how he had done everything by hand, so I started out by puttin' it on my computer."

"It seems your father was a real student," Jesus said, "knew how to conduct research." He looked at the clock, saw it was past 5:30 p.m.

"I am afraid I'll be late for dinner if I don't get moving," he said. "It was a great pleasure getting to know you better, Shantel."

"Likewise," she replied and smiled as they left his office.

By the end of the fifth week, halfway through her program, it became clear that Shantel was stalling out. They got together for the better part of a day to review everything she had done to that point. The software was working, she was able to isolate frequency subsets with significant correlation. Although they did not match exactly with the known frequency coding in the synthetic message, she proceeded anyway to apply every kind of multidimensional analysis and transformation algorithm they could think of in numerous combinations attempting to decode the data, all without success. They knew these methods worked if you used the exact coding in the message, because she had done this as a check before using them on her extracted subsets. The results were even worse when the background noise level was higher.

Shantel also made novel modifications of a couple of the techniques. Again without success. After the review and a lot of discussion on other options, Jesus pushed back his chair and stretched his legs out. He pondered a moment, then spoke.

"Negative results. Welcome to scientific research. You have to get used to them. They will be the major part of your work product, occupy most of your waking thoughts, cause much gray hair. Though I think you do have something to work with from here. You have a way to identify coherent signals. Things fall apart when you try to decode them, because you are not able to extract the frequency subsets exactly in the presence of background noise.

"You made your problem too hard. A lot of time in science, success comes after frustration when we redefine the problem to make it easier. In your case, you created the synthetic signal using many small frequency blocks for the message copies with high levels of random noise to represent the natural background. When you put these things together, you have a signal that is nearly totally incoherent. I would advise three things. First, drastically reduce the level of random background noise. Second, make the frequency blocks bigger and fewer in number. Finally, take a day or two off before starting back on your work."

Shantel drove to Chico. She couldn't go to Reno, Nevada, anymore because she had been tossed out by one of the casinos for card counting. She was no longer welcome at any of the blackjack tables in town, she was getting fed up with being banned. She pledged to herself she would get retribution someday. They called card counting "cheating". She was not using any electronic gear, did not have a partner someplace she was communicating with. It was all in her head, they could not prove otherwise. The casinos didn't like it when a customer refused to lose their money. She could go to the horse book. They would not ban her from there, since they got their cut up front on each transaction and were not affected by how much she won or lost. It would take time to study the performance data, something she did not have a lot of right now. Besides, she had already made enough to cover next year's expenses at Cornell. She went to the mall deciding to see a movie instead.

Halfway through she left. She was back in her cubicle by evening, Jesus saw her coming in as he was leaving for the day.

"Back so soon?" he asked.

"All my wakin' thoughts, Doctor DeNova," she replied as he passed by.

He knew she was hooked, not only on the problem but on research in general. In this sense, they were much the same. Both were relentless when confronted with a problem they could not crack.

Her abrupt return was due to a flash of insight she'd had in the middle of the movie. Decoding the signal concerned searching for meaningful content. Why not try using a Web search algorithm? After all, that is what those algorithms did.

The next two weeks went quickly as Shantel dug into her project. Jesus's suggestions paid off; she could now decode a frequency subset, barely. Up until now, every time she tried to reduce the size of the frequency blocks the result degraded quickly, the signal became indecipherable. Then she tried the Web search algorithm approach. After some adaptation and a few false starts, she started getting consistently useful results. They were not perfect, but were a great improvement over anything else she had tried. Plus their performance was not degraded as much when she decreased the size of the frequency blocks, or added more random background noise.

It was getting close to the end of her stay. She had two weeks left, Jesus thought she had better wrap it up and report her findings. On the whole it had been a good project, she had shown tremendous ability and maturity in her approach.

"Doctor DeNova," she started, "let me try one last set of tests. I want to try my technique one time on real data. I know it doesn't make much sense given the marginal results I have so far, but I would like to see what happens. If the results don't show anything, I won't put them in my report."

Jesus handed her a compact disc.

"In case you asked," he said. "I made this CD last week. It is data from a region of the sky around Alpha Centauri taken a month ago. It is pretty good data, it's the first we've gotten from the new wide-band recording units. Now you know it is from a small patch of the sky, therefore the likelihood of a source being present is very small."

"Yes, that's why I am just gonna run the search algorithm on the signal without trying to correlate the subsets."

Twenty minutes later Jesus got an excited phone call from Shantel asking him to come downstairs to her cubicle. When he got there, she was surrounded by the other students. As they parted for him to get close to the display screen, he saw immediately that there were indications of coherent content for a couple frequency block sizes.

"This is from the data I gave you?" he asked.

"Yup. I'm rerunnin' the test right now to make sure, plus I turned on the correlation."

A minute later the screen refreshed, the same results reappeared. The search algorithm located several frequency subsets that appeared to be coherent. That is, they matched one another to a high degree as if they were copies of the same thing.

"Welcome to the world of scientific discovery," Jesus announced. "See what happens. You get a young upstart in from left field, unexpected things occur."

"They try tackling a seemingly impossible problem, get mixed results at best, then take a stab in the dark with some real data just for the heck of it—presto, a discovery! Isn't it wonderful? Except now, Shantel, I hope you realize you have an even bigger problem on your hands. How do you demonstrate that the coherence is due to intelligent action?" Jesus asked.

The answer was that she couldn't; no one could. Neither could they prove there was no intelligence behind the signals. It would take time plus the work of many others to sort through and understand what, if anything, she had found. She presented her findings, including the final mystery, at the weekly seminar on Thursday, she departed for Cornell the next day.

After Shantel left, Jesus ran the search algorithm on additional data sets and worked on ways to examine and decipher the results. It was an important step forward in the search for extraterrestrial intelligence, the discovery of colored-noise events tantalized the SETI community. But no one had been able to take it further to demonstrate that the colored-noise events truly represented intelligently constructed messages. The possibility that they were one of a number of physical effects was large enough to cast doubt on an intelligent source.

What could not be ignored was the fact that the coherent frequency subsets were only found in data from Alpha Centauri.

Jesus and Shantel published several papers on her work and his follow-up. Then he began doing surveys of smaller sections of the original survey region whenever he could get data from ALMA. He was able to isolate the source exactly at Alpha Centauri. Within the limits of the resolving power of the array, it seemed to be very close to the A star of the pair. That was as far as he could go. There was no way to determine the content of the frequency subsets, if indeed it was intelligently created. Periodic follow-up looks at the source were scheduled to see if anything changed with time. These would go on for the foreseeable future. Otherwise the alternative was to keep working on ways to analyze the signals in the hope that someone would come up with something.

While this was going on, Shantel finished her Ph.D. and went on to a postdoctoral position at Jodrell Bank Observatory in the United Kingdom. She maintained contact with Jesus and helped out occasionally on the algorithms, although she had found her way to the mainstream of astrophysics.

Chapter 42
Mimas
(2115)

When did someone realize that his or her life had changed? Was it possible to actually feel the exact moment it happened? Chris didn't think so, because most changes were really transitions. Of course, traumatic injury or a sudden near miss was practically instantaneous, life could dramatically change from the moment before to the moment after. That was not what was happening here.

She had been married, maybe it was like the transition that happened there. Even though you got to that particular point in the ceremony where one instant you were single then the next you were not, that was a legal issue. Marriage was a process that evolved over time. There was, however, a point at the beginning where you suddenly felt a great excitement. The point at which you realized you had met that special person. This had happened to her shortly after the first time she met her future and now ex-husband.

Mood and setting could have a lot to do with it, she realized. Then there followed that period of tension when you wondered if the other person felt the same, you had all manner of doubts interlaced with moments of euphoria until it finally came out into the open, you both talked about it. You were in love.

Yet the excitement now growing inside her didn't feel the same as being in love. No, she thought; it must be more like what James Marshall had felt when he first noticed flecks of gold in the water of the raceway of John Sutter's sawmill in January 1848. It changed his life completely. One minute he was inspecting the finishing touches of a new sawmill, the next he was holding a nugget between his fingers.

Nevertheless, Marshall could not have imagined the gold rush of 1849 resulting in half a billion dollars of new wealth for a nation that desperately needed it. He was probably excited, but it took time to realize there was a lot of gold in the area. It wasn't until months later that larger-scale mining operations would prove out the initial find. There certainly would have been a lot of excitement, plus uncertainty while assaying the samples, then getting the claims filed, followed by the feeling you had gotten something really big, which at some point turned into reality. That's the moment Chris was wondering about. Both Marshall and Sutter were conscious early on of the potential importance of their discovery, they understood that it would change everything for them, but it did not come in a flash. One man feared it; the other was enraptured by it. Marshall did not survive long enough to see the results of his discovery. Maybe it was just as well, for it ultimately left Sutter, the one who feared it, in ruin.

Yes, she concluded, this was like Sutter and Marshall in California. She had not been looking for it. If it was what she thought it was, it could be the answer to one of the questions of the ages. If so, she would probably not get rich as a result, but as with Neil Armstrong, her name would forever be associated with it, the notoriety would change her life permanently. Like Sutter and Marshall, whose fates had been sealed the August before the gold discovery when the contract to build the mill was signed, her fate had been sealed when she accepted the position of head of the Mimas Crater Survey Project.

As Chris stood in the front of the conference room waiting for the group to arrive, she thought back to the previous day. She had come in the lab feeling sorry for herself. As her mind had wandered between images, she considered how the folks who did the laundry on a cruise ship must feel. Everybody seemed to think it wonderful to have a job in such an exotic setting. At least her friends had said so before she left on the fourteen-month series of trips that had brought her to Saturn.

Chris had been at Titan Observatory Alpha for three years. She was staring at a display screen ten hours a day, five days a week, looking at ice ball impact craters. She might as well have stayed back at her old lab in Houston for all the difference it made. It was boring, repetitive work, and it had to be done up here because the observatories on Earth, Mars, and Jupiter were too remote to direct the orbiters on a real-time basis. Now she was about to share the facts, if not the feelings, she had concerning what she had found.

When her group arrived, she brought the Mimas orbiter image up on the display.

"This is the impact crater I wanted to bring to your attention," Chris commented as she circled the spot on the screen with her light wand. "We spotted it yesterday afternoon from the impacts picked out by the scanners. It's small compared to most of the others we've found, it has a distinct, sharp mound at its center. This is unusual. So far the craters have had no mound or at most a very indistinct hump."

She rotated the dial in the end of the light wand, the image of the mound was enlarged several times.

"Now you can see that the central mound has a conical shape with regular sides and uniform surface texture."

A few turns of the dial brought the image to maximum magnification.

"Here you can see distinct geometrical markings etched on its surface along one part of the side that faces us."

She ended while turning to the small audience in the conference room with a motion that was intended to invite questions, there were none.

Maybe it's the early hour or the fact that it's on a weekend, Chris thought. She launched into familiar background to give her announcement time to sink in.

"Mimas is one of the shepherd moons of Saturn's rings, it's responsible for maintaining the gravitational stability of this part of the ring system. It is eight hundred miles in diameter and has a major impact crater that covers a large part of its surface. The crater makes it look like a galactic bull's-eye. The Mimas orbiter project maps the surface of the moon, surveying its most recent craters in an effort to determine the current rate of impacts. This in turn will help us understand the nature of Mimas's role in maintaining ring stability." *Old news,* she thought; straight from the briefing booklet.

Chris had called together the Observatory management team on a Saturday morning to tell them about an unusual impact crater. She still felt she hadn't gotten their attention, so she turned back to the high resolution image of the object.

"This small crater, unlike the previous ones, was not created by an ice ball impact. It was made by a much harder, rigid object. You can see that the object is symmetric. In fact, it is cone shaped sitting on its base. The sides appear to be smooth and featureless except for the markings mentioned a few minutes ago. We estimate it at five feet high and eight feet in diameter across the base. It is artificial. Initially we suspected stray debris from an earlier orbiter, but we found no evidence in the archives to support this hypothesis. Nothing this size or shape was ever lost from any previous mission anywhere in the vicinity.

"One more thing," she added almost as an afterthought. "It is on the top of the central mound of the moon's large main crater." She finished in her mind: *where I would place a marker if I wanted to get our attention.*

This finally got them going. Herb Lucas, the manager of flight operations, responsible for satellite and spacecraft in the neighborhood of Saturn, spoke up.

"I've been up here for ten years, we've left a lot of junk floating out there around this planet in the last century. I'm not sure I see what the big deal is."

Just as Chris thought she was going to have to draw them a picture, Gene Temple, her senior technical analyst, chimed in.

"You said it was on the central mound. Could you put up a display of the coordinates?"

Chris had been waiting for him to ask this, she breathed a sigh of relief when the request finally came. She had prompted him before the meeting to ask the question in case things got off to a slow start. She quickly put up the display.

"It is at the absolute top, center of the peak," she pointed out. "It could not be higher or better centered if someone had gone out and deliberately placed it there."

Now Ruth Hopkins, the director of the Observatory spoke up. "What do you recommend to this group as a course of action?"

"We should retrieve it," Chris answered. Before she could continue, Lucas interrupted.

"Chris, the next lander scheduled for Mimas is six months from now. How long can this wait?"

"It doesn't have any bearing on our immediate project," Chris said. "Since it is definitely not ice ball related. From that limited point of view, we have no immediate need. Aren't you curious about what it is?"

"Of course I am," he shot back. "I'm just not in favor of changing schedules, interrupting projects with major scientific issues involved to go out and pick up what may turn out to be an old radar cone or a funny shaped meteorite."

"It's a fabricated object," Chris replied, wondering, *don't they see it? Is it only obvious to me? This is not one of ours. It could mean we are not alone.* Maybe she was too close to it, or else these folks weren't tuned in to the possibilities. She would have to tune them in.

"I think we appreciate the possibilities this object represents, we share your interest in finding out where it came from. Although, I think a lot more work has to be done before we jump to any conclusions." Lucas replied.

Director Hopkins asked, "What orbiters do we have near Mimas that might be moved? Specifically, do we have one with something beyond the visible light photo and radar altimeter capabilities of this orbiter?"

"I see what you are getting at," Herb answered. "The one other craft at Mimas is a Hercules orbiter, which has multispectral imager, magnetometer, and microgravity platforms. That might give us clues on the composition of this thing. It can probably be rescheduled to do flyovers of the site within a week."

"Okay," Director Hopkins said. "Absent any objections, let's go ahead with that. I'll insert an item in the director's Monday morning report. Keep me posted. Thank you for coming so early in the day. Chris, thank you for your usual thorough job." Director Hopkins stood up and started for the door.

The others got up and talked amongst themselves for a few minutes, then went on their way. No one seemed anxious to sacrifice any more of their Saturday.

Chris was about to waylay Herb on the way out to grill him on lander schedules, then she thought better of it. He had been cooperative, given the circumstances, his offer had been more than she'd anticipated. No sense in stirring things up, at least not until they had a chance to see the data from the Hercules orbiter. She hurried back to her office. She wanted to call a group meeting for first thing Monday morning to start preparing for the flyovers. There were also a few outsiders she needed to contact and bring into the effort. Her people were not equipped to do the kind of analysis that would be required.

Back in her office, Chris got a cup of coffee then walked over to sit down at her desk. She put the high resolution image of the impact object up on the screen in front of her and rocked back.

I guess I shouldn't have expected everyone to leap out of their chairs, immediately shouting out the implications of this image. She had understood its potential meaning immediately, but realized it would take time for her colleagues to come to terms with the discovery.

Chris waited ten long days before the Hercules data was in and fully analyzed. She did not sleep well during the wait. One part of her wanted to start telling everyone what had been discovered, what it meant. The object was indeed metallic, the mass estimates from the gravity anomalies indicated it was either an extremely low density material that would not have retained its shape on impact, or it was not a completely solid object. It must be hollow inside. Further scans through the databases of past missions near Saturn failed to turn up anything that resembled it. Widening the search to all known objects that had left the vicinity of Earth's orbit also came up empty.

Waiting took a toll on Chris, especially since there was little else she could do without actually getting down to the object itself. "The forty-niners would not have had to wait for approvals up the chain of command," she said wistfully to herself. "They would have immediately gone out and sunk a pick in the ground."

Chris was a modern-day professional explorer. She had always been interested in discovery and read widely on past expeditions to other planets as well as the many missions on

Earth to explore remote regions or find lost treasure. One story that stuck in her mind was the group that had found and salvaged the wreck of the side-wheeler steamship *Central America*. It took ten years of research, planning, fundraising, and outfitting before they could put to sea. Then two years to locate the wreck followed by several years of recovery operations, only to have to plod through ten years of court battles before they could finally take possession of what they had found. They had recovered twenty tons of gold. They probably felt at the end it had been worth it, but how had they maintained their sanity during this interminable process?

Another meeting of the Observatory senior staff was called for the next morning, Chris hoped it would not become her *Central America*.

"Thank you for coming once again," Chris began when the meeting convened. "I won't keep you long. The relevant data are on the display screen, the conclusions of the analysis team are at the bottom. Next to them you will see the statement of negative results from the archivist." She paused, drew a big breath, and continued. "We are recommending an immediate lander mission to begin direct observations leading to retrieval. The object took some intelligence to fabricate. It is apparently *not* one of ours."

Chapter 43
Grand Opening
(2115)

The object was now sitting in a decontamination room off the air lock bay of Titan Observatory Alpha. Technicians were busy examining its exterior with robotic arms. There would be no direct human contact until it had been verified to be free of hazardous bio-agents or other contaminants. It was an exact replica of an old Gemini capsule. At least that was the way it looked from the outside. Corrugated paneling on the sides with a titanium alloy base. No equipment module, just the capsule for the astronauts. Plus the base was not scorched like the ones in the history books. Mimas had no atmosphere, consequently there could be no heating as the capsule headed in for impact. The impact itself had done no obvious damage. The weak gravity of the small moon and the strength of the craft were enough to ensure it survived landing intact.

Chris stood behind Gene for about five minutes, watching him manipulate a pair of robotic arms near one of the entry hatches.

"I'm going to try to open it up," he said without turning or even taking his eyes off the monitor in front of him.

A second monitor on the same table displayed a page of plans for what looked to Chris to be the object. Then she realized they were for an actual Gemini capsule.

"The latches on this thing look exactly like the ones in that schematic," Gene said, "they were designed so the astronauts could exit and re-enter in space for EVAs. I'm glad they chose Gemini and not a Mercury capsule – those had explosive bolts for quick removal of the hatch after splashdown."

The robot arm had a grasper mounted on it, Gene was maneuvering it above one of the latches.

It took him a few minutes to figure out how get into the best position to undo it.

"I'll have the rest of them off in twenty minutes. Why don't you go for a walk, bring us back some coffee?"

Chris hadn't realized how much tension had built up inside her. She suddenly felt drained.

"Was this how Robert Ballard felt when they originally entered the wreck of the *Titanic* with their remotely guided robots?" she asked.

"Who?" Gene responded.

"Not a National Geographic video fan, I take it," said Chris. "I'll go get the coffee."

Gene was down to the last couple of bolts when Chris got back. She rolled a chair next to him, placing the coffees on the table. She was now even tenser than when the first bolt was being drilled. The hatch would be open in a few minutes, soon they would get a look inside.

"That's the last one," Gene stated as he reached for his coffee. "Where is everybody?" he inquired.

"Oh, jeez!" Chris gasped. "I clean forgot about telling Joe and the rest of the team."

She immediately spoke to the console sending out a message.

"They should be here in a few minutes," she said. "I can't believe I forgot! The stress of this is really getting to me. I have half a mind to tell you to go ahead, but that wouldn't be fair to the others." She grabbed her coffee, sat back in the chair, and swiveled around to look at the entry door to the control room.

Thirty seconds later, she spun back to face the screen.

"Oh, God, go on. I can't stand this any longer!"

Gene turned to face the console once again.

"It'll take a while to ease the panel up off the mounts," he said. "They'll be here by the time it's clear of the chassis, then we can all take a look inside."

Chris's team was in the room by the time Gene finished lifting the panel, they crowded in front of the monitors on the table. Each displayed the same thing: a dark rectangular opening in the object. Gene set the hatch on the floor, the robot's arms moved back toward the capsule. One arm had a light attached; the other a video camera. Soon they were peering in at a pair of seats complete with lap belts and shoulder harnesses mounted in front of a set of panels covered with lights and toggle switches. Gene shifted to his second terminal, he began paging through the Gemini manual from the archive. He found a page with an interior shot of the craft and inserted it in the main display for everyone to see.

"Gemini capsule inside too," Chris said. "No surprise, I suppose. The control panels and interior fixtures are exact duplicates of the real thing."

"What is going on here?" Gene asked.

Can this truly be a hoax? Chris thought. The same sentiment was quickly voiced by several team members. In the meantime Gene kept manipulating the camera, looking deeper inside to scan around the floor and beside the seats. He homed in on five cases anchored to the wall next to one of the seats. They appeared to be made of hard plastic with hinged lids. He set the light down on one of the seats and moved the arm back out to get another attachment. He then unfastened one of the cases and lifted it out of the capsule. Everyone stared in silence at the monitors. The case was light, it took Gene a few tries to flip the lid without the base coming up at the same time. Finally they had a look inside, it contained several dozen plastic disks.

Another chorus of "What the hell!" followed.

Chris was now beyond stunned; she was flabbergasted. Was this somebody's idea of a joke? Who would spend the time and money required to build this thing and send it all the way out to Mimas to deliver old CD's? She felt betrayed and foolish at the same time. How was she going to live this down? These thoughts flashed through her mind at once, until she gathered herself and spoke to the group.

"I know what you are thinking," she said, "because I'm thinking it too. However, before we jump to any premature conclusions, let's review all the information we have."

Gail Kranz was the first to chime in.

"Well, it sure looks like a hoax from here. I'm guessing there is some interesting stuff waiting for us on those disks!"

"I hope the perpetrators reveal themselves," another team member said. "If they are still alive, I'd like to track them down."

"And then what?" Chris asked. "No, wait—let's relax. It's going to be a while before we can get our hands on the disks. We have to finish the decontamination procedures before we can touch them. In the interim Gene can disassemble the whole thing. Once we can get at the pieces, we'll run a set of tests on the materials, by then we should be able to try to read the disks. Right now I suggest we keep quiet about this for obvious reasons. I'll make a report to management later today. For now, no leaks to the outside. We have managed to keep things quiet so far, let's hold to that discipline until we have examined the object and gotten a clearer understanding of what this thing is."

She turned and walked out of the room. No one followed because they knew how hard it was going to be on her to talk to the senior staff, it would be better to let her alone.

Chris's report was received without much comment at first, as it turned out in the end, they were completely understanding, actually a little amused. They might have thought they had been hoodwinked, yet they had to admire the quality of the hoax, if that was what it was. There was the metallurgical data on the container that would be available soon, and the contents of the disks to be reviewed. They thought the matter would be settled in the next couple of days.

Data on the composition of the capsule and fabrication techniques used to build it indicated it had been made in a manner identical to the craft it resembled with materials of the same type. Nothing of the capsule's physical composition hinted at an alien hand in its manufacture. It did not rule it out, nor did it rule out a hoax. The disks now became the sole determinant.

When they examined them, the team realized they were similar to computer laser disks made at the end of the previous millennium. A direct match had been made with schematics from archives back on Earth. The problem was they had no actual CD readers, which had long ago become obsolete.

The team was surprised to find so much detail on CD readers in the archive. It would take a week to fabricate something that could do the job. They would have to figure out what format the contents had been written in, then build a program to translate it to a form compatible with current video, audio, and text display devices. Not impossible, but it would take time. Luckily the right people to do the work were available on site. Everyone, including the director, wanted to get this thing resolved, partly because of their curiosity to discover the contents, partly to learn who was responsible. Mostly they wanted to get some answers before word leaked out. Saturn was a long way from Earth, there were not a lot of people at the Observatory. Unfortunately, this would only put off the inevitable. The transmission time delay to home was forty-five minutes, no restrictions were placed on personal communications, anyone could send a message at any time.

Andy Jenkins was the primary hardware guy working on building the reader. Work was going well, but he knew that was just one part of the puzzle.

He figured it would be easier to use original software. It turned out that a common recording format was used for optical disk media at the time. It was compatible with the major computer operating systems. All he had to do was find source code for one of those old operating systems, extract the part he needed, then marry it to their existing system. Otherwise he was going to be in for an extended effort building something from scratch using the format specification.

He narrowed the options down to two dominant technologies of the time. One was an operating system called Windows by a long defunct company named Microsoft. Andy remembered it vaguely from a history of invention article he had read years before. He recalled that the heirs of the exceedingly rich founder were still around. One of them was the current junior senator from Washington State.

The other technology was more familiar. It was a public domain operating system. Though the use of its name had long ago faded away, its legacy lived on to the present. They found eighty-year-old source code from when it had been called Linux. Upon examination, Andy determined it could be adapted for use on their current systems. It would take a few hours to port the input/output interfaces plus key system commands, happily it appeared they could get the guts of the software to function.

Once the disk reader was finished and connected to a computer he did some tests to make sure they could communicate with it. They had no spare CD to do a read/write test, so he stuck the disk labeled '1 of 155' in the drive and asked for a listing of its contents.

Bingo!

He put in a call to Chris and the rest of the team. They would want to be in on the next step.

Fifteen minutes after the notice, everyone was there, including people from the night shift who had been sound asleep.

"What have you found?" Chris asked as she walked up to Andy's console.

"I've started listing the contents of the first CD," he replied. "We should be able to get into the files in short order."

The screen display was not what they were used to seeing. It didn't have a fancy graphical user interface that used voice commands, it was serviceable for someone like Andy who knew his way around the innards of software and hardware as if by instinct.

"We don't have keyboards anymore," he said, "Instead, I jury-rigged a speech-recognition program. It produces simple keystroke commands that the Linux I embedded in our software can recognize. The resulting text will show up at the prompt."

As the others watched over his shoulders, Andy began reading through the CD's contents listing.

"That was easy enough," said Andy. "By the file appends, it seems to be a whole bunch of what were called streaming video files, plus a couple files in a format called Postscript. Those are most likely text with embedded images."

The program listed file names until Andy spotted something that made him ask it to stop.

"There it is—just what I was looking for. A 'readme' file. We still use these simple text files to communicate general information about file directory contents. Anybody remember the name of the editor for this thing?" he asked. Someone answered that the most basic was "vi."

Using it opened the readme file immediately, its contents flashed onto the screen.

"Greetings, Earthlings. Welcome to the outer planets," it began.

"Well, at least the author has a sense of humor," Andy said.

"Disk 1 of 155. The contents of these disks were placed by the authors on the Saturnine moon Mimas in the year 1992 by your reckoning. They contain a record of our visit to your planetary system, our stay at your star, called Sol or Sun, your third planet, Earth, and travels by one of us on that planet's surface starting in 1919. They also include historical video and narratives of our lives prior to arrival. The files are in standard video and text formats of the time." The readme file contents ended with a simple declaration, "Look for further news from:" followed by a series of numbers.

"Regards, John, Vanya and Caleb."

Stunned silence followed.

There was not much else to do except start going through the CDs. Everyone took a bunch and spent the next several days viewing the contents. Most of them contained video with voice-over narrative. Everything was in English. Though the authors had obviously edited the content, much of it appeared to be from a surveillance camera. The subjects seemed unaware they were being recorded. There was footage of the authors where they were definitely looking at the camera. The background was either a generic interior much like those at Saturn Titan Observatory Alpha or outdoor shots with normal looking grass, trees, and buildings. Nothing on the CDs could be called alien. Several sequences were apparently taken in space, such as of stars the authors claimed to be Epsilon Indi and Alpha Centauri A, along with planets they said were members of the two star systems. The planetary shots included distinctive surface scenes, mainly mountain ranges, canyon complexes, or large bodies of water taken from high altitude.

The authors were not making it easy for them. The pictures of the stars were so enlarged that no background stars were visible. As a result, they could not determine the stars' locations. The simplest thing would have been to include spectra, which would allow them to verify the subject stars. As far as they could tell, they could all be two close-up shots of the Sun.

The planetary pictures were more interesting. The Observatory team did know there were planets orbiting the two stars, which was about it. The surface features appeared to be unique. They were similar to features on Earth and Mars but did not directly match any. Since no one from Earth had ever been past Uranus, and they could not directly image inner planets around even nearby stars, there was nothing to base a judgment on.

After viewing all the CD's, no one thought they had run across anything that could be used to prove the disks were of alien creation. It looked more like a hoax than ever, because there was nothing in it they could not have done themselves.

The people looked like people. They had the right features with nothing obviously missing or extra. The narrator spoke English with a neutral accent similar to television and radio broadcasters of the time. None of the other people in the video spoke directly. Although they could see lips moving, the only audio was the author providing commentary.

The CDs were copied to the station library, anyone who wanted to could study them to see if they could spot something out of the ordinary that would make the case one way or the other. After two weeks they were at an impasse. They did not possess the equipment or skills to study them any deeper. It would take forensic capabilities to go further.

Finding the capsule had been reported immediately to Earth as part of routine daily traffic, though no official mention had been made to the public. Regular updates went back with the daily reports, with parts of the CD contents. A few individuals put snippets in personal vmails, rumors were starting to circulate. Director Hopkins could wait no longer; she prepared a full briefing for release to the public and sent it along with the entire CD contents, detailed video of the capsule, and images of the discovery site on Mimas. Further official work at the station came to an end, although Chris, Andy, and a number of others continued to study the recordings in their spare time.

Chapter 44
Decryption
(October 2141)

Twenty-six years had passed since the discovery of the Gemini capsule on Mimas. The numbers in the readme file on the first CD were determined to be celestial coordinates for a location very near to, but not exactly at, Alpha Centauri A. They were found to correspond closely with Shantel's anomaly. CDs containing technical data provided information on how to decode and translate the signal coming from something called the Alpha Centauri HUB. The problem was no one had been able to capture enough signal from the source of Shantel's anomaly to do anything with it. Their instruments were not sensitive enough, yet.

Kevin clicked to page 55 of the online document to look at the coordinates for Alpha and Beta Centauri. He would use the coordinates to calculate aiming parameters from the offsets given in the Mimas disks. He had time scheduled on the International Space Array for the following weekend and was setting up the observing parameters. It would be the first time he used the newly upgraded 45 GHz band receivers. This was where one of the primary sets of alignment channels was supposed to be. They were looking for a signal from the transmitter claimed by the Mimas disks to be stationed at Alpha Centauri. They had been looking since the contents of the disks had been released to the radio astronomy community in 2115.

Though the bulk of popular opinion sided with hoax at the time, funding for research based on the Mimas disk data grew dramatically with time. The SETI segment of the worldwide astronomical community had taken the discovery seriously from the start—none more so than the SETI Institute and Kevin and his colleagues. Over the years they did scan after scan in a band around 45 GHz in the region of the sky between Alpha Centauri A and B, with nothing to show for it. They recorded data across the entire radio spectrum. Each time more sensitive electronics were added to the array, they repeated the search. Several specific marker frequencies were noted in the disk files as reference points to be used for registration and calibration. From those they were supposed to be able to decode the signal.

In addition to improved receivers, antennas were added to expand the size of the array. Together these upgrades doubled resolution and sensitivity.

Something was out there, they were sure. It was not random noise, though the signal was very weak, it was coherent. It had not been deciphered yet. Therefore, they could not say for sure it had an intelligent source. They would have to detect one of the alignment frequencies in order to be able to make sense of the signal.

Years ago the Alpha Centauri double star system had been found by Shantel Jefferson and her successors to be producing a general level of background signal that was not completely random. It was found using a wide-beam array. That is, one where the antennas were close together and the region of the sky from which the data was collected was large. It covered a half degree on a side or one-eighth the size of the full moon. They attempted to focus in on the source location by continually shrinking the area of the sky being observed, but the source was too weak for them to reliably detect coherent signals from it.

Listening for a longer period did not help, either. They were not trying to detect a natural signal that could be built up in strength with time by adding it to that which had already been captured. They were trying to detect what they assumed was a set of intelligently produced messages modulating the carrier frequencies. They had to be able to directly receive data across enough frequencies to extract the message. If extraterrestrials were really out there, they were not making it easy for the Earthlings.

Gabrielle worked in the application software section at the SETI Institute. She was collaborating with Kevin and his team on data processing. This was where the contents of the recorded signals were torn apart, massaged, and reconstructed in an effort to isolate faint sources in the field of view. It took lots of computer time to do the processing, behind which were hundreds of man-years of physics and mathematical research, software development, and hardware engineering.

Gabrielle's specialty involved a broad area of methodologies designed to separate a complex mix of signals into individual components that could be further processed and analyzed. She was anxiously awaiting data from the new 45 GHz band receivers that would provide previously unobtainable sensitivity to weak signals in the 38 to 52 GHz range. It was called the 45 GHz band because that was the center frequency. Three of the markers were in this band, they were about to discover if the signals could at last be reliably detected and understood.

Chapter 45
Worth the Wait
(March 2142)

The SETI Institute was the body that oversaw processing of nonastronomical data from the space array as well as the ground-based Allen Telescope Array in California. The director of the Institute, Andrew Moore, stood before a microphone waiting for the audience to quiet down. Behind him was a large screen showing the Institute's logo.

"As you know by now," Moore started, "secrets being hard to keep in the scientific community, two days ago researchers at the Institute uncovered, and I mean that in its most literal sense because an enormous amount of scientific detective work was involved, what appears to be a set of coherent signals coming from the Alpha Centauri system. The signal is emanating at the marker frequencies given in the Mimas journals, we have started to decipher it.

"Before giving the podium to the folks who did the heavy lifting, I want to say a few words of thanks to all who have backed and believed in the SETI Institute over the years searching for evidence of extraterrestrial life—from our sponsors and benefactors, to the multitudes who downloaded screen savers, to the scientists, engineers, mathematicians, and support staff who have devoted their careers to the search. It appears that this hard work and dedication has finally paid off. The question of the validity of the Mimas journals has been settled. Many believed from the start that it was not a hoax. Although emotions have ebbed and flowed on this question during the twenty-seven years since the discovery of the capsule on Mimas, there were always those who would not quit until the question was answered one way or the other. Today we have gotten that answer. We are not alone."

He paused to let his last four words sink in.

After an extended period of cheering, applause, and general commotion died down, he began again.

"It is now my pleasure to introduce Kevin Snow and Gabrielle Hauser, who will take us through the details," the director concluded.

Kevin called for the first image, it appeared as the auditorium lights dimmed.

"What you see before you," said Kevin, "is an image of a small area near Alpha Centauri made by compositing ten million channels from the 45 GHz band. You will note the obvious, faint source located a short ways outside the limits of the star's habitable zone.

"This next view is an enlargement of the previous image centered on the faint source. Its colored-noise index is five on the Jefferson scale; an extremely high value."

Kevin called for the next picture.

"Here we have displayed three spectral lines centered on the expected marker frequencies. Two of them show significant power above the background. The third is less pronounced. These data are from the narrow-beam scans made on the area centered on the faint source. They do not correspond to any known natural lines, they align perfectly with the Mimas frequencies after accounting for a small amount of Doppler shift due to the relative motion of the Alpha Centauri system with respect to Earth. Starting with the marker frequencies, we have been able to construct message fragments from the encoding information on the disks. The translation key has allowed us to produce several thousand English characters. It is rather mundane so far, but it does make sense."

Kevin called for the auditorium lights to be brought back up, he left the final picture on the screen.

"These results," Kevin remarked, "would not have been possible without the skills of Gabrielle's group, who have produced a number of breakthroughs in the past few years. We'll now open the floor to questions."

The entire audience stood up at once and started shouting, it would take two hours to field the inquiries from the assembled media representatives. Chris, sitting two places to the speaker's right, just smiled.

Epilog

The characters in this story live in a calm and peaceful world free from want and most of the dangers we have to face, without the need to work or even the need for money. They are nurtured and supported from birth in an environment of caring family members, friends, colleagues and shipmates. They are protected from harm, and rescued from illness and injury by the ship's ever present, all seeing systems and robots that also free them from the burden of everyday chores.

Some would contend that this world could never be, it is naïve or unrealistic. I believe that a society similar to the one described that is highly educated, introspective, and open-minded must come to pass if we are ever to gain the perspective necessary to understand our true role in the universe.

I am convinced that what I have described will start to be within our reach given a few hundred additional years of technical development. Much of it is already more a matter of engineering than scientific discovery, the main area of remaining discovery probably being in materials science.

I hope I have also convinced you that we will not be bored in this utopian world, there will still be plenty to do, if you have the desire to keep on learning and discovering new things. We will all have to become explorers and constant learners. I believe this can be done, and that the end result has to be something similar to the society described herein.

About the Author

Tom Morgan has been a practicing research and development scientist for the past forty years. He has a Ph.D. in Geophysics and was employed mainly in seismic exploration for oil and gas with side trips to nondestructive testing, medical ultrasonic imaging, and radio astronomy data processing. He has written and spoken widely during his career on work conducted with academic, commercial, and governmental organizations.

He and his wife reside in upstate New York where he continues to write and do research in the field of data science.

www.ingramcontent.com/pod-product-compliance
Lightning Source LLC
Chambersburg PA
CBHW071305200626
46813CB00015B/51